PRAISE FOR KRISTEN PROBY

"A Kristen Proby book is a guarantee of a fantastic romance. Proby always delivers when it comes to heat, heart, humor, and ALL THE FEELS." —Lauren Blakely, *New York Times* and *USA Today* bestselling author

"No one packs as much passion and romance on each and every single page the way Kristen Proby does." —Jay Crownover, *New York Times* and *USA Today* bestselling author

"Kristen Proby's stories are all sexy, swoonworthy must-reads!" —Laura Kaye, *New York Times* and *USA Today* bestselling author

"Kristen Proby writes contemporary romance like no one else!" —Monica Murphy, *New York Times* and *USA Today* bestselling author

"No one does swoony alphas, strong women, and sexy love stories like Kristen Proby. She truly knows how to write romance with heart." —Laurelin Paige, *New York Times* and *USA Today* bestselling author

"Kristen Proby is a master at creating hot heroes and tender romance. I love her books!" —Jennifer Probst, *New York Times* and *USA Today* bestselling author

LISTEN

to

ME

Also by Kristen Proby

Easy Love
Easy Charm
Easy Melody
Easy Kisses

Come Away with Me
Under the Mistletoe with Me
Fight with Me
Play with Me
Rock with Me
Safe with Me
Tied with Me
Breathe with Me
Forever with Me
Easy with You

Loving Cara
Seducing Lauren
Falling for Jillian

LISTEN

to

ME

A Fusion Novel

Kristen Proby

WILLIAM MORROW

An Imprint of HarperCollins*Publishers*

HarperCollins books may be purchased for educational, business, or sales promotional use. For information please e-mail the Special Markets Department at SPsales@harpercollins.com.

FIRST EDITION

Designed by Diahann Sturge

Library of Congress Cataloging-in-Publication Data has been applied for.

ISBN 978-0-06-243475-3

16 17 18 19 20   OV/RRD   10 9 8 7 6 5 4 3 2 1

This book is dedicated to Jay Crownover.
Thank you for your friendship,
for inspiring one of the scenes in this book,
and for being you. I love you, friend.

Acknowledgments

This series has been brewing in my head for a while. I love the concept of five best friends who are also business partners. I feel like I have women like this in my life as well. I couldn't do this job without the amazing team that supports me.

I need to say a heartfelt thank you to Kevan Lyon, my agent, for your unwavering confidence and support. You are simply the best there is, and I can't tell you how grateful I am to have you.

To my editor, Amanda Bergeron, thank you so much for taking a chance on me and this series, and for being so patient with all of my questions and requests. You have made this experience fun and exciting. Thank you for all you do!

A special thanks goes out to Brad Yunek and Dan Keseloff, the writers of *If I Had Never Met You*. Thank you for the many hours you've dedicated to this project, and for sharing your incredible talent with me. I absolutely love the finished product, and couldn't have asked for a better song to fit Jake and Addie's story.

And finally, to Sarah Post, the chef who developed the recipes for Jake and Addie's date night. You have been a joy to work with! Thank you for sharing your talent with me.

LISTEN

to

ME

Chapter One

Addison

"'In summary,'" Cami, one of my very best friends, and a business partner, reads from the *Portland Tribune*, "'Seduction is a restaurant unlike any other I've experienced. The food is delicious, the wine bar impressive, and the ambiance so sexy, it will take your breath away. I highly recommend this restaurant for your next date night.'"

"I want to send that reviewer flowers," Mia says with a wide smile. "Who would have thought that just six months after opening this place, we'd already have a review like this?"

"Well, it's a no-brainer that they'd love the food," I reply, and reach for the paper so I can read it again for the fifteenth time. "You're a genius in the kitchen, Mia. We've known that since we were in high school."

"I still get nervous, especially now that I never know who the customers are going to be. We didn't even get a heads-up that this guy was going to be here." Mia bites the cuticle on her thumb and frowns. "Maybe I should add to the menu."

"The menu is perfect," Cami replies with a shake of her blond head. "He loved us."

We smile at each other, and finally I do a little happy dance in my seat. We haven't opened for the day yet. Kat and Riley, the final two business partners in our fivesome, haven't arrived. But Mia, Cami, and I have read this article over and over again, smiling and dancing.

Rejoicing.

Because damn it, we've worked our asses off since we opened the doors six months ago. All of our eggs are in *this* basket. We can't fail.

And we won't.

We hear the front door open and close, and I expect to see either Riley or Kat, but instead Jeremy saunters into the dining room, looking all rumpled and messy from sleep. His eyelids are still heavy. His chin is scruffy. His blond hair is standing on end, still in chaos from my fingers last night.

Jesus, this man makes my hormones work overtime.

He grins and kisses my head, then picks up my coffee and sits next to me.

"Why are you here?" Cami asks with a frown. "I'm in too good of a mood to have to pretend to like you."

I glare at my best friend, but she just shrugs.

"My girlfriend is here," Jeremy replies and sips my coffee. "I missed her."

"Please," Mia whispers with a roll of the eyes. My friends used to like Jeremy, in the beginning, but now they make it no secret that they don't care for him. But they are just over-protective. They don't want to see me get hurt. Sure, he's a musician. Not a particularly gifted one at that, but he does well, booking gigs for his band, Hells Roses, regularly.

And, oh my God, what the man can do in the bedroom should be a felony. He makes me laugh, and despite his arrogant persona around everyone else, he has moments of real vulnerability and sweetness when we're alone.

Is he *the one*? Probably not, but I'm pretty much convinced that *the one* was invented by romance novelists and Disney.

"Be nice," I snap and continue to read the paper. "We got a kick-ass review in the *Tribune*," I inform Jeremy with a grin.

"Of course you did," he replies and kisses my cheek. "Are the music reviews in there too?" He snatches the paper and shifts through the pages, then reads through the reviews of the music and club scene in Portland. "Not one fucking mention?"

Cami catches my gaze, then crosses her eyes in annoyance. I simply shrug. He's not in the restaurant business. He wouldn't understand what a big deal this is for us.

"I've been thinking," I begin, and lean my elbows on the table. "Now that business is picking up, I think we should add live music on the weekends."

"Sorry, cupcake," Jeremy says with a sigh. "We're booked."

Thank God. Jeremy's band isn't the one I'd want for my place. But rather than jab at his ego, I simply smile and kiss his shoulder.

"I know, babe. But I'd still like to bring in someone.

Maybe just a one-person act, just a microphone and a stool, you know?"

"We can afford it," Cami replies with a thoughtful frown. Cami is our chief financial officer. She handles all things money, and she's a wizard at adding up figures in her head. "Who are you thinking?"

"I don't know." I reach for my coffee mug and frown when I see that Jeremy has sucked down every last drop. "Babe, will you please run over to Starbucks and get us more coffee?"

"I forgot my wallet," he replies with a scowl. I reach into my bag and pass him a twenty. "You got it."

"Thank you."

"Oh, and one place you might look for a musician," he adds as he steps away from the table, "is the open-mic night at Crush this Saturday. There are usually some good acts there. I'd bet you'd find what you're looking for."

I grin at my sexy boyfriend and blow him a kiss. "Thank you."

He winks and saunters out of the restaurant. When the door closes behind him, Mia shakes her head at me. "Seriously?"

"Open mic night is a brilliant idea," I inform her.

"That's not what she's talking about," Cami says. "Jeremy is a douche bag."

"He is not." I roll my eyes and sit back in my chair. Okay, maybe he has douchey moments. "He's sweet. And sexy."

"And mooching off of you. His wallet was in his back

pocket," Mia argues. "And I'll bet all of this month's chocolate budget that he's staying with you too."

"His roommate moved out, and he couldn't afford his place alone."

"Addie." Cami reaches for my hand. "You are not a doormat."

"He doesn't treat me like a doormat."

"Yes. He does." Mia sighs and takes my other hand. "You deserve so much better."

"I love you both," I begin, my stomach heaving. "I know you just want to protect me. Jeremy is a good guy. I like him."

"Okay." Cami sips her coffee, then shrugs one slim shoulder. "But when he breaks your heart, we'll be here."

"Let's talk about this open-mic night. Who's going with me?"

Mia and Cami exchange glances.

"I'll be working," Mia says. "I have some new Saturday night specials I want to try."

"I don't want to," Cami says honestly. "I trust you to find exactly what we need."

"I'll take Kat." I chew my lip, ideas already swirling in my head. "She's a good judge of these things."

"Good idea."

The door opens again.

"Oh good. Mr. Wonderful is back," Cami mutters.

"How DO YOU do that to your hair?" Riley asks from her perch on my vanity stool, eating Chunky Monkey ice cream from the carton as I twist my hair into chunky ringlets. I've streaked it with purple tonight.

"It's not hard. It just takes practice, but once you get it down, it goes fast."

"I like the purple," she says with a grin. "And the painted-on jeans. You have a great ass."

I grin and turn to the side, eyeing my ass in these jeans. She's right. My ass isn't bad. I could do without the hips, but what are you gonna do?

"Should I wear a jacket over this top?" It's a flowy, black camisole, showing off my cleavage, but not hugging my *problem areas*.

"No. It's hot. You'll either find a hot singer for the restaurant, or a date."

"I have a date." I glance up to the heavens. "Give me strength."

"Jeremy isn't a date," Riley replies as she scrapes the bottom of the ice cream carton. "He's someone to fuck."

"Riley!"

"Truth," she says with a shrug. "And nothing wrong with it either, as long as you know the score."

"Well, the sex doesn't suck." There's a sharp knock on my bedroom door, and then Kat walks in, looking tall and gorgeous and freaking *badass*. Her red hair is pinned up. She's in a sleeveless top, showing off her awesome ink, and she's in mile-high pink stilettos.

"It should be illegal to look that hot," Riley says with a sigh. "You're both hot."

"Why aren't you coming with us?" Kat asks.

"Because I have a new marketing plan to come up with for this new music act."

"Excuse," Kat says, watching me apply my makeup. "And speaking of a hottie, hello, bombshell."

I grin at her in the mirror. "You're the hottest date I've had in a long time."

"Back at you." She winks. "Okay, what are we looking for tonight? Addie, this is your show, I'm just here to help."

"It's *our* show," I reply.

"The front of the house is yours, and you do an awesome job with it." Riley slicks some of my lipstick on her full lips, checks herself out, then vigorously wipes it off. "I can't do lipstick."

"I want to find a one- or two-person act." I tease my hair, until it falls just the way I want it to. "Someone with a sexy voice. I'm thinking Gavin DeGraw–ish."

"Hot." Kat nods in agreement. "How much can we spend?"

"Let's try to keep it around five hundred a night," Riley replies. "Cami said that's how much we can comfortably spend."

"That's not bad. Let's just hope we find someone. I already put a sign in the window too. It doesn't hurt."

"Okay. Let's do this." Kat leads us out of the apartment.

"Have fun," Riley says and waves as she walks to her car.

"This is gonna be fun," Kat says, then fist-bumps me and leads me to her car.

"CAN I GET you another chardonnay?" the waitress asks Kat, who shakes her head no.

"I'll just take a Diet Coke."

"Same for me."

The waitress nods and moves on.

"Wine not good here?" I ask Kat with a grin.

"Tastes like piss," she replies. "I totally understand wanting to serve an inexpensive bottle, and there are some delicious ones out there. There's no excuse for serving subpar wine."

My smile grows. "It turns me on when you turn on your wine-speak."

"It's what I do."

"And you do it well." And she does. Kat is the best sommelier in the Pacific Northwest. She knows wine.

"What do you think so far?"

We are seated at a high table, near the stage, in the center of the room, so it's easy to see the acts. Right now a young woman is singing a Trisha Yearwood song off-key.

"I haven't heard anything to write home about."

Kat nods in agreement, then glares at the man who just grabbed her ass as he walked by. "Keep your hands to yourself, buddy."

He shrugs and smiles unapologetically, then keeps walking.

"Men are gross," Kat mutters.

They sure can be.

The off-key girl finishes her song and we applaud. Next up is a throwback from 1967. Except the guy is young—

maybe twenty-two. His dreadlocks fall to the middle of his back. He has a beard. His clothes are dirty.

He's probably a homeless guy who usually sings on the street.

But then he starts to sing, and oh my word. He has the voice of an angel, singing "Hallelujah" as if he were singing it from heaven. We're mesmerized as he plays his guitar and sings.

He's amazing.

When he finishes, the applause is deafening.

"Wow." Kat turns her wide blue eyes to me. "Did you hear that?"

I nod. "We'll get his contact info. If we could clean him up, he could be perfect."

"If he'd be willing to clean up," Kat replies. "This could be what he wants."

Several more lukewarm acts play, then a duo take the stage. A man and woman, who look at each other with stars in their eyes, and sing a love ballad. Their harmonies are smooth as silk.

"I like them," Kat says as she leans my way. "They have the right look. And they're in love, which will bring a sexy chemistry to our place."

"I agree."

I want them. Like, *want them.* They'd be absolutely perfect.

"I'm going to go talk to them." Kat nods, turning her attention to another act already singing.

They're not nearly as good as the duo who just finished.

"Excuse me." They turn to me, and I paste on my best

smile. "I'm Addison. I'm the co-owner of Seduction, a new restaurant in town, and I'd love to talk with you about a possible weekend job at my place."

They glance at each other and grin. "Thank you. I'm Rebecca." The small blonde shakes my hand. "And this is my husband, Paul."

"You're both very talented."

"It's all her," Paul replies and stares down at Rebecca with heart eyes.

"I need an act for Friday and Saturday nights. I'm paying five hundred a night."

"Five hundred each?" Rebecca asks, her eyes suddenly shrewd.

"No." I shake my head. "For the act."

They glance at each other again, and Paul shakes his head. "Sorry. We're worth more than that."

"What do you normally charge?"

"Oh, we haven't taken any jobs yet. We're new to the area."

I raise a brow. "You're worth what someone is willing to pay. It was nice to meet you."

Without glancing back, I return to our table. "Egos," I say simply and shrug.

"Bummer."

"It happens."

A man walks onto the stage and sits on the stool, strums his guitar. The MC didn't announce his name.

The singer is wearing a black T-shirt and jeans. No shoes. A hat is pulled down his forehead, shadowing his face.

But I'd recognize those tattoos anywhere.

"Oh my God, I think that's Jake Knox," I whisper to Kat in disbelief.

"The tattoos," she breathes and I roll my eyes. "God, I used to be in love with him. I had his posters on my walls when I was in high school."

"Most did," I reply and watch as his fingers play the strings on his guitar as if he's making love to a woman. "God, he can play."

"What's he doing at an open-mic night?" Kat turns wide eyes to me. "Does he live here?"

I nod. "Yeah, I heard somewhere that he lives nearby. Maybe he needs an ego boost?"

But then he begins to sing a familiar Lifehouse song, and my chest tightens. I love this song. I love his voice. It's raw and rich and just a little bit raspy. It's pure sex.

"He'd be absolutely perfect." Kat's voice is a whisper. She probably didn't mean to say it out loud.

"I know we can't afford him. He probably plays at celebrity weddings and shit."

Jake glances up, showing his face and those amazing green eyes for the first time, and aims them right at me. He sings at least five lines, holding my gaze, then winks and lowers his head again.

Arrogant.

"Speaking of egos," I murmur. "That would be a hot mess."

"A sexy-as-fuck hot mess," Kat replies. "God, look at the way his muscles bunch as he plays."

Trust me, I noticed. You'd have to be blind with an IQ of minus 20 to not notice the way Jake Knox moves. He makes everything in me come awake. Which makes sense because he's probably been trained to do that. He has to sell music, after all.

He finishes the song and leaves the stage. There are murmurs in the audience. We obviously weren't the only ones to recognize him. Let's be honest, Jake Knox is one of the biggest rock stars there is.

Or, was. I don't think he's released any new music in the past few years.

I wonder why.

"I don't think we're going to find our act here," Kat says with a sigh. "We've seen at least twenty people in the past two hours. The only ones we liked were a homeless guy, an egomaniac couple, and a rock star."

"You're right. Let's go." We gather our handbags and walk out into the cool spring evening. Walking ahead of us, away from the club, is a man with his guitar case. I'd recognize that shape, that walk, anywhere.

Jake Knox.

What is up with me being so damn attracted to the bad-boy musician type? It never fails. If there's a bad-boy musician within a thirty-mile radius, my girl parts are on high alert. Every. Single. Time. Ever since I lost my virginity to Todd Perkins in the eleventh grade. Todd was the lead singer of a garage band and happened to seduce me out of my pants in said garage, right behind the drums.

And dump me the next day.

"He even walks sexy," Kat whispers into my ear.

"Mm," I reply.

"Don't act all nonchalant with me," she says, shoving my shoulder. "He turns *me* on, and you're the one who loves the bad boys. You have ever since I met you freshman year."

I shrug. She's right.

"Let's go to the restaurant. I want to see how Jamie is doing behind the bar," Kat finally says when it's apparent that I'm not going to talk about my penchant for musicians.

"I'll check on the waitstaff, and we can both make Mia go home."

"Mia's working?" Kat asks with a frown.

"Of course Mia's working. She's not sleeping."

"She needs an intervention."

"I'll TAKE A glass of that," Mia says as she joins Kat and me at the bar after closing. Kat and I each handled our own staff for the rest of the evening, juggled a few mishaps, then sent everyone on their way and decided to unwind with a glass of wine before we head home.

"I can't believe you're still here," I say to Mia. "You've been here since this morning."

"Back at you," she replies with a sigh as she sits on a stool beside me and rolls her head back and forth on her shoulders, stretching. "It was a good day."

"You're taking tomorrow off," I say, not looking her in the face.

"You're not the boss of me."

"Yes, we are," Kat replies and passes two glasses of wine

to Mia. "Of all of us, you work the longest hours. The kitchen will survive for one day without you."

"What does one do on a day off?" Mia asks.

"Clean your bathroom. Go to the coast and put your feet in the water. Get laid. Just don't come here."

"Maybe." Mia shrugs. "Did you find us an act?"

"No." I shake my head and sip the crisp, dry wine.

"But you both look so hot. No one threw themselves at you?"

"Kat had her ass grabbed a time or two."

"I want to grab Kat's ass," Mia replies. "Ever since we met her in college we've wanted to grab her ass."

"And you have," Kat replies with a salute and takes a shot of tequila.

"And you loved it," Mia replies. "Tell me about tonight?"

"There's not much to tell. We found one couple that would be good but they wanted a ton of money."

"We also found Jake Knox," Kat says with a satisfied grin.

"What?" Mia shrieks. "You did not!"

"We did. He sang one song."

"Why? He's famous. He doesn't have to go to those things."

"Trust me, I wasn't questioning his motives." Kat tops off our glasses again. "I was simply thankful to be sitting roughly ten feet away from him."

"I'm so jealous! I had Hard Knox posters all over my bedroom!"

Kat reaches out a fist for a bump. "Me too."

"Hard Knox was a good band." I sip my wine. "They broke up, you know."

"So sad." Mia shakes her head. "You got to see Jake Knox."

"But we didn't find an act for here." I feel defeated. I so wanted to wrap that up tonight.

"We'll find one," Kat says. "Have Jeremy ask around."

"He doesn't really play the kind of music I want for us."

"You mean the *good* kind?" Mia asks sarcastically.

"Okay, so he's no Daughtry. He's not horrible."

Both Kat and Mia just raise a brow at me and smile.

"Okay, he's not good."

We all giggle and fall into a comfortable silence. Finally, Mia whimpers and lays her head down on the bar. "So tired."

"Day off tomorrow, Mia. I mean it." I rub her back in big circles. "You need to sleep."

"Okay. But if anything happens, you call me."

"We will," Kat says. We look at each other while I continue to rub Mia's back and we don't need to speak aloud to know what the other is thinking.

The place would have to be on fire before we'd call Mia tomorrow.

Chapter Two

Jake

"You're quiet."

My head jerks up at the sound of her voice, pulling me from some damn daydream, and I frown. "Sorry, I don't mean to be."

"What's on your mind?"

I chew on my bacon and watch my best friend of more than fifteen years across the table from me at this dive diner that serves the best breakfast in Portland. Christina has been with me through fame and money, and some of the shittiest moments of my life. She's watched as I hit bottom and clawed my way out of the darkness again.

She's the only person in the world that I know I can trust without blinking.

"Music's always on my mind," I reply and take a sip of coffee. She rolls her pretty brown eyes and tosses her brown hair over her shoulder the way she does when she's annoyed.

"You've been invited to—"

"Not interested," I reply, cutting her off. "I lived it, and I don't need it anymore."

"You miss it. You sang at that open-mic-night thing last weekend and you nailed it."

I shrug one shoulder and don't deny that she's right. I do miss it.

Not playing music for people hurts as bad as if I were missing a leg, but playing at that open gig the other night was a big mistake. Because now I crave it again.

But I don't deserve it.

Because Christina *is* missing a leg.

Because of me.

"I loved the song you wrote for Nash that just released last week."

I manage a grin. "Thanks."

"Why did you do it?" she asks unexpectedly.

"What?"

"Open-mic night."

I rub my hand over my lips and sigh. "I just . . . God, I miss it, C."

Her eyes soften. "I know."

"So, I sang and I got it out of my system. Case closed." A complete lie, but I won't admit that to her.

"Working this afternoon?" she asks.

"Yeah, Max and I will be in the studio this afternoon, finishing a couple of songs for Daughtry."

She nods thoughtfully. "Must really suck to be you, with your own production company, and fancy studio at your house, and famous people flying in to work with you and all of that."

"Yes, it sucks to be me," I reply dryly.

"You're writing, and producing, still making a difference in the music world, just not performing." She tilts her head to the side and runs her pink-tipped finger over her bottom lip, in thought.

"You already know this."

"Excuse me?"

We both turn to the pretty blonde standing beside our table, wringing her hands nervously.

"Hi," I reply with a smile.

"Aren't you Jake Knox?" she asks and I immediately switch gears. My smile is cocky, and I lean back in the chair, assuming the role.

"I sure am. What's your name, sweetheart?"

"M-Michelle," she replies with a slight stutter, and her cheeks blush. More than five years out of the limelight and this still happens at least once a week. "I'd heard a rumor that you lived in Portland now."

I raise an eyebrow and glance at Christina, who's hiding her smile behind her coffee mug.

"I live in the area," I reply. "What can I do for you?"

"Oh! I'm sorry. Could I maybe just get a selfie with you?" She pulls her phone out of her pocket and smiles shyly.

"Sure." I stand, wrap my arm around her shoulders, and

take her phone from her, aiming it high. I paste my signature smirk on my face and take the picture.

"Wow, thanks. I love your music. Are you going to put a new album out soon?"

Now Christina frowns and glances down at her empty plate.

"Thank you. No, the band broke up. I'm more behind the scenes now."

"Aww, that's a shame," Michelle says with a frown. "Thanks for the photo."

"You're welcome."

Michelle leaves, happily staring at her phone, and I return to my seat.

"That wasn't too painful," I say and take another bite of bacon.

"It *is* a shame," Chris says.

"Don't start, C." I toss the bacon on my plate and push it away.

"All I'm saying is—"

"The same thing you've been saying for years. I don't want to live a public life anymore. It just fucks things up."

"You don't have to live a public life to play music." She shakes her head, cutting me off when I would speak. "Just listen. Kevin took me to a new restaurant the other night. It's *awesome*." She leans in, her brown eyes shining with excitement. "It's sexy."

"The restaurant is sexy?"

"Yes, and it's amazing. So, these women have opened

this place in downtown Portland called Seduction. There are aphrodisiacs on the menu, sexy music and atmosphere, amazing wine cellar. Did you know that asparagus is an aphrodisiac?"

"I had no idea."

"Me either! Until we went there. It's so great for couples, and it looks like it's making quite a name for itself."

"What the fuck does it have to do with me?" I ask mildly and sip more coffee.

"There was a sign in the window advertising for a weekend musician."

I stare at her, blinking.

"So?"

"So you should go apply!"

She slaps her hand on the table and leans back with a satisfied smile, proud of herself.

"Fuck no."

"Why not?"

"Jake Knox doesn't perform anymore."

"Jake Keller could."

I tilt my head, suddenly intrigued.

"You don't have to go in there and be a rock star, you know. You could just go in with your guitar and play music. You don't have to do the old Hard Knox stuff, unless you want to try some acoustic arrangements. You could just do covers, if that's what you wanted. Or new stuff you're writing."

Suddenly the yearning in my gut is so intense I can barely breathe. I love producing and writing music. Hell, I spent a month up in Seattle last fall cowriting and producing with Leo Nash, an old friend of mine, for his band's new album. It's fulfilling.

But fuck me, how I miss performing. And it's really not about the screaming women, the lights, the louder-than-fuck music.

It's just the music itself. Performing and watching the crowd sing along.

There's just nothing like it. And the other night, when I sat on that stage and sang, it was like visiting an old friend.

But I gave it up on a rainy night five years ago when Christina was almost killed and lost her leg, all because of me.

I shake my head and clench my jaw. "No."

"God, you're so fucking stubborn," she growls and clenches her tiny fist. "I don't expect you to never perform again because of something stupid that happened long ago."

"That's not it."

"Cut the bullshit." She leans in and narrows her eyes at me. "My accident wasn't your fault, J. I don't know how many times I have to say it before you'll believe it."

"If we hadn't fought—"

"I'm going to beat you up. Hard."

"Yeah, I'd like to see you try with your one leg." I smirk, but my chest hurts at the words. "I don't know what I would ever do without you, C."

"Then do me a favor and go apply for this job. I want to watch you sing again. I miss it. And the one song the other night wasn't enough. I know it wasn't."

"I'll bring my guitar over tonight."

She smirks and shakes her head. "Just go apply. They might not hire you. Maybe you suck now."

I smirk. "Baby, I've never sucked at music."

"So prove it."

"God, you're a pain in my ass."

She laughs. "I know. I have to go to the doctor now." She scrunches up her nose and sighs. "I swear, all of Portland has seen my hoo-haw."

"Your what?" I ask, raising a brow. "Are you eight?"

She throws an orange wedge at me. "This whole pregnancy thing needs to resolve itself. Lying with your feet in stirrups is not sexy or fun."

"Do you find out today if it worked?" Christina and her husband, Kevin, have been trying to get pregnant for three years. They want this more than anything in the world, and it's just another thing that the accident has robbed her of.

Another thing that *I've* robbed her of.

"Yes," she says with a smile. "So cross your fingers."

"And my toes."

"Can I help you?" A young woman greets me as I enter Seduction, nestled in the heart of the Pearl District, one of the trendiest areas of Portland. From the outside, it looks like an old warehouse.

On the inside, it's pure sex. But not the kind of seedy sex that you'll find in any of the many sex or strip clubs in the city. This is classy sex.

"I'd like to speak with your manager, please."

"That's Addison," she replies with a bright smile. "I believe she's in the bar." She points to the back of the house. I nod and walk through a sea of black tables with wide-backed, plush gray chairs and teal blue table linens. Along the back wall are inviting booths, giving a feel of privacy with pretty gray curtains hanging at the side of each booth.

The room is arranged to face a small stage that currently sits empty. It's only lunchtime, so instead of live music, Adele is crooning through the speakers about chasing pavements. I hum along with the song as I enter the bar area, similar in color scheme but a bit more edgy.

A wall of wine barrels rises behind the bar, with bottles of wine lying inside. There must be a thousand bottles on that wall. Under the countertop is the largest wine fridge I've ever seen, also packed full of bottles.

So they do wine well.

"You need more for lunch than a glass of wine," a woman announces. She has deep red, almost burgundy, hair, wide blue eyes, and is wearing a pair of jeans that was made for her ass along with a white tank top that shows off some pretty amazing ink. Her face is made up to look like a pinup model, and her red lips tip up in a grin as the blonde with her back to me takes a sip of her glass of wine.

"Wine comes from grapes, which is fruit. I'm having a fruit salad for lunch," she says and sips her glass. "God, this is good."

"Of course it is," Red says with a smirk, then sees me leaning against the archway leading into the bar. "Can we help you?"

"I'm looking for the manager. I was told I'd find her in here."

"And you have," Blondie says and turns on her bar stool to look at me.

And suddenly the air is stolen from my lungs. This is the woman I saw the other night at the club. The one I couldn't take my eyes off of. The one that made the rest of the room fade away.

The only word I have for her is *bombshell,* and I've never used that word in my life.

She slides off her seat, perfectly at home in her mile-high black heels, and strides quickly and confidently over to me. She's in a high-waisted, black pencil skirt with a white button-down tucked into it. Her sleeves are rolled, the top few buttons unfastened on her shirt, giving me a glimpse at the most impressive cleavage I've ever seen.

Her blond hair is piled high on her head, in lazy curls. Her makeup is simple and flawless.

And she's wearing black-rimmed glasses.

Fuck me.

I swallow hard and hold my hand out to shake hers, but she comes to an abrupt halt about two feet too far to take it.

"You're—"

"Jake Keller," I interrupt and close the gap to shake her hand. Hers is warm and slender, but her grip is firm. Her eyes narrow.

"Jake Knox," she corrects me. "My friends all had your posters on their walls."

"You didn't?" I ask with a cocky smirk, already enjoying her.

"No, I wasn't particularly smitten with you." She pulls her glasses off her nose, much to my disappointment, and tucks them on top of her head in her hair.

God, I'm such a sucker for a beautiful woman in glasses.

"Shame," I reply and continue to smile at her.

"How can I help you?"

"I'm here about the job."

She frowns. "You want to be a busboy? Are times really that bad, Mr. Knox?"

"Keller," I correct her. "Actually, just call me Jake. And I'm here about the weekend music gig. Although, I can clear tables if need be."

She tilts her head, hooks a stray strand of hair behind her ear, and smiles, and my heart stops. Fucking hell, where did this woman come from?

And where the hell are these thoughts coming from?

"I'm quite sure I can't afford you, Mr. Keller." She turns to walk away, but I catch her elbow, turning her back to me.

"It's not about the money," I say quickly. "I'd really just like to play."

"Your whole band?" she asks with a frown.

"No, just me. I'll bring my guitar and all I'll need you to provide is a mic and a stool, but I'm sure I can come up with a mic if you don't already have one."

She blinks at me, as if I'm not speaking English, then finally says, "Okay, where are the cameras?" She looks around the room and points at Red behind the bar. "Did you stage this? Seriously, you guys are bitches for doing this to me."

Red laughs and shakes her head. "No tricks here, Addie. But send him over to me when you're done with him."

Addie turns back to me with skeptical eyes. "She was one of my friends with your poster on her wall."

"And I'm not afraid to admit it," Red says loudly as she stocks more wine.

"So, the job." I cross my arms over my chest and watch her eyes dilate when they land on the sleeve tattoo on my right arm.

She's not immune to me.

"Do you seriously want to sing here for peanuts?"

"I'd prefer popcorn, but I'll take the peanuts."

I smile and she chews her bottom lip and crosses her own arms, mirroring me. All that accomplishes is pushing her tits together, giving me a prime view of the best body I've seen in . . . *ever*.

Her curves have curves, and she owns every one of them, packaging them nicely in an outfit that screams *class*. In this moment, all I want to do is take her in my hands and feast on her.

But, one thing at a time.

"The job is for Friday and Saturday nights, from ten to close."

"What time do you close?"

"Midnight."

"I can work with that."

She nods and then tips her head back and laughs. Her voice is raspy and just as sexy as the rest of her.

"Did I just hire Jake Knox?"

"No, ma'am, you just hired Jake Keller." I sigh and rub my hand over my mouth, remembering that I haven't shaved in about a week. I must look real professional, walking in here in questionably clean jeans and black T-shirt, unshaven, hair a fucking mess because I'm pretty sure I just ran my fingers through it before I left the house this morning.

But Addie just chews that lip again, then nods. "Okay, you can start this Friday and we'll see how it goes."

"Is this an audition?" I ask with surprise.

"Everyone auditions, Mr. Keller," she replies and rests her hands on her hips. "But it's a mutual audition. I'll see if you're a fit for us, and you'll see if we're a fit for you."

Oh, I'm pretty sure the fit will be just fine, sweetheart.

"Sounds good. I'll be here at nine thirty on Friday night to set up."

"Great. You can just come back here to the bar. I'll meet you here and show you around."

I nod and shove my hands in my pockets, suddenly nervous for the first time since I was a kid, which kind of annoys me and makes me smile all at the same time.

"Now that that's settled," I say and hold her pretty blue eyes with mine. "How about if I take you out for a drink after closing Friday night?"

She blinks for a moment, not moving, then shakes her head and laughs, looks at her shoes and then back up at me.

"Let me make something perfectly clear," she begins, speaking clearly. "I'm not a part of this offer. Nor will I ever be. I'm your boss, that's it. Not to mention, I am in a relationship."

"Idiot woman," Red mutters behind the bar, but Addie ignores her.

"Understood," I reply respectfully, but can't help but feel a moment of regret.

Addison is one beautiful woman.

I have a feeling she's much more than that, but she belongs to someone else, so it doesn't really matter.

And why in the fuck does it matter to me anyway? Jesus, has it really been that long since I got laid?

"I'll see you Friday night."

"Yes, you will," she replies and immediately turns her back on me, sauntering back to the bar in those amazing fuck-me heels, her ass swaying the whole way.

I can't wait to see her Friday night.

I wave at Red and walk back out the way I came. The restaurant is filling up with lunch patrons. When I hit the sidewalk outside, I call Christina.

"Miss me already?" There's a smile in her voice.

"Desperately. And, I think I just got a job."

"You went?" She squeals and then relays the information to her husband, Kevin, before returning to me. "And you got the job?"

"Of course I got the job."

"Did the manager recognize you?"

"Yes, but something tells me I got the job despite my music history, not because of it."

"Interesting. I like her already."

"So do I."

THE DRIVE TO my home west of Portland via the Sunset Highway only takes about thirty minutes from downtown. That's one of the things that I love about this city: you can go from bustling city to lazy suburb in just half an hour.

I bought a house on three acres in the rolling hills outside of Hillsboro about four years ago. It's gated, and monitored closely by security. The main house is bigger than I'll ever need, but it was the pool and, most important, the pool house that made me fall in love with it.

I love to swim, and I work out in the pool every single day I'm home. My best friend, and cofounder of Hard Knox, Max Bishop and I converted the pool house into a full studio and partnered up to begin Hard Knox Productions. Since starting business two years ago, I've had everyone from U2 to Usher in my studio, laying down tracks, writing songs.

Making music.

The music feeds my soul and has since I was nine and got my first guitar for Christmas. It's a magic I haven't been able to duplicate or replace with anything else. And for a little while, when I thought I'd abandon music altogether, it felt like I was living in purgatory.

A necessary purgatory, but fuck, how it hurt.

I park and jog around back, bypassing the house altogether, and am not surprised to find Max already at work when I walk into the studio.

"You're late," he mutters, then bites his pencil and tickles the keys of the baby grand in the corner that looks out over the pool.

"I got a job," I announce and lean on the piano, reading the music lying in front of Max.

"Who's coming now? I thought Maroon 5 had to postpone, since Adam has to tape the auditions for his show."

"No, a regular gig job."

His head jerks up, and for just a moment, there is so much hope in his eyes, it makes my chest hurt. "You got the band a gig?"

"No." I shake my head and stare at the top of the piano. "There's a new restaurant in town that needs a weekend musician. I'm going to do it."

Max doesn't say anything for a long moment. "Who are you?"

"I was thinking it might be fun for you to come with me sometimes. We can perform some acoustic versions of some of the old songs. Show off our harmonies."

"Are you sick? Should I call an ambulance?"

"Fuck you," I reply and turn to walk away. I don't need his shit. I should probably call Addie and tell her I've changed my mind. This is a ridiculous idea.

"Jake," he says. "Talk to me. You hate to perform."

"No, I just *can't* perform the way we did," I reply and turn around, hands in my pockets. "It almost destroyed my life once. And I'm sorry that when I lost it, so did you."

"I didn't have to," he replies matter-of-factly. "I've been offered other lead guitar gigs in other bands. You know that. I don't want to do it without you."

"Let's not talk about our feelings. We're dudes."

"Tell me about this gig. What made you decide to look into it?"

"Christina told me about it and asked me to." I drop into a leather couch and sigh, my head leaned back on the cushion, and stare at the ceiling. "I love producing and writing with you. I don't miss touring. I don't miss the booze or the girls. We still have the same friends, and we still make music, so I have nothing to complain about."

"What *do* you miss?" Max asks.

I chew my lip, and immediately remember Addie doing the same, and wonder what it would be like to feel her full lips under mine. To feel her full *everything* beneath me.

"I miss singing." I glance over at Max and see him nod. "I miss watching the crowd sing along with our songs. I miss the feeling I get when I'm singing so hard and long that my lungs are screaming and my throat feels raw, but I don't even care because it's just the music that matters."

"I know."

"And when I did the open-mic thing last weekend, it just hammered home how much I really do miss it."

"I know."

"So, for a couple hours a week, I want to sit in a room of people and strum my guitar and sing."

"I think that's awesome." He grins. "And I can't wait to show off our harmonies. Because we kick fucking ass."

"Of course we do." I sober and link my fingers behind my head. "So, tell me straight. You don't think it's a bad idea?"

"I think it might be the best thing you've done for yourself since you quit the band."

I nod thoughtfully, but then shake my head no. "This studio is the best thing I've done."

"It's a great thing, and it's making us a shit-ton of money, and we love it, but I think the music, singing, is going to heal you. And I don't think you've done that quite yet."

"Have you?"

"I was never broken, friend. That was your journey. And it makes me fucking happy as hell to see you in this place, because I haven't seen it in a long time, and I've missed it."

"Feelings. No feelings."

"Yeah, yeah. If you've finished being lazy, you can help me with this song. I can't figure out the second verse."

I stand and return to the piano, feeling better after hashing the Seduction gig over with Max. He's right. I need it.

"We talked about the second verse building in intensity, and then falling abruptly at the end. That'll make the chorus that much more powerful, remember?"

"That's right," he says and swears under his breath as he erases what he wrote earlier. "You think you're so damn smart."

I smirk. I'm not smart, or special. I just know music.

Chapter Three

Addison

"This asparagus wasn't grilled long enough," Mia announces and wrinkles her cute nose. Since she's not in the kitchen tonight, her long, dark hair is loose around her shoulders and down her back in long, natural curls. Her makeup is done and her curvy body is rocking in a fun little outfit. Riley grabs Mia's hand and shakes her head.

"You're not going in the kitchen tonight," she says with authority, making the rest of us smile. "We're having fun."

"I know," Mia replies and takes a deep breath. "I'm holding myself back. But I'll be having another meeting with my chefs on Monday. I wish I could work every day, all day."

"You'd kill yourself, and we won't allow that," Cami says and takes a bite from her plate. "Does anyone else find it ironic that we're all sitting here, eating aphrodisiacs, and not one of us is getting laid tonight?"

We're sitting at the table right in front of the stage, eating dinner, waiting for Jake to show up. When the rest of the girls found out that I'd hired Jake to be the weekend entertainment, you'd have thought we were fifteen again. So of course we're all here, front and center, for his opening night.

And we're all dressed to the nines.

Because I hired Jake freaking Knox.

I mean, Jake Keller.

"Two girls got very lucky last night," I reply, the words still bitter in my mouth.

"Okay, I didn't hear the story yet," Kat says and sips her wine.

"Yes, tell it again," Mia says. "And then I'll add the part where I'm going to rip Jeremy's balls out."

"It's just the typical story," I begin. "I went home early last night, and walked into the house to find him fucking two girls in my living room."

Riley's eyes narrow. "I never liked him."

"What did you do?" Cami asks and adjusts her silver, shimmery tank top.

"Well, by the time they finally noticed me standing there, I'd had time to go from shock to sadness to blinding rage, so I just smiled politely—"

"Uh-oh, that's never a good sign," Cami mutters.

"And I told them all to get the fuck out of my house."

"And Jeremy?" Kat asks.

"Jeremy tried to make excuses, but I just stared at him, impassively—"

"Another bad sign," Mia adds.

"And told him that I never wanted to see his disgusting, small-dicked, cheating face again. And he left."

Of course, I don't mention that I curled up into a ball on my bed and cried for a few hours, and questioned myself and why men seem to think it's okay to walk all over me like a doormat.

Because no one will ever see that side of me.

"My man picker is broken," I announce and take a big bite of roasted grape and brie crostini with honey and sea salt and immediately—and silently—praise Mia's culinary genius. "Which is fine, because I'm done with men."

"It's not broken, it's off-kilter," Riley says with a smile. "Maybe you need a break from men for a while. You didn't take much time after the split with Craig before Jeremy got his meat hooks into you."

I frown, surprised that the ache that used to come when someone mentioned Craig's name isn't there anymore.

"I still want to punch Craig," Kat mutters into her glass. "I was pulling for him."

"Another musician," Riley says with a shrug. "Granted, one that we all thought was a descent human being, and was with you for the better part of eight years, but still. A musician."

"It was never going to work out with Craig," I reply with a sigh. "Even though we both tried for a long time. Longer than we should have. I'm needy. I want to be with a man on a regular basis, not just hear their voice over the phone, and he was always touring."

"You'll find a non-musician, non–bad boy," Mia says with confidence.

"Yes, for the love of all that's holy, stop dating the bad boys," Cami adds. "Although, with the outfit you're wearing, you'll attract every boy—bad or otherwise—in a ten-mile radius."

I glance down at my black skinny jeans, red camisole, and black leather vest, then back at Cami. "What's wrong with my outfit?"

"Not one thing," Kat replies with a grin. "And those red heels are to die for. Not to mention the red streaks in your hair."

"You never look the same two days in a row," Riley says. "I love it."

I shrug. "The way I look doesn't seem to have anything to do with men being faithful to me."

"That's because you pick idiots." Mia takes another bite of asparagus and frowns at her fork.

"I know what you need," Riley announces. "You need a sexcation man."

I swallow the wine in my mouth and frown at my friend. "A what?"

"You need to find a guy that you can just call up like once a month and go see him—"

"But he doesn't live here," Cami adds, surprising the hell out of me. "You have to travel to see him."

"Right, because you don't need him to be hanging around, mooching off of you, or generally just annoying the hell out of you," Kat says with a nod.

"Exactly," Riley says and grins. "So, he lives in like Seattle or maybe San Francisco, 'cause that's just a short flight. And you go see him for a couple days, have a lot of crazy sex, then come home and get back to your life. Everyone's happy. No strings."

I feel like I'm watching some sort of sports game as I look from friend to friend, trying to follow this crazy conversation.

And it's even crazier because I kind of like this idea.

"But he can't be a musician," Mia adds.

"No way," I reply, getting into the spirit. "Been there, regretted that. But he has to have a good job. A really good job. And he's really smart."

"And knows his way around the bedroom," Kat says.

"Or kitchen," Cami says with a smirk.

"Or bathroom. Water play is fun," Mia adds.

"Or balcony," Riley says, raising her glass in salute.

I can't stop laughing. Oh my God, these girls are so funny.

"This is why we're friends," I say, wiping a tear from the corner of my eye. "Also, he has to have awesome abs. Like, abs for *days*. And maybe blond hair. Blue eyes. Green? No, blue."

I'm babbling now, and the girls are all smiling, but just watching me, letting me ramble.

"I like tattoos, but they're not a deal breaker. He has to be tall. Taller than me for sure. And he can do this thing with his—"

I glance up and notice Cami look over my shoulder and smile wider and I stop midsentence.

"Oh God. Who's behind me?"

"Hi, Jake," Mia says and wiggles her fingers in a wave.

I drop my chin to my chest and mutter, "Fuck me."

Suddenly, warm lips are next to my ear, and Jake whispers, "Yes, I think that's what would be involved in this sexcation thing."

Kat snorts and I do my best to pull my dignity around me, along with my big-girl panties, and clear my throat.

"Hello, Jake." I stand and gesture to the girls around the table. "You remember Kat from the other day."

Kat waves hello.

"This is Mia, our master chef." Mia smiles.

"Cami is our CPA, and Riley is in charge of marketing and publicity. And the five of us are all co-owners of Seduction."

"It's a pleasure to meet all of you. You're an intimidating bunch, aren't you?"

"What do you mean?" Riley asks.

"Gorgeous, intelligent, powerful." Jake shrugs. "Pretty amazing."

"I like him," Kat says. "He can stay."

Jake winks at her, and I turn to lead him away. He's charming. And looks better than anyone should in his torn jeans and simple gray T-shirt. The tattoos on his arms are just . . . *God.* And his body is firm.

Get a grip, Addison!

"This is a pretty simple setup," I begin, glancing over my shoulder to make sure he's following me, and catch him eyeing my ass. "Don't look at my ass."

"No, ma'am," he replies with a cocky grin.

That smile makes a whole zoo take up residence in my stomach. The first time he smiled at me the other day, my immediate thought was *Oh shit.*

Because he could bring me to my knees with that smile.

No way.

"I'm taller than you, you know. And I have tats. I know that wasn't a deal breaker, but it's a bonus."

I shake my head.

"I have brown hair, but I could lighten it. And I think you settled on blue eyes, but I heard green mentioned, and . . . bingo." He bats his eyes at me and before I know what's happening, he lifts the hem of his shirt.

Oh, sweet Jesus.

"And I'm not one to brag, but, abs."

"The mic and stool are here as you requested." I turn away, doing my best to calm down my breathing and ignore him. "You are welcome to drink whatever you like as you play. Just let the server know what you want and she'll make sure you have it all night."

He nods and toes off his shoes, making me frown.

"I always sing barefoot," he says. "It's been a habit since the early days."

"Why?"

"I have no idea." He laughs and shakes his head. "I guess it's just comfortable."

And your feet are sexy.

Figures.

"I can't believe you're really doing this!" A brunette

launches herself into Jake's arms and holds on tight. She's gorgeous, tall, and clearly very attached to Jake. He grins widely and wraps his arms around her tenderly.

"I told you I would."

"I know. It's just so great. I'm so proud of you."

Someone should tell this poor girl that her boyfriend was just hitting on someone else. Typical.

Motherfucking typical.

What in the hell is wrong with men?

Jake sets the woman aside and offers his hand to shake to a man I didn't see come up behind us. "Hey, man," Jake says. "Thanks for coming."

"Like we'd miss it," the tall, handsome man replies and pulls Jake to him for the man-hug thing that I'll never quite understand.

Just like the cheating thing and the mooching thing and the leaving-the-toilet-seat-up thing.

It's all a bloody mystery to me.

"We are so rude!" The woman smiles politely at me. "I'm Christina, and this is my husband, Kevin."

"Christina has been my best friend since high school," Jake adds with a grin. "I'm stuck with her."

"He is," she nods happily.

"I'm Addison, part owner here. Welcome." I smile warmly and move to walk away, but Christina snatches my hand.

"Will you sit with us for a few minutes? I would love to chat with you."

"Of course," I reply immediately, and silently curse myself. I'm too conditioned to giving the customer anything they want. But Christina smiles widely and then hugs Jake once more.

"Break a leg, J."

Kevin leads us to a table in the center of the room. When my waitress arrives, I tell her to bring anything these two want, on the house, for the whole evening.

"You don't have to do that," Kevin says after the server leaves.

"My pleasure." I smooth the tablecloth with my hand and glance over at Jake as he pulls his guitar out of its case and strums it, making sure it's in tune. He talks to his waitress, then settles on the stool, adjusts the mic, and strums the guitar again.

"Good evening," he begins and smiles at the crowd. But this smile is different than the one he aimed at me earlier. It's detached. Professional.

He has his game face on.

Fascinating.

"This is my first night here at Seduction. I'm Jake Keller." He aims a look at Christina, who offers him a thumbs-up and an encouraging smile. "Be gentle."

The audience laughs, and suddenly there is whispering and commotion. "Aren't you Jake Knox?" someone calls out from the crowd.

Jake's smile never falters. "I used to be. But tonight, I'm just some guy with a guitar."

And with that he breaks into a fast-tempo cover song. His voice is smooth as caramel, with just a little rasp at the right spot.

It's sex.

"What's up?" I ask Christina.

"I just wanted to say thank you for giving Jake this job. It may seem like a little thing, but it's important to him." She watches him with love-filled eyes. "It's important to me."

Kevin takes his wife's hand and kisses it tenderly.

"I was shocked when he walked in here the other day," I admit.

"I bet," she says with a laugh. "You'd never know he's nervous, would you?"

I turn my gaze to Jake and watch him play with confidence, his fingers moving effortlessly over the guitar, as though it's simply part of him. The notes coming from his mouth are perfect and smooth.

"No," I reply.

"He's terrified," she replies seriously. "He hasn't performed in front of people in five years."

"I saw him the other night." I frown at Christina. "He sang at an open-mic night. I was looking for talent to fill the position."

"He sang one song," Christina says with a nod. "And that was the first time, which made him crave it again, I think. Although he won't admit it."

"Didn't I hear that he still writes and produces?"

"Yes, but singing for a room of four of his friends is very different from this," she says. "So, thanks."

"My pleasure." My eyes scan the room, happy to see the customers enjoying their food, singing along with Jake, smiling at him. "He's made my customers very happy."

"And he'll continue to do so," Kevin says, earning a kiss on the cheek from Christina.

"How did you two meet?"

"I had an accident a few years ago and needed physical therapy," Christina replies.

"And I was her therapist," Kevin finishes for her.

I grin. "That's pretty awesome. And romantic."

"We think so too."

Just then Jake switches to a slower song. My favorite song. It's currently sitting on the charts, and every time I hear it, my heart simply weeps.

Because it's all about everything that I'm convinced I'll never have.

Jake holds my gaze as he sings the song, never looking away, and I can't tear my eyes away from his either. Christina is talking next to me, but I don't hear her.

It's only him.

When he gets to the chorus, asking me to love him like I do, I blink and look down, then make myself stand, excuse myself and hurry to the bathroom, lock the door, and lean my hands on the countertop, staring at myself in the mirror.

What the fuck is wrong with me?

At least my makeup is holding up. Smoky eyes stare back at me. I watch my glossy lips as I begin my pep talk.

"You are not attracted to musicians. You are going to find a CPA, or a real estate agent or a lawyer, with no tattoos. He will be devoted to *you*. He does not have women throwing themselves at him. He's a good guy. Sure, he has a great smile because I have a thing about teeth, but he's not a cheater. And he doesn't lie. And he will be proud of you and you will be his priority.

"Granted, he might be a little boring, but boring is *good*. He's not a manipulator, and he would kill himself before he would ever hurt you."

I stand straight and smooth my hands down my leather vest and over my skinny jeans at my hips, then jab my finger at my reflection.

"Jake is not hot. You're not interested. Get over it."

I give myself the stink eye before marching out of the bathroom, with my new armor intact.

SEDUCTION IS PRETTY much empty now. Jake's set went amazingly well, and if he's willing, we'll keep him on as the weekend performer for as long as he wants it.

I can hear some movement in the kitchen, most likely the chef prepping for tomorrow. The last of the servers just left, with wide smiles on their faces thanks to tonight's heavy tippers. Cami, Riley, and Mia left right after Jake finished, and Kat just walked out the door.

"Buy you a drink?"

I spin, surprised to see that Jake is still here.

"I told you no before. Are you senile?"

"It's just a drink, Addie. I suspect you've had a long day."

I shrug. "I won't deny that. Okay, I'll join you." *What the fuck, Addison?* This is so not professional! I mentally shake my head, resigned to being an idiot who can't seem to say no.

I lead him into the bar and walk behind it to pour us

each a drink. "What have you been drinking tonight? Jack and Coke?"

"Just the Coke," he replies. "I don't need the Jack."

I pour his drink, surprised to hear that he didn't drink any alcohol while he played, but I don't ask him about it. I pour myself a glass of wine, and reach over the bar to clink glasses with him.

"To your first night."

"Cheers." His eyes smile at me over the rim of his glass as he takes a sip of his drink. "Come sit with me. Get off those killer heels."

"I'm used to the heels," I reply as I circle around the bar and settle into a stool next to him. "But I've been on them all day."

"You worked all day, and stayed tonight too?"

"Of course. It was your first night."

"My audition," he says with a nod. "I don't think I've ever auditioned for anything."

"Well, you passed. You're welcome to play here for as long as you like."

His amazing green eyes warm as he smiles at me. "Thank you. I like it. It's an intimate crowd, and the room has great acoustics. I'd like to bring Max with me sometimes so we can play some of the old songs, sing some harmonies, if that's okay."

If that's okay?

Duh.

"Sounds fine to me." I taste my wine.

It's quiet in here now, and the silence is too loud. He's staring down at his drink, his eyes a deep green in the low light of the bar. A crease forms between his eyebrows in a frown, and then he shakes his head, just a tiny bit. Jake sips his drink, and I can't help but wonder what he's thinking.

And I'm a woman, so I ask.

Because who ever heeded the whole *don't ask the question if you don't want the answer* warning?

"What are you thinking?" I ask softly.

He chuckles and shakes his head.

"You don't want to know."

"I asked."

He swivels in the stool, facing me, and rests his hand on the arm of my own stool, leaning into me, and it takes everything in me not to back away. His eyes lower to my lips.

I lick them, and watch his eyes dilate.

This is a very bad idea.

I swallow hard as he continues to watch my mouth.

"It's quiet in here," he says evenly.

"I was thinking the same."

"Are you comfortable in the quiet, Addie?"

I frown and feel my nipples pucker when he reaches up and tucks my hair behind my ear. His fingers are warm.

And when he's this close, I can't help but breathe him in and enjoy the scent of him.

"Why shouldn't I be?"

"Some aren't. Some need chaos, noise. The quiet makes them nervous."

You make me nervous.

I lick my lips again.

"I don't mind quiet. You?"

"I love the quiet."

I smirk. "You're a musician."

"And I love music too. But the quiet is where the truth lives."

I blink once, twice.

"Where the truth lives?" I'm whispering now.

He simply nods. "There's no distraction. No way to deny what is. It's honest."

"And you claim to be honest?"

"To a fault," he confirms. "I'd also love to hear more about this sexcation you're scheming."

I feel my cheeks flush and turn away, taking another sip of my wine.

"I was simply being silly with my friends, Jake. Drop it."

He doesn't answer. Damn the fucking quiet.

I risk a peek at him, only to find him still watching me, lust heavy in his eyes. "Why are you staring at me?"

"I'm not staring. But you're fucking gorgeous when you blush and I can't help but wonder how far down that blush goes."

My jaw drops, then I quickly close it again.

"I guess you *are* honest."

He smiles, that damn cocky smile, and I'm just . . . *mad.*

"Guilty."

"And too charming for your own good."

"Charming isn't a bad thing."

I laugh, but not in an *oh, you're so funny* way, and his face sobers.

"Do you really think you're getting in my pants with this? Buy me a drink, say sexy things, use the impossible-to-say-no-to body language?"

"It's just a drink and conversation, Addie."

"Right. I don't buy it. I've been down this road before with men like you, Jake, on a motorcycle with no helmet going way too fast, and all that it leads to is a fiery crash."

"Look—"

"No, *you* look." I slide off the stool and pace away, too much energy flowing through my body. Too much frustration. My heels echo in the silent room. "I've dated a dozen of you, and you're all the same."

"No. We're not." I turn to find his jaw clenched and eyes narrowed.

"Oh, really? Are you telling me that you haven't been with countless women?" I cross my arms, cock my hip to the side, and watch him clench his hands into fists.

But he doesn't deny it.

"Are you going to deny ever having some poor girl think she means something to you, but all the while you were with someone else in the same night?"

He swallows hard and stands, but still doesn't say anything.

"Don't try to tell me that you're not a man-whore, Jake, because I *know* differently. I've dated the bad boy my whole life. And I've read the tabloids. I know your past." His face transforms for just a split second into pure pain, then it's gone and all that's left is . . . nothing.

After what feels like ten minutes of silence, he simply nods and says, "Well, I guess you just have it all figured out, don't you?" He looks me up and down, then turns and walks out of the bar.

Not two seconds later, Mia comes out of the kitchen, surprising me.

"What are you still doing here?"

"He didn't deserve that, Addie."

I blink rapidly and march behind the bar to pour myself another glass of wine.

"They're all the same, Mia, and it was insulting to both of us for him to deny it. I'm sick of being lied to. I'm sick of being hit on by men who only want to get up my skirt, but don't give a flying fuck about my feelings."

"He was being nice to you."

"Of course he was."

"Addie, Jake isn't the one you walked in on last night fucking two other women."

My gaze whips over to hers and I frown. "I wasn't taking that out on Jake."

"Bullshit."

Tears gather in my eyes and I turn away, embarrassed, and not a little ashamed because Mia's right; he didn't deserve it.

"I'm a bitch."

"You're not a bitch, you're hurt, and you don't want to be attracted to him."

"I'm not attracted to him."

Mia smirks and shakes her head. "Okay."

"Fine, I'm attracted to him, but I'm trying really hard not to be."

"Not every person is the same, Addie."

"I just deserve so much more, Mia. I don't understand what it is about me that screams, *Fuck me over. Hurt me. I like it.*"

The tears want to flow, but I swallow and hold them back.

"Your luck with men has just been shitty," she says. "I guess you could say that about all of us."

"Boy, you're not kidding."

Suddenly we hear the front door open and close.

"We're alone," Mia says soothingly. "It's okay to cry, you know."

"No it's not. It doesn't accomplish anything."

"Oh, Addie. You don't have to be strong all the time. It's just you and me. You can be vulnerable for five minutes and let it out. I won't tell."

She puts her arm around my shoulders, and I cave. I lean my head on her shoulder and cry, thankful that I have someone, four someones really, that I can be weak with. Because God knows I learned long ago that showing anyone else weakness will only get your heart torn out and shredded.

And I'm never going down that road again, on a motorcycle or otherwise.

Chapter Four

Jake

$\mathcal{I}$t's been a month since I started playing at Seduction on the weekends. These gigs have been more fun for me than any other I've performed, and I've played at all the major awards shows, celebrity weddings, and the biggest arenas in the world.

Yet, sitting on this stool with my guitar, playing new and old songs for a room full of maybe a hundred people fulfills me more than any of those other performances did. Because this is on *my* terms. It's just me and the music, in its most raw form, and I crave it more strongly than I ever thought I did.

It's addicting.

"Ashley, you can go after you finish wrapping that silverware," Addie says to her lead server, who's currently counting out her tips.

Speaking of craving.

Addison is one hell of a woman. Yes, she's gorgeous on the outside. Tall and blond with curves in all the right places, she makes everything male in me stand up and take notice. But she's so fucking smart too. She has this place running like a well-oiled machine. Her staff respects and likes her, and the customers are always her priority. It's not a hardship in the least to watch her mingle from table to table as I sing, catching her gaze once in a while.

Watching her lips twitch into a reluctant smile before she turns and walks away, always makes my heart beat just a little faster.

And I never know how she's going to look when I get here each night. She changes her style more than most people change underwear, and she looks amazing every time. Whether she looks classic or edgy, or anywhere in between, it's always a surprise.

The best damn surprise I've had in years.

Now the place is quiet. The staff is wrapping things up for the night as I fiddle with my guitar, adjusting the tuning.

If I'm honest, the guitar was already perfectly tuned. I just want to watch Addie move about the room.

And that's fucking pathetic. She doesn't want to have anything to do with me. She's made it clear, which pisses me off and amuses me at the same time.

I've never been good at taking no for an answer.

And I can't help but wonder if that's what this attraction is all about: the challenge.

"Can we discuss my schedule?" Ashley asks. "I have a

family dinner for my dad's birthday next weekend. I'd like to switch with someone, if that's okay."

"Sure," Addie replies, then frowns in thought. "Shit, I left my iPad in the car. I'll be right back."

"I'll meet you in the bar," Ashley says.

Good idea.

I don't drink much, not anymore, but I could use one now.

"Great set tonight, Jake," Kat says from behind the bar. Her lips are deep red, almost matching her hair. She's in a ripped AC/DC tank top tonight and tight jeans, showing off her ink.

"Thanks," I reply with a smile.

"What can I get you? Your usual?"

"I have a usual?" I ask with a raised brow, keeping an eye on the back door that leads to the alley. Where is she? It seems to be taking her too long to grab her iPad, but then again, I'm probably being ridiculous.

"Coke." Kat chuckles. "I'm a bartender, Jake. That's my job."

"You're more than that," I reply seriously. "You run this place very well."

"I know." Her smile is confident, inspiring more respect from me. These women are all fucking amazing. "I have a thing for booze."

"You sound like a wino," Mia says as she comes out of the kitchen and takes a stool next to me. "She's not really."

"Being good at alcohol doesn't make anyone an alcoholic," I reply, starting to worry about Addie. "It's an art form."

"I like you," Kat says and blows me a kiss.

"Where's Addie?" Mia asks. "Did you send her screaming into the night?"

"That's not how women usually react to me, no." Kat slides a drink over to me and I sip it.

"She ran out to her car to grab her iPad," Ashley says as she scrolls through her phone.

"It's been a while. I'm going to go check on her."

"I really like him," Kat says as I walk through the kitchen and out the back door. I stop and listen, not sure where Addie parked.

"You are a worthless piece of shit," someone yells, and I immediately run in that direction. I turn a corner and see red.

A man, not much taller than Addie, has her back pinned against her car, and his hand is wrapped around her thin neck. Her eyes are wide with fear as she pushes on his chest, but she can't budge him.

He pulls his other hand back, fist clenched, when I reach them and yank him off her.

"What the fuck?" he yells, then doesn't say anything when my fist connects with his jaw.

"Jake!" Addie's voice is rough, and I barely feel her hand on my arm as I stand over the piece of shit that had his hands on her. "Jake, stop."

"Stay behind me."

"Who is this asshole?" the fucker yells from the ground, wiping blood from the corner of his mouth. "Are you fucking him too?"

"Shut the fuck up." My voice is steel. "I suggest you leave, right now, before I call the cops."

"What for? We were just talking." He staggers to his feet and looks up at me. He's clearly drunk. Probably high.

"You were assaulting her."

"This is none of your business."

"Just leave, Jeremy," Addie says from behind me. Her voice is firm, but she's still holding on to my arm, and her hand is shaking, pissing me off more.

Something tells me that it takes a lot to scare this woman.

"You heard her."

Jeremy glares at me, then spits and turns away, stumbling out of the alley. When he's gone, I spin and pull her into my arms, holding her tight against me. She's trembling, but she's not crying.

"Are you okay?"

"I'm fine."

"Who was that asshole?"

"An ex," she mutters. "No one important."

Important enough to come looking for her. But I keep that thought to myself. "Do you want me to call the cops?"

"No. He didn't hit me."

"I'm going to hold you for a minute."

"Good plan." She's clinging to me, her fingertips gripping my back, her face pressed to my chest. She fits. There's no other way to describe it. I wrap my arms around her firmly and lean my face down and bury my nose in her hair, breathing her in. She smells like peaches. She's beautiful tonight in a black blouse that falls off one shoulder and a tight, red skirt.

Finally, she pushes away from me and swallows. "Thanks

for that. I haven't seen Jeremy since I threw him out of my apartment more than a month ago. I don't know what he was doing here tonight."

"So he doesn't threaten you on a regular basis?"

"No." She straightens her shoulders and lifts her chin. *Good girl.*

"Okay. Let's get you home."

"What?" She frowns. "Why?"

"Because you were just attacked in the alley, Addie."

"I have work to finish." She reaches into her car to re-trieve her iPad and walks toward the restaurant. "I can't go home."

And the stubborn woman is back.

I follow her in, watching her like a hawk. She marches right over to Ashley, firing up her tablet, but her fingers are a bit shaky.

I should scoop her up and take her home, but she wouldn't let me get three steps away without giving me what-for.

She's so freaking hot.

"What's going on?" Kat asks, watching both of us.

"Addie—" I begin, but Addie cuts me off with a glare.

"Nothing." She turns to Ashley and the two proceed to discuss the schedule for next weekend.

"What's up?" Mia asks. "Is everything okay?"

"Jeremy was in the alley," Addie admits, not looking anyone in the eyes. "He was being a drunk idiot, and Jake scared him off."

She's purposefully leaving out the part where he was about to beat the shit out of her.

But, none of my business.

I simply shrug and down my drink, then push the glass over to Kat, gesturing for another.

"Thanks so much," Ashley says with a smile and then heads out, leaving the four of us alone.

"You gonna tell us what happened?" Kat asks Addie, who has yet to look up from her iPad.

"What happened with what?" Addie replies.

"God, she's stubborn," Mia mutters, then lets her long, dark hair down. She scratches her scalp and sighs in ecstasy. "That feels better."

"You have beautiful hair," I say. I'm usually attracted to brunettes, and Mia is a very pretty woman. She's also curvy, a little curvier than Addie, and much shorter, with long, dark hair and gorgeous dark eyes. The smile that tickles her lips is one of pure female satisfaction.

"Thank you."

"If you're done flirting with the owners, you can leave," Addie says. I glance up to find her scowling at me, which only makes me smirk.

"I'm leaving when you leave, beautiful."

"He *is* flirty," Kat says to Mia, as if I'm not sitting right here.

"I am not."

"Okay, *beautiful*," Kat replies with a smug smile.

"Well, I'm leaving now," Addie says and flips her iPad closed, then marches off to the office to collect her things.

"Is she okay?" Mia asks. "Honestly."

"She is now."

Kat and Mia both glare at me, but before they can say anything else, Addie returns.

"You don't have to walk me out."

"Hmm." I lift my guitar and don't comment further as Addie leads me out the back, into the alley, toward her car.

I just happen to be parked next to her.

Wordlessly, she slips into her late-model Jetta, just as I lower myself into my Mustang. I pull out behind her and we drive through downtown, which is still very active on a Saturday night, and through the hills of west Portland, to a nice, gated community of apartments. I follow her through the gate, and once she pulls into her garage, I park behind her and get out of the car.

"Why are you following me?"

"I wanted to make sure that asshole didn't follow you," I reply, my fingers itching to tuck a stray piece of her hair behind her ear. "And I want to make sure you're okay."

"I'm fine."

"You need to tell the others that he assaulted you."

She doesn't even try to pretend that she doesn't understand. "They don't need to worry."

"They need to know, in case that asshole comes to the restaurant." She frowns and looks down, but I'm a persistent asshole. "Addie."

"Fine, I'll tell them. But you're being silly. I'm fine."

But she swallows hard and her eyes still look scared.

"Invite me in."

"Excuse me?" She crosses her arms, facing off with me in the middle of her garage. And now I can't stand it anymore.

I step forward and gently tuck the hair behind her ear, then drag my fingertip down her neck to her bare shoulder.

"You have sexy shoulders."

"I can't have you here."

My gaze finds her ice-blue one. "Do you have a curfew?"

She doesn't smile. "I think I'm going to fall apart, and I can't have you see that."

"Ah, baby."

"I don't want you to see me fall apart."

"Okay." I sigh. "But I need to make sure you get inside okay, and I need to get you settled."

And I don't even understand *why*. Why the need to comfort and protect her is so damn strong. I've never felt this way about anyone besides Christina before, and even that isn't this strong.

But I can't stop it.

"I don't need anyone to take care of me."

"Just humor me."

She rolls her eyes and turns away, slaps the button to lower the garage door, then leads me inside and up the stairs to the apartment. The rooms are big, open. New. And the furniture is trendy, yet comfortable.

Addie drops her purse and keys on her dining room table, then turns to me. "Okay. I'm in safely."

I step to her, unable to turn away and walk back out of here, and wrap her in my arms, the same way I did in the alley, rocking her back and forth.

"Scared me," I whisper.

"What did?"

"Seeing him with his hand wrapped around your neck." *The thought of him hurting you. The thought of losing you, and you're not even mine.*

"I didn't enjoy it either."

I smile softly, my lips brushing back and forth over her hair. God, she smells like heaven, and having her sexier-than-fuck body pressed to me feels like pure sin.

The best kind of sin.

"Are you sure you don't want me to call the cops?"

"I'm sure."

"Go change," I whisper and pull back. "Get comfortable."

She sighs, watching me, then turns and walks to what I assume is her bedroom, her heels clicking on her hardwood floors. When she shuts the door, I turn back to the room. The walls and trim are white. The kitchen cabinets are white as well, with black granite countertops. The windows are wide, and I bet she has a beautiful view during the day.

I'm drawn to the mantel over the fireplace and examine the photos on display. There are shots of all of the owners of Seduction, at different ages. It looks like Addie knew Mia and Cami when they were young, and as they got older, Riley and Kat are added to the photos.

Next to the fireplace is a bookcase, filled with books from floor to ceiling. She has cookbooks, novels, biographies . . . *everything*. But one book, with nothing written on the spine, catches my eye.

It's a big book, the kind most people keep on their coffee table. And when I open it, I'm floored to find it full of photos of Addie.

Addison was a model.

There are runway shots, fashion shots, swimsuit shots. Smiling, flirty, serious. Jesus, she's beautiful. And so painfully young in these photos. She was a bit slimmer then, but still had her curves.

"What are you doing?"

I turn slowly and smile over at her. "I thought I recognized your face."

Her eyes drop to the book in my hands, then whip up to mine. "That's private."

My heart stills as I look her over, from head to toe. She's in an old white T-shirt and men's boxer shorts. Her long hair is piled on top of her head in a knot. And her face is completely clean of makeup.

I've never seen her look more beautiful, and I've seen her in a dozen different looks. But this, right here, is *Addie*, and she's so stunning, she takes my breath away.

"Are you going to speak, or are you just going to stare at me?"

"You're so fucking incredible."

She stumbles, blinking rapidly. "Excuse me?"

"You're beautiful."

"Why are you being nice to me?" she asks, bewildered. "I've been horrible to you."

I close the book and return it to the shelf, then cross to her, take her hand, and lead her to the overstuffed couch. I sit and guide her next to me.

I want to pull her into my lap, but I'm not so sure she'd allow that.

She pulls her legs up and leans her cheek against my shoulder, holding on to my bicep with her hands.

"I can take it," I whisper and resist the urge to kiss the top of her head. "You were perfectly professional."

"I'm cold."

"You were hurt."

She snorts.

"And you like me, and that scares you."

She immediately pushes away, shaking her head. "You wish."

I smile and tug her into my lap now, holding her to me. Her lips are turned up, but her blue eyes are cautious, just as they should be.

But I'm not going to talk my way into her bed. Not tonight. Tonight she needs a friend, and she needs to be held.

I would never admit it, but after seeing her in danger earlier tonight, maybe so do I.

"Admit it, you like me."

"I like it when you leave." She smiles widely and bats her eyelashes.

"You're a smart-ass."

"Absolutely."

"Good."

"Good?" She leans her cheek on my chest and traces imaginary circles on my shirt. "It usually pisses people off."

"I'm a smart-ass too, so I speak the language."

"I like that you're tall."

"Why?"

"Because I'm tall."

And you fit.

"Tell me about the modeling."

"I don't do it anymore."

"You're kidding." My voice is dry as I drag my hand down her back, over her soft shirt, to her ass, then up again. "Care to elaborate on that?"

She sighs. "Girls with curves don't last too long in that industry. I was a size eight, which is way too big to be a runway model."

"Bullshit."

"No, it's true."

"I know it's true, I just think it's bullshit."

She shrugs. "It is what it is. I'm bigger than that now, so those days are long behind me. But I love fashion. I love playing with different looks. I always have."

"I've noticed. It's sexy as hell."

"It's fun."

"Who gave you the book?"

"It was a gift from my stylist, Cici. We met early on, and I took her everywhere with me. She's the best hair and makeup person out there. She still does my hair. All five of us, actually."

"She lives here in Portland?"

"Yeah. She moved here with her husband and kids a few years ago. We do a girls' night once a month and get our hair done, waxed, nails, the whole enchilada."

"That sounds . . . terrifying," I reply with a laugh, but

can't help but wonder what, exactly, she has waxed. The thought has my dick twitching, so I take a deep breath and think about puppies and baseball, because NO SEX.

"Well, then it's a good thing you aren't invited to join us."

"Do you miss it?"

She shrugs again, still brushing her manicured fingertip over my chest. If she doesn't stop touching me like that, I won't be responsible for my actions.

Like bending her over the back of the couch.

Jesus, get a grip, Keller.

"I miss the clothes. God, the clothes were so fucking fun. And I miss the hair and makeup too."

"You do that for yourself every day."

"It's not the same," she replies, almost sadly. "I miss the people. Some of the designers and photographers. But I don't miss being told that I'm fat."

"You're *not* fat."

"In that world I was. I'm a curvy woman, that's just how my body is made, and I can't change it."

"Nor should you."

"When you're young, it can really mess with your head. I'm so thankful that I had the experience, and I still have friendships from that life, but I'm fine with it being over."

God, I can relate to that.

"Why did the band break up?" she asks softly.

"Because I'm a jackass."

She pulls back so she can look up at me. "The bandmates don't like you either?"

"*Either?*"

"Like me."

"Oh, you like me."

She simply raises a brow, making me laugh. "Of course they like me."

"So tell me about your jackassery."

"This is a story better suited for another time. First, I want you to talk to me about Jeremy."

"You know everything."

She buries her face in my chest again, hiding.

"Does he have a key to your apartment?"

"I'll have the locks changed tomorrow."

"Why didn't you do that already?"

"I didn't think he'd do anything. He was gone."

I'm not leaving here tonight.

"Have the gate code changed too."

"I will." She's quiet for a long moment. "He was going to hit me."

My gut clenches all over again and I wish he were here so I could beat the fuck out of him. "No, he wasn't. I wouldn't have let him."

"If you hadn't been there, he would have. I wasn't the one who cheated on him. I didn't do anything wrong, but he was going to hit me."

"He doesn't matter," I whisper, and kiss her head as I lift her into my arms and walk to her bedroom. I toe off my shoes, pull the covers back, and lay her on the bed, then with all of my clothes still on, I climb in after her.

"What are you doing?" *Excellent question, sweetheart.* I believe this is called comforting without the expectation of sex afterward.

And it's a completely new experience for me.

"Curing cancer." I tug her to me, tangle our legs, and wrap my arms around her as she rests her head on my chest. "We could both use some comforting, I think."

"Why do you need comforting?"

Oh, sweetness, for so many reasons that if I laid them all out for you, you'd run from this room screaming.

"Because I hit a guy tonight and bruised my hand."

"Oh!" She grabs my fist in her hands and kisses my knuckles, making the breath hiss out between my teeth. "I'm sorry."

"You should kiss it again."

She does, gently pressing her sexy, full lips against my skin, and then to my utter surprise, she uncurls my fingers and tucks her cheek in my palm, holding my hand to her face. "Thank you."

"For what?" I whisper.

"For saving me from that douche bag. For being so nice to me even though I've been an utter bitch to you."

"You're not a bitch. You just like me."

"Do not."

I smile and hold her close, staring at the shadows from her window on the ceiling. The room is dark and cool. Perfect sleeping conditions.

"You like me. It's okay, I have that effect on women."

She stiffens for a moment, then relaxes again. "I'm sure you do."

I tip her face up, so I can see her eyes in the moonlight. "It was a joke, Addie."

"It doesn't matter."

"Yes, I think with you, it does."

Her eyes drop to my lips as she licks her own and it takes all of my willpower not to roll her under me and take her right here and now. But then she looks back up at me and presses her lips to my chin. "Thank you."

"You already thanked me."

"It was worth saying twice." And with that she settles in against me, and mere minutes later, she's breathing the long, deep breaths of slumber.

I've fought insomnia for years, so I settle in for a long night of staring at Addie's ceiling, but as she breathes long and slow against me, her arms wrapped around my waist and legs tangled with mine, I find myself drifting with her.

She just fits.

Chapter Five

Addison

*H*e's not gone.

I haven't opened my eyes yet, but I can feel the heat from his body next to me. I can hear his even breathing. Of course Jake Knox doesn't snore.

I do. Which is only the most mortifying thing in the world.

I open one eye, and sure enough, there he is, still in his clothes from last night, looking all rumpled and sexy as hell. He's on his back, and I'm on my side next to him, and we aren't touching.

But with the heat and sexy vibes rolling off of him, we may as well be. God, he's hot. Like, if you look up *hot* in the dictionary, there's Jake's picture. And when he smiles, all bets are off. He's been melting my panties off for a month with that cocky smile.

It was nice of him to make excuses for me last night, but I know the truth. I *have* been horrible to him. Because I'm so damn attracted to him, and my man picker isn't just broken: I'm pretty sure it doesn't exist.

My heart just can't take any more bruises.

Last night, my face almost gained a few bruises, and my stomach clenches again at the thought. What the ever loving fuck was that all about? I'd just reached my car when Jeremy scared the fuck out of me, coming up behind me and spinning me around, pinning me in place and yelling about how he has nowhere to go, and it's all my fault.

I'm no shrinking violet, so I gave it right back to him, calling him a loser who needs to get his shit together.

He didn't take kindly to that.

But I never would have believed that he would have hurt me. Jeremy is a lot of things, but an abuser isn't something that was on my radar.

And then Jake came to the rescue. I've never felt such relief as I did when he pulled Jeremy away from me. He was my savior.

And that's just corny as hell.

Lying here in the early morning sunshine, I can't help but admit that he's sexy, and surprisingly has a sweet side.

And it's not just the way he looks that has me attracted. Don't get me wrong, my fingertips itch to trace the tattoos on his arm, to feel his hair in my hands. But I've also come to learn this past month that Jake is a *nice guy*.

And I'm mature enough to admit that he scares me more than a little.

Now it's the morning after. Nothing happened, yet it feels like it was way more intimate than getting naked together.

I roll onto my back, bite my lip, and try to sneak out of the bed, but suddenly a strong arm wraps around my stomach and Jake pulls me tightly against his chest.

"Where are you going?" he rasps into my ear.

"It's morning."

His hand slips under the hem of my T-shirt and his fingertips begin to draw circles on my skin.

Holy mother of God, that feels good.

"I'm not having sex with you," I say primly and try to inch away from him.

"I didn't invite you to. Stop squirming." He nuzzles my neck, making my eyes cross, and continues to play my stomach like a freaking guitar. Then he pushes more firmly against me, making me giggle.

"Whatever it is that's pressed to my ass disagrees with you."

"That's nothing. Just a flashlight."

I burst out laughing. "Do you carry a flashlight in your pocket often?"

"Mostly just in the morning," he replies seriously and kisses my neck, right under my ear, and my hips circle involuntarily. My nipples are puckered, and I know my panties are soaked.

This man is *potent.*

Dangerous.

So fucking hot.

"Seriously, Jake, I am *not* having sex with you."

"Seriously, Addie, I am not even attracted to you. Stop trying to have sex with me."

I giggle some more, grip his hand in mine, and raise it to my lips.

And bite.

"Ah, she's a biter."

"I'm not attracted to you either."

"Let's not get crazy, sweetheart. Yes you are. You like me."

"You're delusional."

He tugs me onto my back, smiling down at me. He drags his fingertips down my cheek, then tucks a strand of hair behind my ear.

And hello, morning breath.

Not him, of course. But I'm quite sure my breath could rival a dragon's right now, so I tug the sheet up and over my mouth, as Jake's eyes smile down at me.

"Making sure I won't kiss you?"

"Making sure I don't kill you with my morning breath."

He chuckles and leans in to nuzzle my temple. "You smell so good."

"Right. Don't you have somewhere you need to be?"

"It's Sunday, Addison," he whispers.

"So? Maybe you need to go to the grocery store. Or the gym. Or church."

He chuckles. "None of that is on my list today."

"Well, some of it is on my list." His hand takes a journey up my shirt again, and those talented fingers skim my skin.

"You make me crazy when you bite your lip like that," he whispers as the sheet is tugged down around my chin.

His green eyes are on fire as he continues to nuzzle me, cuddle me.

When was the last time I was just cuddled? I don't even remember.

Probably because I hate to snuggle.

Hate.

"You're overthinking," he says.

"I am not."

"You've been overthinking for the past thirty minutes," he says simply. "As someone who shares that affliction, I'm here to tell you to stop. It'll make you crazy."

"You make me crazy."

"I know. You're wild about me. It's embarrassing, really."

I giggle, unable to stop myself. This playful side of him is just . . . *fun.* My chest feels lighter with the entertaining banter, making me relax. Maybe he's right, maybe I do over-think everything.

"You really need an ego check."

"Oh, I have plenty of those," he replies and kisses my forehead. "But you were right, I do have things to do today."

Damn. Not that I had any intention of keeping him to myself today, but this just feels *so good.* I don't want it to end.

"Where is your phone?" he asks.

"Over there." I point to the bedside table on his side, and suddenly he moves away, grabs it, then returns to me and pulls his phone out of his pocket. "We don't need to text, Jake. I'm right here."

"I don't have your number. I only have the restaurant

number." He wakes his phone up, then waits expectantly for me.

"That's the only number you need."

"No, it's not." He leans in and nuzzles my nose. "Because I want to see you outside of Seduction."

"Are you sure?"

"Been sure since the first moment I saw you, sweetness."

I swallow hard and frown. "I don't just hand my private number out."

He looks a little hurt for a split second, which brings some tightness back to my chest, and then his lips spread in that cocky grin.

"Addison, will you please give me your number?"

God, he's cocky. And I know I'm not going to tell him no. I mean, I can always choose to just not answer the phone. I rattle off my number for him. A few moments later, my phone pings with a text from him.

You are beautiful.

"You're too charming for your own good," I reply, rolling my eyes.

"Doesn't change the fact that you look good in the morning."

I grin shyly, then bury my face in my hands. He chuckles and nudges my hands away. His lips are just inches from mine.

"Addie, I want to kiss you."

"Okay. I'm okay with that."

"If I kiss you, we won't leave this bed. So I'm going to save it." Disappointment sits heavily in my belly as he simply kisses my forehead, then hugs me again, burying his face in my neck. "Are you okay?"

"Yes." I smile as he pulls back. "I'm okay."

"Good. Now, I need you to stop snuggling me and let me go. I have to work today."

I raise a brow and let go of him, but he pulls my arms around him again and sighs, as though he's frustrated.

"Seriously, Addie, I have to go. God, you're clingy."

"You're not all that, you know." I chuckle and sit up, then gasp when I see the time. "Holy shit, we slept until almost eleven!"

"You did. I've been awake for a while. Did you know that you snore?"

"Damn." I bury my face in my hands again. "I was hoping I wouldn't do that."

"It's kind of cute, actually. And it means that you slept well. I didn't mind."

I drop my hands and stare over at him. "You're very nice to me."

"I have moments." He kisses my cheek and then climbs out of bed, scratches his head, making his hair even messier, then grins down at me. "I'm outta here. Call me if you need me."

If I need him for what?

"Have a good day."

"What? No *call me if you need me too?*"

"What could you possibly need me for?"

His eyes sober and he sighs as he watches me, as though he wants to climb back into this bed and take us for a tumble.

And I'm not so sure I'd turn him down if he did.

"That's a list we'll talk about later. Have a good day."

And with that, he's gone.

Did that just happen? I drag my hand over the bed, and sure enough, it's still warm where he was lying.

Deciding to get my ass out of bed, I pad into the bathroom and start the shower and sigh in happiness when the hot water hits my shoulders and back.

Jake is *funny*. This morning could have been very, very bad.

But instead he made me feel at ease. He made me feel cared for.

He's good at the morning-after thing.

And then it hits me: *he's good at the morning-after thing.*

Which means he's done it a lot. It's old hat to him.

Crap.

I hurry through the rest of my shower and reach for my phone. I need some girl time. Mia and Kat are probably still sleeping, so they're out. Riley would be way too logical.

Cami. She's sweet, but also logical, and she has to be up by now. So I call her.

"What's up, buttercup?"

"Hey, I need you to go to the gym with me." I pull on yoga shorts, jumping in place to get them over my ass, then reach for a sports bra. I kind of did the whole shower-and-gym thing backward, but that's what happens when you need an emergency heart-to-heart with a best friend and have too much energy to sit still.

"What did I do? Are you mad at me?"

I smile softly. God, I love Cami. "No, silly. I need to talk, and I need to get on the treadmill, so we might as well do both at the same time."

"I don't want to." Her voice is just a little whiny.

"Come on. It'll be fun. And you're my person, and I need to talk."

"You have three other *persons,* Addie. Riley likes the gym."

"I want you. I need to talk about Jake."

"Jake?" That perked her up. "I'll meet you there in fifteen."

"YOU KNOW, YOU have a membership to this gym," I remind Cami as we begin walking side by side on the treadmills. She's glaring at hers, as though it's an evil entity.

"I know. And I came here, once."

"Once?" I chuckle and increase my speed.

"I had these horrible side effects. I got sweaty. I was out of breath. My legs were shaky. I'm pretty sure that all means that this is *not* good for me. I mean, I couldn't *breathe,* Addie."

"You are a hot mess." I laugh loudly as I increase the speed to a slow jog.

"Okay, I'm on this machine of destruction. Talk."

"I spent the night with Jake last night."

Cami stumbles, almost falling off the back end of the treadmill, then coughs hysterically. The hot guy at the customer service counter watches with concern, his finger hovering over the speed-dial button for 911, I'm sure.

"What?"

"You heard me."

"You had sex with Jake Knox?"

"No."

She frowns. "Wait. What?"

"He stayed with me last night, but we didn't have sex."

"What did you do? Play Parcheesi?"

I relay the story of Jeremy cornering me at my car last night, but leave out the part about Jake saving me from having my first black eye.

That'll only freak her out, and it *didn't* happen. He's gone. Probably already moved on to the next poor girl.

She can have him.

"I knew I hated that guy."

"Yeah, I should have listened."

"So how did you end up with Jake?"

"He followed me home to make sure I was safe."

"Hello, swoon," she says with a sigh. "And then?"

"And then he held me most of the night."

She stares at me for a long minute. "And that's it?"

"Yep."

"And you let him hold you? You're not a snuggler."

"I know. It felt good." I shrug and wipe the sweat from my forehead. "I don't remember the last time I snuggled with someone."

"That's because you're not a snuggler," she says again. "I'm quite sure you've always been anti-snuggle."

Yeah, because that was before I'd been snuggled by Jake.

"He wants to see me again."

"Good."

"Not good."

"I'm so confused." Cami shakes her head, her honey-blond hair bouncing as she walks quickly beside me. "Why is it bad? You enjoyed the snuggling. He rescued you from the ex–douche bag. He's nice to you, Addie. This is a *good* thing."

"He's too good at it. He made this morning easy and funny and relaxing."

"That bastard! You're right. Stay away from him." She rolls her eyes.

"Look, smart-ass, I'm saying that he's *too good at it*. Like, he's good at it because he's done it so much already. I'm not special. I'm just another woman that he's woken up next to."

"Okay, number one, that's kind of a bitchy thing to say. He didn't have to go to your place at all. And he certainly didn't have to stay the night. Just because he didn't want this morning to be weird doesn't mean that he does it every day."

"Except, he's a rock star, so he probably does."

She glares at me for a minute. "He's an ex–rock star. He hasn't been in the limelight for five years, Addie. People change a lot in five years. And that leads me to number two. He's a good guy. He's always really nice to all the staff at the restaurant. He's quick to give a sweet compliment, but he's not overly flirty. Except with *you*."

I frown, listening to Cami, and thinking about how Jake has been over the past month. She's right, he's kind, but not superflirty.

"I really think you're overthinking this."

"You're not the first person to say that to me." I slow the pace down to a quick walk now. "I guess it's in my nature to overthink."

"Of course it is. You're a woman." Cami also slows her pace. "Holy shit, look at that."

Across the room is a man lifting weights. His muscles are *crazy* big. He's not bad on the eyes at all.

"I'm telling you," Cami says, her eyes still on Mr. Beefcake. "They should have an observation deck here, where we can sit with a glass of wine and watch the show. I'd come to the gym every day."

"I can get behind this idea," I reply thoughtfully. "We should put it in the suggestion box."

"I'm totally gonna do that."

"Great. Now that that's solved, what am I going to do about Jake?"

"You're going to see him. If this all bothers you too much, talk to him. Ask him if this is just a fun time in bed for a while, or if he wants more. And if his answer makes you happy, go for it. If it doesn't, don't see him."

"You make it sound simple."

"It is, Addie. It's really simple. Don't make it harder than it needs to be."

She's right. I don't know if I want to have that conversation with him, but it doesn't have to be difficult.

"I need to have my roots done," Cami says with a sigh as we both stop our machines and climb off to head to the showers.

"Let's call Cici and schedule a girls' night for this week."

"That sounds like heaven. There are few things better than being pampered by Cici."

Being pampered by Jake Keller doesn't suck, friend.

"YOU WENT TOO long between cuts," Cici scolds Mia as she trims her hair. "You should have been in here weeks ago."

"I don't know if you know this," Mia replies sarcastically, "but I have a kitchen to run."

"That's no excuse to neglect your scalp."

Cici is short and stick thin, despite having four kids. She keeps her bleach-blond hair in a pixie cut, and her makeup is always flawless.

Her makeup was flawless when she gave birth, for crying out loud.

"When did you get the new Chanel bag?" she asks me.

"Last week." I pet the black leather with pure joy. "Isn't she pretty?"

"I prefer Gucci," Riley says as she reads *People* magazine, waiting for the color to do its job on her head. "There are some new brown heels out this season that I'm dying for."

Kat is lying on a facial bed with a mask on her face and cucumber on her eyes. Her hands are folded over her stomach. "Y'all spend too much money on accessories," she mutters.

"You enjoy tattoos," Cami replies, snuggling Cici's youngest baby in her arms. She is only three months old, and we all love snuggling her. "They like bags and shoes."

"What do you like?" Mia asks Cami.

"Saving my money," Cami says with a grin, then kisses the baby's head.

"Mom! Mom! Mom!" Two little boys come running through Cici's basement, wielding foam swords. Their faces are smeared with chocolate. "Daddy won't let us stay up to watch TV!"

"You're supposed to stay upstairs," Cici says with a scowl. "Where is your sister?"

"On the phone. As usual." The boys shrug, have a long, dramatic sword fight in the middle of the room, then run back upstairs as quickly as they came down.

"You know I love you, Cici," Kat says. "But the best birth control in the world is one night a month at your house."

"Oh please, learn from my mistakes, friends. Not that they're *mistakes,* and I wouldn't trade any of them for anything, but they're a handful."

"I'll just come over and share your handful for a while," Cami says with a soft smile on her pretty face. She looks so at home with that baby in her arms. Cami's going to be an awesome mom someday.

My phone pings in my hand with an incoming text. I grin when I see that it's from Jake. I haven't seen him since Sunday morning, but he's texted me several times a day, every day. I never know what they're going to say. Sometimes he's flirty. Sometimes he sends silly selfies, and sometimes he's just sharing something that happened that day. It's only Wednesday, but I miss his face.

> Thinking of you. What are you up to tonight?

"Who's that?" Mia asks with a frown. "All of us are here."

"Is it Jake?" Cami asks innocently, but I narrow my eyes at her.

> I'm getting pampered with the girls this evening. What
> are you up to?

"Why would Jake be texting you?" Riley asks. "What aren't you telling us?"

"And why does Cami know and the rest of us don't?" Kat asks as she peels the cucumbers off her eyes.

> Good. You deserve to be pampered. I'm writing a song
> with Max tonight. Take you to dinner tomorrow night?

"Addie. Start talking," Mia demands.

"Can't I have two minutes to respond to messages?" I bite my lip, and type my response.

> Okay, but don't get any ideas about me being at-
> tracted to you or anything.

"Is she seeing Jake?" Riley finally asks Cami.

"Not my story to tell."

"Addie!"

Stop fawning all over me. I'll go out with you. Geez.
Have a good night.

"Everyone calm down." I shove my phone in my pocket
and take a deep breath, then relay the same story I told
Cami the other day. Everyone has stopped what they were
doing to listen to the story. Cici has even stopped trimming
Mia's hair.

"I haven't even seen him since Sunday."

"When *are* you going to see him again?" Kat asks with a
grin. "And also, I approve of this. I like him."

"He's taking me out for dinner tomorrow."

"And after-dinner sex." Riley does a happy dance, then
fist-bumps Kat.

"Maybe."

"Maybe?" Cici rolls her eyes and snips at Mia's hair. "Girl,
he's gorgeous. And sexy. And a *rock star*. You better hit that."

"*Hit that?*" I laugh out loud. "Since when do you speak
like that?"

"I don't know, it just came out," Cici says with a laugh.
"And you know we're going to want details."

"No details."

"You're no fun." Riley pouts and crosses her arms over
her chest.

"You've never wanted details before," I point out.

"You've never had sex with Jake Knox before," Mia says.

"Keller," I reply automatically.

They all blink at me for a minute, then look at each other.

"She's got it bad," Kat says. "Not that I blame her."

"He's the trifecta," Cami says. "Music, hot body, and personality."

"I'm jealous," Cici says with a sigh.

"You have an awesome husband," I reply with a roll of my eyes. "And he worships the ground you walk on."

"True. But he's not a rock star."

"No, he's just a literal rocket scientist," Riley replies. "You don't ever get to complain."

"I'm not complaining. I'm coveting."

"We're all coveting," Mia says. "But I'm so damn happy for you."

"And if he hurts you, we get to kill him and hide the body," Kat says as she pops a frozen grape in her mouth. "We've always threatened to do that, but now we'd get to make good on it."

"We can still kill Jeremy and hide the body," Riley suggests. "And speaking of that, what was he doing in the alley, Addie? That doesn't make any sense."

"He was just drunk, and being stupid. It's really no big deal." If any one of them lied to me about something like this, I'd be *pissed*. But I don't want them to worry. It's over. Jeremy's too lazy to come back for more. He's most likely moved on to someone new now. And good luck to her.

"I don't think Jeremy's worth potential jail time," Mia says.

"And Jake is?" I ask with a laugh.

"Hell yes. Jake's the real deal. He could seriously do some damage."

That's what I'm terrified of.

"Or he could be the best thing that ever happens to you," Cami says thoughtfully. "Just lead with your head and not your heart. 'Cause your heart's an asshole."

"They all are," Kat agrees with a sympathetic smile. I nod and chew my lip. Cami's advice is exactly what I needed to hear. And being with my girls tonight is exactly what I needed for my soul.

Chapter Six

Jake

*M*ax and I are in the studio, finishing up a song and checking our schedule for the next week.

We're swamped. And damn if that doesn't make me happy. When we started the business, I was terrified that we'd fuck it up. That artists wouldn't want to work with us.

But it seemed that from the minute Max came to me with the idea and we set it in motion, it had a life of its own.

We have to turn people away.

"I know you don't like to work on Sundays," I say to Max while examining the schedule, "but it's the only day we can get Steve in the studio, and I'm not willing to turn a musical legend down."

"Agreed," Max says with a nod. "It's fine. Maybe I'll just bring Tiffany along. She'd get a kick out of it."

Max and Tiffany have been together for more than ten years, with no sign of marriage in sight. She's been through *everything* with him. Sundays are their one day off a week together.

"Good idea." *I wonder if I can talk Addie into coming too.*

What am I thinking? This isn't a backyard barbecue. This is work.

"Wanna start that new song for Starla tonight?"

I shake my head and close the laptop. "I can't. I have to get ready to go."

"Go where?" Max asks with a raised brow.

"I have a date." I grin, but don't look him in the eye. He's going to give me shit. If I don't look him in the eye, maybe he'll leave me alone.

"A date? With who?"

And maybe not.

"With Addie."

Silence. Finally, I glance up to find him watching me, hands on his hips, a frown between his eyebrows.

"Addie from the restaurant?"

"That's the only Addie I know."

"So, you have a girlfriend?"

"No." She's not a girl, she's an incredible woman.

"So, you're gonna bang her?"

"You're starting to piss me off, man." I cross my arms and stare Max down, eye to eye now.

"I'm confused. You don't date. You work and you sulk, and sometimes you get laid because you're Jake fucking Knox, but you don't *date*."

I sigh and rub my hands over my face. "What's your point?"

"That's pretty much it."

"I like her," I reply with a shrug. "I want to hang out with her. It's really that simple. There's no need to make a big deal out of it."

"She's beautiful."

I narrow my eyes on my friend.

"Come on, man," he says with a chuckle. "I may be taken, but I'm not six feet under. She's a beautiful woman. Smart. Too smart to waste her time with a bozo like you."

"I love you too."

"Do we need to have *the talk*?" His grin has turned pure evil now. He loves flinging shit at me.

"Fuck you."

"Be safe. Condoms are important."

"Stop talking."

"No means no."

"Shut the fuck up, Max." But I can't help but laugh. God, he's a bastard.

"Be a gentleman. Open doors, pull out her chair, and all that happy horseshit. Oh! Do you need money for dinner?" He reaches for his wallet. "She shouldn't pay for dinner."

"I'm going to deck you."

Max is laughing in earnest now, almost doubled over at my expense.

Asshole.

I turn away and walk to the door, not looking back at him.

"Compliment her shoes!" he calls out behind me. "Girls like that!"

I flip him off, then jog to the house to quickly shower and change clothes, and just as I pull out of my driveway, my phone rings.

"Keller."

"Hey, handsome."

Christina.

"Did Max call you and tell you to give me shit about my date tonight?"

"I don't know what any of those words meant," she replies. "I haven't talked to Max."

Well shit.

"But now I want to know everything."

"Of course you do. Why are you calling?"

"Oh no," she says with a laugh. "You're not changing the subject. Spill it."

I take a deep breath and merge onto the freeway. "I have a date with Addie tonight. And before you start," I say, interrupting her, "Max already gave me a bunch of shit."

"I like her."

"You do?"

"Sure. What's not to like. Hold on." She doesn't bother pulling the phone away from her face as she talks to her husband. "Jake's going out with Addie tonight. Yes, on a real date. I know, I like her too. I told him that. Oh, you think she's pretty?"

"Chris, do you want me to let you go so you guys can talk about Addie, or was there a point to this call?"

"Sorry. We both approve."

"Thank goodness," I reply sarcastically. "Otherwise, I'd have to call and cancel."

"So, now that you have a girlfriend, does this mean I won't see you as often?"

My hands tighten on the steering wheel. I knew she'd tease me. "No, you won't see me anymore because you annoy the shit out of me."

"Aww, you're so sweet," she says with a smile in her voice. "If you talk to Addie like that tonight, you'll get laid for sure."

"Why is everyone so damn worried about me getting laid?"

"Well, everyone *should* get laid," she says, as though I'm a slow child.

"Getting laid isn't my objective tonight," I mutter.

"What *is* the objective?" Christina asks.

"To have dinner. To spend time with her. To get to know her."

"You're seriously going out on a date." Her voice is heavy with surprise, and that just pisses me off.

"I've gone out on dates before."

"Okay, all joking aside," she says, her voice excited, but sincere. "I really like her, Jake. She's smart and funny, and she runs her business brilliantly."

Hell yes she does.

"You look good together," she adds.

"Is that part of the criteria?" I ask with a laugh.

"Of course. And you make a beautiful couple."

"It's all her," I reply softly. "Anyone would look good standing next to her."

"Wow," she whispers. "That might be the sweetest thing I've ever heard you say about a woman."

"I like her."

"I'm glad. Have fun tonight, friend. Call me tomorrow and fill me in, after you get home of course."

"I'll be home tonight."

"Jake, if you're taking her out on a date, you really should stay the night after you have sex with her. It's the right thing to do."

"I'm not having sex with her tonight."

Christina is quiet on the other end so long I think I've dropped the call.

"Chris?"

"This one is different," she says.

"Are you *crying*?"

"No." She sniffles and I roll my eyes. "I'm just so happy for you."

"Oh my God, C. Stop crying. It's a date, not a wedding."

"You deserve to find someone like Addie who's smart and pretty and likes you."

"I'm not so sure she likes me," I reply honestly. "Or if she does, she doesn't want to."

"Trust me, J, if she didn't like you, she wouldn't be going out with you tonight."

I nod, then remember she can't see me. "Good point."

"I have to go."

"Why did you call in the first place?"

"Oh! I almost forgot. I have news."

"Okay."

She sniffles again, and my stomach drops. "What's wrong, C?"

"I'm not going to have a baby. It didn't take this month."

My own eyes get misty. "Wow." My voice is gruff with emotion. "I'm so sorry, sweetheart."

"I know."

"Are you okay?"

"I think so. Kev and I are a little sad, but we'll try again next month," she says, trying to sound better than I know she feels. "I wanted to tell you. Because you're my person."

"I love you, C. This is going to happen." I hope. I pray.

"Thank you. Now, you go enjoy your date, and call me tomorrow."

"Yes, ma'am." I grin as we hang up, and pull through Addie's gate, ready to see my girl.

"I'VE NEVER BEEN here before," Addie says with a grin as she dips her bread into cheese dip.

"How have you never had fondue before?" I ask, watching her eat. God, that mouth makes everything in me sit up and take notice.

"I dunno," she says with a shrug, which makes the black blouse that lays off of one shoulder slide farther down her arm. She has gorgeous shoulders. "Just never got around to it. Here, you have to try this."

She holds a piece of bread, dripping with cheese, out for me to take. I oblige her.

It's delicious.

"Good?" she asks with a smile.

"Good."

She immediately dives in for more and it occurs to me that I've never seen her eat before. The way she enjoys her food is *fun*.

"Did you grow up in Portland?" I ask and finally dig in with my own skewer. If I keep watching her, I'll walk out of here with an embarrassing hard-on.

"Yep," she replies and licks cheese off her lips. Maybe fondue wasn't a great idea. "Mia, Cami, and I all grew up here, and have been friends since we were little."

"That's cool," I reply, remembering the photos on her mantel. "Are your parents still married?"

"They are, and they live in Hawaii."

"What took them there?"

"A job. My dad is a college professor, and he took a job there so Mom could work there as a marine biologist. She got her degree in her forties."

"Wow, that's amazing."

Addie nods and smiles. "She had me very young. It was a huge scandal." She leans forward, as though she's telling me new family gossip, making me smile. "She took my father's advanced physics class when she was a senior in college, and they had an affair. She got pregnant"—she points to herself—"and they got married."

"Wow, that *is* scandalous."

Addie nods and shoves more bread in her mouth. "She hid the pregnancy until the end of the semester so my dad wouldn't lose his job, and then they got married."

"Is he a lot older than her?"

"About ten years," she replies. "He was a child prodigy in math and science. He was a college professor at the age of twenty-two."

"That explains why you're so damn smart."

She snorts and rolls her eyes. "He'd disagree with you, I'm sure. Anyway, Mom stayed home, raising me and being a housewife, and she never complained about it. She liked it. But when I went away to college, she decided to finish college herself, and now works as a marine biologist, with a love of all things sharks."

"Sharks?" I ask with a laugh. "Is she a thrill seeker?"

"She got pregnant by her college professor. I would say so."

"Do you see them often?"

"No." She shakes her head, her eyes suddenly sad. "They're busy, I'm busy. We talk on the phone about once a month."

I tilt my head, chewing, watching the change in her. "That's a sore spot for you."

She shrugs again. "A little."

The waitress exchanges our appetizer cheese and bread with the main course of different meats and vegetables.

"How about you?" Addie asks before I can question her further. "Are you from here?"

"I thought you read the tabloids," I reply with a raised brow. "My life story is out there for everyone to see."

"I only read the juicy stuff about women who'd been done wrong." Her pink lips tip up in a half smile, but her eyes are shrewd, watching for any reaction.

"You do realize that most of that is made up, right? It sells magazines, but it's not the truth."

"So, you didn't get a woman pregnant with twins and then send her away to Bermuda to have the babies and make her give them up for adoption, paying her ten million dollars to not talk about it?"

My jaw drops as I watch her tell this story.

"If I paid her ten million to shut up, how did the story get out?"

"So you admit it?"

I laugh and shake my head. "No, Addie. None of that is true. Jesus, that's one I missed."

"I made it up," she admits with a giggle. "But it would be a fun story."

"Let's get this straight, right now, so we can move on without any suspicions. The band broke up five years ago, and since then I've had one girlfriend that lasted roughly one year before I discovered that she was more interested in my money and what my name could get her than in me, and I've slept with a few women since then."

"And before the band split up?" she asks, watching me intently.

"I was a jackass," I reply. "I let the fame and the attention go to my head. I slept with more than my share of women. I enjoyed the booze. Too much. I abused cocaine, because it, combined with the booze, was the best high there is, and I will never go down that road again. It nearly cost me the most important person in my life. So I walked away from all of it."

She blinks, holding my gaze, then picks up her skewer and stabs a piece of chicken. "So, where did you grow up?"

"You don't want to continue talking about my sordid past?"

"No, I don't." She reaches across the table and takes my hand in hers. "We've all made mistakes, Jake. Especially when we were younger. I slept with men I shouldn't have in my modeling days."

I don't want to know this.

"I want to know who you are now."

"Who I was then affects who I am now."

She nods slowly. "True. And maybe, with time, we'll talk about that more. But for now, I'm content to talk about other things."

"Minnesota."

"Excuse me?" She releases my hand to eat more of her meal.

"I'm from Minnesota. My parents divorced when I was nine. Mom remarried and lives in Texas with her husband. I stayed in Minnesota with Dad."

"Did he remarry?"

I shake my head and eat a carrot. "He was kind of heartbroken when Mom left. He passed away a few years ago."

"I'm sorry." Her eyes are sad.

"Not your fault." I shrug, the familiar pain I get in my chest settling in when I think of my dad. "I miss him too. And I might feel a little guilty."

"Why?"

"It kind of goes back to the jackassery. When I was with Hard Knox, we toured constantly. I was wrapped up in the band, and I didn't see him or speak to him as much as I should have."

"I'm sure he was very proud of you," she says with a soft smile.

"I think he was." *God, I hope he was.*

"How did you end up in Portland?"

"Max is from here," I reply. "When the band broke up and he came back here, I decided to come with him. I bought a place just outside of Hillsboro."

"Do you like it here?"

"I'm liking it more and more," I reply truthfully, holding her blue gaze in mine. "It helps that you're crazy about me."

"You're just crazy," she replies primly.

"Seriously, you're embarrassing me. Stop fawning all over me."

She rolls her eyes, but she's grinning, and I know she enjoys the banter as much as I do. "What's your favorite kind of music?"

I tip my head to the side. "I love all music."

"But there must be a favorite. A band, or a genre."

"Can I get you dessert?" the waitress asks, but I quickly shake my head no, and she leaves.

"Maybe I want dessert," Addie says with a raised brow.

"I do too, but we're going to get it somewhere else."

"Fun." She smiles.

"Um, baby, you have something in your teeth." I point to the spot, and she frowns as she searches for it, making me laugh. "You got it."

"Thanks."

I pay the check, then take Addie's hand and lead her out into the warm early summer evening, leading her toward my favorite ice cream place.

"So, you didn't answer my question," she says.

"You answer it first, and then I will."

"You just want to copy my answer to make me think that we have stuff in common."

God, she's funny.

"You caught me. Just humor me."

I glance down and watch her move next to me. She's in killer red heels with her matching red toes poking out the end, and a black skirt, but she's walking as easily as if she was wearing sneakers.

Amazing.

"Johnny Cash," she replies, surprising the fuck out of me.

"Excuse me?"

"I love Johnny Cash. Especially the old stuff."

"You're shitting me."

"No," she says and giggles, then shocks the hell out of me by linking her fingers with mine. "He was amazing. I also like newer stuff like Daughtry and I've always loved the Goo Goo Dolls."

"What about Hard Knox?" I ask, unable to help myself.

She looks up at me with narrowed eyes. "I didn't have your posters on my walls."

"I don't give a fuck about posters," I reply honestly. "It was never about that shit for me."

"I loved your music," she replies softly and stops us, right here, on the sidewalk so she can look up at me. " 'Simply Red' is my favorite song, but I knew them all. Your voice gives me goose bumps. But that's not why I'm here tonight."

"Why are you here?"

She glances down, but I catch her chin with my finger and make her look me in the eye.

"I'm here because I can't seem to say no to you, even though I *want* to say no to you. I don't have a good history with musicians."

"Dated a few?" I ask, feeling my gut clench. I know how musicians can be in relationships. Hell, I know how *men* can be.

"My share," she says with a nod. "So, I'm not here because you're a successful musician, Jake, I'm here in spite of it. I'm here because I feel the chemistry between us."

"And because you like me."

"I didn't say that." She smiles now, relief in her eyes. "I'm still deciding on that."

I take her hand and continue leading her down the sidewalk to Sweet Treats. "How can I tip the scales in my favor?"

"Tell me what kind of damn music you like already."

"I like the bands you mentioned," I reply thoughtfully.

"Of course you do." Sarcasm drips off of every word, making me laugh.

"But I also love B. B. King. Sarah McLachlan. Alan Jackson. Maroon 5. Sugarland."

"Wow, that's quite a range of sounds."

"I told you, I love *music*. I respect it all. It all evokes different emotions, feelings."

She nods. "Where did it start for you? The music?"

"Birth." I laugh and pull her to the side as a bicyclist zooms past us. "My dad played the guitar, and loved music. The radio was always on."

"Did he teach you to play?" she asks as we walk into Sweet Treats and start staring at the menu.

"He did."

"Should I get a milk shake?" she asks thoughtfully.

"Baby, my boys are already in your yard," I reply, eyeing the brownie sundae.

She blinks, then bursts out laughing. "Now I have to get a milk shake."

We place our order and, treats in hand, walk slowly back toward my car.

"How's your shake?" I ask.

"Chocolatey," she says, and then sighs. "Damn you, Jake!"

"What?"

"Now I have that damn song in my head!" She starts to dance, moving her shoulders and ass. *"My milk shake brings all the boys to the yard . . ."*

I stop and watch, laughing at her as she sings all the words, moving that sexier-than-fuck body.

I'm a first-class idiot for taking sex off the menu tonight.

"THANKS FOR DINNER," Addie says as she unlocks her door. "And dessert. And putting that song in my head. It'll be there for weeks."

"You're welcome." I grip her shoulders and turn her to face me, then smile down at her softly. "It was all my pleasure."

She's staring up at me, biting her lip, her blue eyes wide and maybe a little scared.

I understand that completely. She scares the fuck out of me too.

I cage her in against her door and tug her lip out of her teeth with my thumb, then brush it over the plump skin.

"You make me crazy when you bite your lip like that," I whisper.

"So you've said," she replies, watching my own mouth. "Jake?"

"Yes, sweetheart."

"Kissing me now would be nice."

"Bossy little thing, aren't you?"

"I'm not little."

"Just bossy then." I cup her cheek in my hand, loving the softness of her skin, the way she's breathing just a bit harder, the way the pulse in her throat thrums against my wrist. I brush my nose across hers, just barely skimming my lips over hers. She inhales sharply as my lips gently nibble hers.

Fuck me, she's sweet.

Her hands grip my shirt at my hips as she presses closer

to me, and I kiss her earnestly now. She tastes like chocolate, and what I'm quite sure is simply *Addie*. The kiss is slow and thorough, taking her all in. Her lithe, long body is pressed to mine, her arms wrapped around my back now, her nails barely gripping on to my skin through my shirt.

God, I can't control myself with her. My body, my emotions.

She devastates me.

I pull back, breathing hard. "Sleep well, baby."

She shakes her head, as if clearing the lust from it so she can think straight. "You're not coming in?"

I drag my fingertips down her cheek, her neck, then tip my forehead down against hers. "Trust me, I want to. I want you more than anything I've ever wanted in my life, Addison. But this isn't a sprint, it's a marathon."

"Did you just use a running analogy?"

I grin and kiss her softly. "Yes."

"Okay." She plants her hand on my chest and pushes me away, then opens the door to her back. "Good night."

"Sleep well."

She smiles and closes the door and I have to take a deep breath before walking back to my car. The drive home is fast, as there is little traffic at this time of night. My house is quiet as I walk through to the kitchen and drink orange juice out of the jug, then saunter into the living room and sit behind the piano.

Max is usually the one who writes music on the piano. I prefer the guitar. But the melody running through my head is piano.

So I sit and play, thinking of a certain stylish, funny-as-hell blonde. The sound of her laughter. The way her body moved as she sang on the sidewalk.

I play through the melody three times, committing it to memory, before walking up to my bedroom.

I miss her.

Jesus, I'm ridiculous. I just saw her an hour ago. And I was the idiot that chose to leave rather than take the invitation to come inside and bury myself in her for the rest of the night.

I'm a moron.

I don't know what the fuck is happening to me. What is it about *this* woman that has me all tied in knots? Maybe I should stay away from her. Slow down. Give her some space.

Fuck that.

Finally, I reach for my phone and call her.

"Hello?"

"Hey."

"Are you okay?" She doesn't sound sleepy, so I know I didn't wake her up.

"I'm fine. I was just thinking about you."

Silence.

"Why does that confuse you?" I ask.

"It doesn't," she lies and I can hear rustling. "Aren't you supposed to wait three days to call the girl after a date?"

"This isn't a game, Addie," I reply, suddenly irritated. "We aren't in high school. If I want to hear your voice, I'll call you."

"All you had to say was *I miss you, Addie*."

I snort. "I just saw you."

"You missed me," she repeats confidently. God, her mouth turns me on. In a million different ways.

"Okay, I missed you."

"Now say, *You're always right, Addie*."

"Not a chance," I reply with a laugh.

"A girl can try."

"I had a good time tonight," I murmur.

"Me too. Thanks again."

"What are you wearing?"

"A smile." I can hear it in her voice, and then more rustling around. "And a sheet."

"Damn."

"What are you wearing?"

"A hard-on," I reply.

"At least you're honest." She giggles. "I kind of like that you're all turned on over there."

"You've been turning me on since the moment I first laid eyes on you."

"Please." I can almost hear her roll her baby blues. "You did not find me attractive when I told you you'd have to audition for the position at Seduction."

"Actually, I did. But that's not the first time I saw you. You were at that open-mic night with Kat the weekend before."

"You remember that?"

"You were all I could see in that audience."

"Yeah, the lights were bright."

I turn on my side and laugh. "No, sweetheart, you were so beautiful that you were all I could see."

"Oh."

"Yeah, oh."

"That's kind of sweet."

"I have moments," I reply, soaking in the sound of her voice. "When do I get to see you again?"

"You're singing on Friday," she reminds me. "And I'm working a full day tomorrow."

"Friday it is then," I reply softly. "Sleep well, baby."

"Good night, Jake."

Chapter Seven

Addison

"The back of that top is adorable," Kat says as she walks past me. I'm sitting at the bar, going over next week's schedule. "And you're humming."

"Hmm," I agree with a slight smile. It's a good day. Jake played last night, and we had the best head count we've had so far at Seduction.

And Saturdays are always busier, so tonight should set another record.

"Earth to Addie," Kat whispers, leaning over the bar toward me.

"What do you want?" I ask with a laugh.

"Why are you so chipper? Wait." She shakes her head and resumes taking stock of the white wines in the cooler. "I don't want to know."

"It's not that," I reply.

"Still haven't slept with him, huh?"

"Not yet," I say with a sigh and pray that changes very quickly. The man has every nerve in my body on high alert and he's not even *here*.

It's so weird.

And, I admit, it's pretty fun.

"Our numbers were very good last night." I sip my latte.

"I know," she says with a grin. "They were good back here too. Your boy sure brings in the crowd."

"And they're coming back because they like *us*," I say confidently. "When I make my rounds through the dining room, customers rave about the food and the cool atmosphere."

"Same back here too," Kat replies and stands to jot down notes. "It's good."

"It's fucking awesome." We grin happily at each other, then fist bump, just as Marcy, one of my daytime waitresses, walks into the bar.

"I have a question," Marcy says, a frown on her pretty young face. She's only twenty-two, but she has the work ethic of someone twice her age, and she's freaking adorable with her slim figure, big brown eyes, and deep auburn hair, so she makes great tips.

"Shoot," Kat says.

"Who is Brian Tallman?"

Kat and I glance at each other and then roll our eyes.

"Did Cami give you his number?" I ask, then glare at the woman herself as she bounces happily into the room, then stops short when she sees us staring at her.

"What?" Her blue eyes widen innocently, but I know better. She isn't innocent. "What did I do?"

"Did you seriously give Marcy your ex-husband's phone number?" Kat demands.

"He's your *ex-husband*?" Marcy asks with disgust. "Ew!"

"Like I told you, he's a really nice guy," Cami says. "He's just looking for the right girl."

"*You* do not need to be the one to find him that nice girl," I tell her for the hundredth time since their divorce last year. "There's no reason to try to set him up, Cam. He's good looking, has a stable job, and isn't a complete asshole. Those are most women's requirements right there."

"I know, but his women picker is so skewed," she replies with a frown, and Kat and I both gape at her.

"Uh, Cami, he picked *you*," Kat reminds her.

"Exactly!" Cami throws her hands up and paces in front of the bar in agitation.

"Is she okay?" Marcy whispers to me. I simply nod, then shrug.

Because she's a bit wacky when it comes to Brian.

"I was *not* right for him."

"Does that mean your man picker is skewed too? You married him," Marcy points out, earning a sober stare from Cami.

"I shouldn't have married him. But he's a great person. He deserves someone beautiful and sweet and loving."

"And he will find her," Kat says as she wipes down the bar. "It's just not your job to find her for him."

"I'm going back to work," Marcy says before returning to the dining room.

"Seriously, Cam," I say, "stop trying to pawn off your ex-husband on my waitresses."

"And my bartenders." Kat points at Cami, driving her point home.

"Fine." She sits on the stool next to mine. "The back of your top is pretty. Only you can pull something like this off."

I grin at my friend. "Thanks." The front of the gray top is quite modest, showing little cleavage, although it is clingy. But the back is wide open, hanging down in a swoop to the top of the small of my back. The sides are held together by three spaghetti straps in the center.

"I have to know," Cami says softly, leaning in. "How do you keep your boobs up? You're too busty to not wear a bra."

"I want to know too," Kat says with a nod.

"It's a stick-on bra," I inform them with a smile. "It holds me up, with stickies on the sides and underneath."

"That's like ripping duct tape off your skin." Cami recoils and cringes. "Ouch."

"Watch your nipples," Kat says with both brows raised. "You don't need to rip those off when you take it off."

"I've done this before," I assure them with a laugh and pull my hair back, covering most of what the top shows. Oh my God, my friends are funny. "And it's not as strong as duct tape. But even if it were, it doesn't cover the nipples."

"Did I just hear you talking about your nipples?" a voice asks from behind me, making every hair on my body stand on end.

God, I fucking love his voice.

"We're looking out for you," Kat informs him. "She's trying to rip them off."

I roll my eyes and spin on my stool to face him. "I'm not trying to rip them off."

"Good. I have plans for them later." His green eyes smolder as he looks me over from my hair, which I have down in wavy curls, to my navy blue heels.

"I just bet he does," Cami says to Kat. I ignore her, but the nipples in question pucker at the thought.

Jesus, I hope he has plans for them sooner rather than later!

He steps to me and cages me in against the bar, his face inches from mine. He smells like his shower gel, and I want to just wrap my arms around him and bury my nose in his neck.

So I do. I hear both Kat and Cami's *awws*, but I ignore them, soaking him in. I just saw him last night, but I didn't get any alone time with him.

And I'm not alone with him now.

But I just need to feel him against me, just for a minute.

"Are you okay, baby?" he whispers into my ear, only for me to hear.

"I'm so okay," I reply and pull back, but his hands stay on me, stroking up and down my back, not helping the puckered-nipple situation in the least.

"You're missing half of your shirt," he says mildly, but his eyes are on fire. I'm not the only one turned on.

"I'll look for it later."

I WAS RIGHT. Last night was busy, but tonight is busier, and there is a one-hour waiting time for seating.

And Jake is singing his heart out onstage. The older Matchbox Twenty song is perfect for his raspy voice. He glances up and pins me with those eyes, then offers me a slow, wide smile, making my toes curl in these heels.

God, he turns me inside out.

"Miss?" A woman flags me down from her table.

"How can I help you?" I ask politely, trying to ignore the sexy rock star onstage.

"We placed our order already, but I wanted to make sure the waitress noted the no pine nuts on my husband's salad. He's severely allergic."

"I'll double-check for you," I tell her and walk into the kitchen, where Mia is barking orders and bustling about like crazy.

"That steak is overcooked," she says to her sous chef. "I won't serve it like that. When the customer says medium, they want medium."

"Everything okay in here?" I ask with a wide smile, ready to get the beatdown from Mia.

"Why are you in my kitchen?"

"I'm double-checking to make sure that table nineteen's order came in with the instructions to not put any pine nuts on his salad. He's allergic."

Mia searches for the ticket, finds it under a plate ready to go out, and scowls when she looks at the salad.

"There are pine nuts on this salad. Who plated it?"

She whips around to stare her staff down, scowling when the sous chef hangs his head in defeat.

"Did you not read the ticket?"

"Obviously not close enough," he replies.

"You're fired!" she shouts, then points to the door. "Get the hell out of my kitchen."

"Chef—" he begins, but she cuts him off.

"No. You almost *killed* a customer. Get. Out."

His nostrils flare as he stares at Mia. The rest of the kitchen staff keep their heads down, assembling plates as quickly as possible. Finally, after a long moment, he unties his apron, throws it on the floor, and marches out of the kitchen.

"Mia—"

"Addie, thanks for the heads-up, but I want you out of my kitchen too. We are swamped tonight and I have to concentrate."

I nod. "Fair enough."

When I return to the dining room, the customers are laughing at something Jake said. His gaze finds mine.

"So, as I was saying," he says into the mic, watching me with that panty-dropping smile. "There is this special woman in my life right now and I'd like to sing a song that tells her exactly how I feel about her."

I stop near the back of the room and raise a brow.

This should be good.

Instead of a slow ballad, he breaks out into a fast, upbeat song. I recognize it. One of my favorite artists, Matt Nathanson, sings it. The song is supersexy, all about how much he wants her.

And Jake's voice makes it nothing but pure, unadulterated sin.

Jesus, I want to rush the stage and climb him. Right here, right now.

I can't help but tap my toe with the music and smile at the blatantly sexual lyrics. It's such a fun song.

The rest of the evening flies by. Jake's set goes perfectly, and the customers are happy.

When he's done singing, he puts his guitar in its case, then crosses to me and takes my hand, raises it to his lips to press a kiss to my palm, then, with his eyes pinned to mine, drags his teeth down to the sensitive skin on my wrist and nibbles. The straggling customers are watching so I lead him back to the office and close the door.

"I taste like sunlight, do I?" I ask, quoting the song.

"And strawberry bubble gum," he replies with a cocky smile. This is the rock star side of him. He's confident and maybe a little arrogant, and damn if it isn't sexy.

"If I invite you back to my place, are you gonna kiss me and leave me by my door again?"

Because if you are, you can forget it, buddy. I know he didn't mean it to be, but it was humiliating.

"I don't know. Have you earned anything more than that?"

Now it's my turn to offer him a cocky grin. Have I earned it? I don't even try to answer that question. Instead I turn and head for the door, pulling my hair over my shoulder so my back is on display.

I hear him suck in a deep breath, and then he lets out a long, low groan.

Yes, this shirt is awesome.

Before I can open the door, I'm spun around and pinned to it, and Jake's mouth is on mine. Hot, hard, demanding. He grips my ass in his hands and boosts me up, propping me against the door and simply devouring me.

"I want you," he whispers against my lips. "I've been fighting to take this slow, Addison, but I'm a son of a bitch, and *I want you.*"

"I'm right here."

"No." He backs away, helping me to the floor, shaking his head, swallowing hard. He starts to say something, but has to swallow again, his neck muscles working and his hands clenched in fists. "This isn't happening here, against the door of your office. I need to get you home so I can take my time with you."

I blink at him, trying to gather my wits.

"Come on." He takes my hand and leads me into the bar. "I'm taking Addie home."

"I have to close up—" I begin, but Kat simply smiles at Jake and nods.

"We have this handled," she replies. "Have a good night."

"Thanks." Jake waves, leads me back into the dining room to grab his guitar, then practically pulls me outside to his car.

"I have a car here too," I remind him.

"I'll bring you back here in the morning to get it."

I frown. "I didn't say you could stay the night."

He shoves his guitar into the backseat, then turns to me and pulls me into his arms, hugging me close. He buries his face in my hair and takes a deep breath.

"I need to be with you tonight. The whole night," he whispers. "Let me stay."

How can I refuse him? I don't want to refuse him. I've been hot for him for a long, long time.

I pull out of his embrace, and his shoulders sag in defeat.

"I understand," he says.

Before he can turn away, I grab his hand and kiss his palm the way he did mine earlier. "Will you come home with me?"

His gaze whips up to mine. "If I do, I'm not leaving you until morning."

I kiss his palm again, then nod. "I'd like for you to stay."

He inhales sharply before leading me to the passenger side of his car. The ride to my place is quiet, the sexual tension hanging thick around us. Now I'm getting nervous. Having sex on the spur of the moment is one thing, but when it's premeditated, well . . . that's daunting.

I haven't showered since this morning and I've been working all day. I can't smell great. What if he wants to go *downtown*? Oh God, maybe I should tell him to wait for me while I shower.

And reshave my legs, because I shaved them yesterday and I was too lazy to do it this morning.

Maybe this is a bad idea.

"Stop it," he mutters and kisses my hand.

"Stop what?"

"Overthinking."

I frown at him. "Are you a mind reader?"

"I don't have to be, sweetness. You're thinking so hard over there, there's practically smoke coming out of your ears."

"I'm sure that's not true," I reply primly. "And being a thinker isn't a bad thing."

"No, it's not. Except when you start second-guessing yourself, and you have no reason to."

"I didn't shave my legs," I admit, ashamed. I bury my face in my hands, embarrassed.

"Oh no. Well, this can't happen then." Sarcasm drips off of every word as he parks, gets out of the car, and opens my door, pulling me out next to him. "Look at me."

I giggle at my own ridiculousness as I peek at him from behind my hands.

"I don't give a fuck when the last time you shaved your legs was," he says, cupping my face in his hands and staring at me with eyes on fire. "If I don't get you under me, quickly, I'm going to die of sexual frustration."

"Oh, well that's a relief," I reply, and walk ahead of him to my condo.

"What is?"

I can feel his eyes on my ass.

"Are you watching my behind?" I ask without looking at him.

"Of course I am."

I smirk and unlock my door, then turn to him. "Here's your chance to kiss me and leave me all hot and bothered again."

His lips twitch as he leans into me, his forearm braced on the door over my head. "What's a relief, Addison?"

"That I'm not the only one sexually frustrated." My voice is a shaky whisper as I stare at his lips just inches from mine.

He leans in and brushes those lips over my forehead. "Are you frustrated?"

I hum and close my eyes, soaking him in. He opens the door and leads me inside, then closes and locks the door behind us, perfectly calm.

There is no frazzled rushing. No clinging to each other and knocking things over in a race to the bedroom.

Instead, his face is perfectly calm as he turns to me and slowly moves forward, urging me to back up, walking with him through my living room. I grip the hem of his T-shirt in my hands and urge it up, until he finally takes matters into his own hands, whipping it over his head in that way men do with one hand that is so damn sexy.

And my first live glimpse of Jake shirtless is something to freaking write home about. Dear sweet Jesus, the smooth skin. The light spattering of hair.

The long, sinewy muscles that flex in his arms and chest.

God blessed him with maybe the best set of abs I've ever seen. And he has that sexier than hell V in his hips, leading down into his low-riding jeans.

Jeans that barely hide the root of his cock.

I'm salivating.

"You're good for my ego, sweetheart," he murmurs, catching my attention.

"You're—" I swallow hard, unable to finish the sentence.

"My thoughts exactly," he replies with that cocky grin back in place. I'm surprised to discover that we're already in my bedroom. Jake leans down and flicks the bedside lamp on, then turns to me, but rather than pull my clothes off, he tugs me into his arms and hugs me tight, rocking us back and forth. His bare skin under my hands is *incredible*.

I can't stop touching him. My hands are everywhere, roaming over his back, his arms, then up over his shoulders and into his hair.

Finally, he pushes his hands under my top and pulls it up over my head, dropping it to the floor. His eyes narrow and darken as he takes in the makeshift bra that holds the girls up.

But rather than try to remove it, he makes quick work of my slacks and shoes, leaving me in just my underwear.

I reach out to help him out of his jeans, but he stops me with a quick shake of the head.

"Wait."

"You're behind." I cock a brow and reach for him again, but he stops me.

"What are we waiting for?" I rest my hands on my hips and tip my head to the side. "If you leave now, I'll dismember you."

"Wild horses couldn't drag me out of here," he replies

softly, his eyes roaming up and down my body. "Jesus, Addison, you are so fucking beautiful."

Everything in me *softens*. His voice is rough. He looks . . . devastated.

"Are you okay?" I step to him and cup his face in my hands. "Jake?"

He brushes his knuckles down my cheek, then his thumb across my lower lip. He tips his forehead down to rest on mine.

"Admit it," he whispers. "You can't resist me."

There he is.

"I can resist anything," I reply with a laugh. "But you're very tempting."

"Just tempting? I'm going for irresistible here."

"You're close," I reply and reach for his jeans again. He doesn't resist me this time. He shuffles out of them, and stands before me naked.

Gloriously freaking naked.

"Now I'm behind," I whisper. He's completely aroused, and I'm itching to get my hands on his cock.

So I do.

I stroke him twice, making him curse beneath his breath.

"How do I get this bra off of you without hurting you?" he asks.

"Very carefully," I reply with a grin and simply peel it off myself. It's uncomfortable, but it doesn't hurt. I drop it to the floor, and finally, *finally*, his hands skim down my torso and back up to my breasts. He cups them gently, skimming his thumbs over the tips. He backs me up until my legs meet the bed, then pushes me back, covering me with his incredible body.

"You're so beautiful," he breathes, kissing me tenderly. His hands are everywhere, all over my body. He hooks his thumbs in my panties and guides them down my legs, then skims his palms back up them, grinning at me. "Except these Sasquatch legs of yours."

"They aren't that bad." I giggle, not at all uncomfortable with him now. The apprehension I felt in the car is long gone.

And now there is just *him*.

"You have gorgeous legs," he says, serious now. His lips follow his hands up my legs, and I'm mortified.

I haven't had a shower in more than twelve hours.

"Why did you just stiffen up?" he asks softly.

"Because I'm not exactly shower-fresh," I reply honestly.

"You smell amazing," he replies. His nose brushes over my smooth pubis. "And I love that you wax this clean."

He blows on my skin, making my back arch. His hands glide up the back of my thighs, to my ass, and he tilts my hips so I'm on display for him, like his own private buffet.

"Your pussy is so pink," he whispers as he lowers his face and gently swipes the flat of his tongue from my opening, over my lips, to my clit.

"Oh God."

"And you smell like you can't wait for me to fuck you."

"It's accurate then," I reply breathlessly. My hands have found their way into his hair, gripping tightly as he continues to lick me. He's not applying any pressure; he's just lazily brushing that amazing tongue up and down my folds, making me freaking crazy.

"Jake," I breathe.

"Right here?" he asks, and tickles my lips with the tip of his tongue. "Does that feel good?"

"So good."

"What about this?" He pulls one hand from my ass and circles my clit with his fingertip, then pushes it inside me, making me clench down on him *hard*.

"Fuck!"

"I'm going to assume that means you like it."

He's such a smart-ass.

"You're amazing, Addie. Every fucking inch of you makes me crazy."

"I want every inch of you to make me crazy too," I reply between pants. He chuckles and bites the inside of my thigh, making me moan.

"You like it when I bite you?"

"I like it all," I reply truthfully. "As long as you're the one doing it."

"Fucking right," he growls, and kisses his way up my body, pausing to pay special attention to my breasts. He bites each nipple, tugs it, then laves it with the flat of his tongue, making me squirm like crazy beneath him.

"Jake, please sink inside me now."

"Oh God," he mutters and clenches his eyes shut. "Addie, I don't have any condoms with me."

"I'm going to assume you were never a Boy Scout," I complain.

"No," he replies and shakes his head in disgust. "God, baby, I'm so sorry."

"I have an IUD," I say as I drag my fingertips up his arm, tracing the ink there. "And I'm healthy."

"I haven't been with anyone since before my last checkup," he admits and smiles slowly. "So does that mean that you still want me inside you?"

"Let me think about it."

But before I can, he settles between my legs, and rubs the head of his cock over my folds, up over my clit, and then pushes slowly inside me, making me gasp loudly.

"Hurting you?" he whispers.

"In the best way," I confirm. He stops cold, and when he would pull out, I stop him. "You're a big man, Jake, but I'm fine. Just give me a second to adjust."

"I don't want to hurt you," he whispers and brushes a strand of hair off my cheek. "I never want to hurt you."

"This is the best hurt there is," I reply, circling my hips. He clenches his eyes shut and curses under his breath.

"Addie, if you keep that up, I won't be able to stay still. God, you're fucking wet."

"Just looking at your hard body makes me wet. But add your mouth on me in the mix, and I'm dripping wet."

"God, baby." His hips begin to move now, slowly, in and out, and it's the best fucking thing I've ever felt. "Your pussy hugs my cock perfectly."

I grin and clench down, delighted when his eyes cross.

"I kind of love turning you on," I gasp.

"I'm past turned on," he growls, and lays his lips against

mine, kissing me deep and slow as his body makes love to me. He's sped up, his hips rocking against mine, his pubis hitting my clit with every thrust.

"God, Jake, I'm gonna come."

"Good." He grins against my mouth. His eyes are open and watching me. "Come, Addison."

I can only watch him as he picks up the speed again, thrusting in earnest. Every nerve in my body is on high alert, and I feel the explosion building at the base of my spine, until I can't hold it back anymore. I arch my back, curling my toes, digging my nails into the skin of his arms, as I fall apart.

"So goddamn amazing," he growls and pushes twice more before stopping, balls deep, and comes hard, groaning in my ear.

We are an exhausted, panting, sweaty mess as he rolls away, but he keeps me with him, still inside me, pulling me on top of him.

"I'm too heavy to stay on top of you, and I want to stay inside you," he says and hugs me tight. "Thank you."

"For what?" I frown up at him.

"I'm *inside you*. And I'm grateful."

I smile and kiss his chin, then push up against his chest so I can kiss his lips thoroughly. I can't help but circle my hips at the same time, and smile widely as I feel him begin to stiffen inside me again.

"Round two," I mutter and slide back and forth. He grips my hips tightly in his hands, most likely leaving little fingertip-size bruises, and that makes me almost giddy.

I can't wait to see them later.

"You have a naughty smile on that gorgeous face," he says, then moans when I reach down and circle my clit as I ride him.

"I'm a naughty girl," I reply before biting my lip.

"So noted."

Chapter Eight

Jake

$\mathcal{I}$ reach for her, but where she should be tucked up against me is cold. She's been out of bed for a while, thwarting my intentions to fuck her into the mattress this morning.

Which is fine. I'll just find her and carry her back here. I lie still and listen, hoping to hear her in the shower. Some playtime in the water could also be fun, but the condo is quiet.

And then it occurs to me: I smell food.

She's making breakfast.

I'm going to marry her. Today.

I slide from the bed and pull on my boxer briefs, then pad out of the bedroom to the kitchen, rubbing the sleep from my eyes.

And then I come to a complete stop, staring in wonder at the gorgeous woman in the kitchen. Her back is to me. She's piled her hair on top of her head, with messy, loose tendrils falling out of it. She's in my T-shirt from last night, which hangs only low enough to cover the majority of her ass, but the very bottom of it where her ass and thighs meet, and her black panties, show, making my morning semi an official hard-on.

She's swaying her hips side to side as she mixes something in a bowl. A waffle iron is set up next to her, heating.

And she's humming.

Completely off-key.

God, she's adorable.

She turns toward the sink that sits in the island separating us, her lip sunk between her perfect teeth, then yelps when she sees me standing here.

"Didn't mean to startle you," I say quietly, all of my emotions suddenly a jumbled mess. Her face is clean of any makeup, that blond hair a halo around her face. My T-shirt looks amazing on her.

And she's cooking for me. I don't remember a woman I've been intimate with ever cooking for me. Certainly not breakfast, because I'm sure to rush out as soon as I can. But seeing this woman, cooking for me, makes my heart ache in the sweetest way.

God, I've become such a softie. Max would have a field day if he heard my thoughts.

"It's okay, I was deep in thought." She sighs, washes her hands, and offers me a sweet smile. "I hope you're hungry 'cause I'm making waffles."

"I'm starving." *For you.* I want her under me, over me, any way I can get her right now, as long as I'm inside her.

But I sit on a stool at the breakfast bar and watch her bustle about the kitchen.

"Bacon too?" I ask in surprise as she lays strips of the meat on a cookie sheet.

"Of course. Isn't it illegal to have breakfast without bacon?"

"Watch out, you'll make me feel special."

She snorts and shakes her head, returning to her bowl of waffle mix.

"What time do you have to work today?" I ask.

"I've been trying to take Sundays off. I have an idea!" She spins, her blue eyes round with excitement. "Let's stay in bed all day and trade sexual favors for trips to the fridge."

My lips tilt up into a smile. "That sounds like the best idea I've heard in years. But, I can't. I have to work today."

"Oh." Her shoulders sag as her lower lip sticks out in a cute pout, then she turns to pour mix into the waffle iron.

"I'd like to bring you with me."

"What?" She leans her hips against the counter and crosses her arms. "Where? To work?"

I nod.

"I'll just be in the way."

"No you won't."

"What will you be doing?" She tilts her head to the side, and I want to bury my face in her neck and kiss her there.

"Max and I have some work to finish up today," I reply,

purposefully evading. I don't want to tell her who will be in the studio with us today. She might get nervous and decide she doesn't want to go.

And for reasons I'm not entirely sure of right now, I don't just want her there today. I need her.

"I want to show you my studio."

A naughty, slow grin spreads over her face. "Is that what they're calling it these days?"

I smirk and let my eyes noticeably travel up and down her body, fucking her with my eyes. When my gaze finds hers again, she's breathing harder, and her right hand is white-knuckled on the granite. Her eyes are a little glassy.

I want her. The several bouts of lovemaking through the night did nothing to assuage that.

But I also want to show her my life. Because I have a feeling she's about to become a very big part of it, and as new and confusing as that is, it also feels really good.

"Come with me today," I say simply.

"Okay." She smiles softly before plating a waffle and passing it to me, along with butter and syrup. "But first, we eat."

"I'm going to eat this," I begin, stuffing a bite in my mouth and groaning in ecstasy. Jesus, she can cook. "And then I'm going to put you in the shower, clean you up, then take you back to the bed and eat you."

Her eyes whip up to mine. Her nipples are puckered against my shirt.

"And you didn't ask to borrow that."

"My bad."

I grin. "It's okay. I'll take it back after breakfast."

She grins in return, then simply pulls it over her head, folds the shirt, and passes it to me. She's left standing there in nothing but little black panties.

Jesus fucking Christ.

"No need to wait," she replies sweetly and takes a bite of her waffle. "It's a soft shirt."

"I've had it awhile." God, is that my voice? I sound like an adolescent, only making her smile widen.

She sets her plate down and stretches her arms high about her head, then bends and touches her toes, giving me a prime view of that amazing body, and I can't stand it anymore. I march around the island, put her over my shoulder, and head for her bathroom.

"What's happening?" She's giggling now, making me smile too.

"I know what you were doing, and it worked, sweetness. You have my undivided attention, and you're about to have much more than that."

"Promises, promises," she replies, only laughing more when I slap her ass.

"We might be a little late for work."

"So that's the house," I say as I lead Addie around to the back of it. "I'll give you the grand tour later. This is better."

"Better than the house?" she asks. "Because the house is pretty great from the outside."

"The back is better," I assure her, and grin when the pool comes into view. "This is what sold me on the place."

"The pool?"

I nod. "I like to swim."

"Makes sense," she says with a nod. "You have a swimmer's body."

I grin down at her. "You love my body."

"I said you have a swimmer's body. There was no mention of how I feel about it." She quirks an eyebrow.

"You can't get enough of me," I reply confidently, remembering how crazy I made her after our shower this morning.

So crazy we needed another shower.

I cup her face in my hands and kiss her silly, until she melts against me and grips my shirt at my hips, in that way that makes *me* silly.

"I still have to show you the best part," I murmur against her lips.

"I thought the pool was the best part."

I nuzzle her nose with mine, then back away. "Nope. It's this." I gesture to the guesthouse turned studio and grin. "Welcome to Knox Productions."

"This is the studio?"

"Yep." I lead her inside and close the door quietly behind me, in case someone is already recording, but Max and Steve are sitting at the piano, bickering.

"You decided to show up," Max says with a frown, then his eyes brighten when he sees Addie. "Well hi there."

"Hi," she says calmly. There's a music legend sitting in this room, and she's cool as a cucumber.

Good girl.

"You've met Addie," I say to Max, then hug Steve as he stands. "It's good to see you, Steve."

"You too, mate," he says, his English accent thick. "Who is this magnificent woman?" he asks, his sunglass-covered gaze raking up and down her body. She's in khaki shorts and a white button-down, tied at the waist.

Her legs go on for days.

"Steve, this is Addison. Addie, I'd like to introduce you to Steve."

"Hello," she replies, holding her hand out for his. "It's a pleasure to see you again. I had the honor of meeting you a couple of years ago when my ex-boyfriend's band, Philadelphia Story, performed at the Grammys."

"I remember." He lifts her hand to his mouth and kisses her knuckles, one by one, making me raise a brow. Steve's known to be a womanizer. "You were with Craig Parker then."

Addie nods and shifts her eyes to me uncertainly. I've met Craig Parker before. He's not a bad guy.

We'll talk about this later.

"If your voice is half as amazing as your face, you'll be a mega-superstar, love."

"I'm not a singer," Addie replies with a chuckle.

"Addie owns a restaurant in Portland," I inform him. My jaw clenches as he tucks Addie's hand into the crook of his arm and escorts her back to the piano.

"Please tell me you'll be here while I record today. I could use a beautiful muse."

"Oh my goodness, Mr. Jennings." She chuckles again and pats his shoulder. "You are absolutely charming, and it truly is an honor to see you again." Her blue gaze catches mine for just a moment before she continues. "I grew up listening to your music. My parents are big fans."

"I have a few talents you'd be a fan of, darling."

Okay. He's just taken it too far, but before I can step in, Addie laughs, pats his cheek, and says, "You're so funny."

"Funny?" Steve repeats as Addie crosses to me. "Times sure have changed. Used to be, a beautiful woman never would have called me funny. Charming maybe, but not funny."

Addie grins and simply links her fingers with mine. "Where can I sit that I'll be out of the way?"

"You're not in my way," I reply and kiss her cheek, then whisper in her ear. "Well done."

"Tiffany's on her way with lunch," Max says as he noodles the keys.

"Tiffany?" Addie asks curiously. "You mean, I don't have to be the only woman in the middle of all this testosterone today?"

"Tiff is my girlfriend," Max says.

"And he's lucky to have me," Tiffany says as she closes the door behind her. She's carrying bags of sandwiches and drinks from a local deli. "You must be Addie."

"The one and only," Addie confirms with a grin and joins Tiffany. "Let me help."

"We're going the simple route today," Tiffany says. "Sandwiches, salads, and drinks. We'll just set up on Jake's desk."

"Perfect," Addie replies and begins asking Tiffany a wide range of questions, pulling the other woman into an easy conversation. I join Steve and Max at the piano.

"I like her," Steve says quietly.

"I couldn't tell," I reply sarcastically. "I didn't know that she dated Craig."

"You and I both know that was a test," he says with a smile. "I love you. I want to know that the woman you've chosen to bring into your life, whether it be for a week or twenty years, isn't a—"

"She isn't," I interrupt.

"No," Steve agrees. "She isn't. Craig is a lot of things, but he loved her. He said good things about her. Shame that he fucked around and lost her."

Typical.

"Can we stop talking about women now and get down to business?" Max asks. "We have four songs to record today."

"I thought we were recording three," I reply, and smile at Addie as she hands me a sandwich.

"I found a fourth," Steve says, all business now. "It's brilliant, and could even be the first single from the album."

"Let's hear it," I reply. Max cues the demo up and plays it as we munch our lunches. Steve's right, the song is amazing, and perfect for his voice. It's hip, but has a vintage edge to it, which will appeal to his older fan base. "I love it. Play it again."

By the time we've all finished our lunches, we've heard the new song five times, and I've memorized the lyrics.

"We already have music tracks laid for the other three," Max says. "This new song will have to be done from scratch."

"So, let's go ahead and record those three, then we'll see

where we're sitting for time. I can have studio musicians in here tomorrow to record this new one."

"Perfect," Steve says with a grin. "I'll stay in Portland one more day. Maybe your girlfriend will come to her senses and decide that I'm the better man after all."

We all look over at the two women sitting at my desk, eating their lunch. Addie is long, curvy, and blond. Her makeup is minimal today, making her look young and fresh. Tiffany is shorter, with less curves and dark hair cut short. She's wearing her signature red lipstick, and a smile that brightens the room.

They're quickly becoming friends.

"Yeah, I don't think that's going to happen, buddy." I clap Steve on the shoulder.

"Pity."

IT'S BEEN A long day, but we're finally finished with the three songs we originally wanted to record today. I have musicians lined up for tomorrow, and Steve has left for the night.

The girls moved their little party out beside the pool about an hour ago while we wrapped things up. Addie seemed to enjoy the studio time. I loved having her here. I loved answering her questions, and watching her face when Steve sang.

Even with as many years as he has under his belt, the man can still sing.

"Hey, guys," Tiffany says as she walks into the room. "Can I have a minute with Max?"

There's something going on. I narrow my eyes at her, but she just smiles, silently reassuring me.

"Is Addie by the pool?"

"Yep. We've been talking about you."

"Great." I laugh and walk out the door, closing it behind me, and immediately see Addie sitting in a chaise under a wide, red umbrella. "How are you, baby?"

"I'm great."

"Why do I get the feeling that Tiffany has a secret?"

"Because she does."

I scoop Addie up, then sit with her in my lap. "What is it?"

She shrugs and settles against me, burying her face in my neck.

"Do you know?" I ask and kiss her head.

"Of course. What do you think we've been talking about?"

"But you're not going to tell me?"

"Not my secret to tell," she replies simply.

"Okay, tell me about Craig instead."

She doesn't stiffen, or look uncomfortable. She simply kisses my neck. "He's the past, Jake. We were together for a long time, but we couldn't make it work."

"Steven says he heard that Craig cheated on you."

"I've heard the same rumor," she replies softly.

Suddenly, the door to the studio bursts open and Max comes running out, his eyes wide and excited, and if I'm not mistaken, wet.

"What's wrong?" I ask as I stand and set Addie on her feet next to me.

"Not one thing," he replies and pulls me in for a hug. The kind of hug that usually makes men very uncomfortable. "I'm gonna be a daddy."

"What?" I pull away and grip his shoulders in my hands. "Seriously?"

"I'm pretty sure the dozen or so tests I took aren't wrong," Tiffany says as she joins us. Max whoops and lifts Tiffany into the air, laughing and crying at the same time.

And I join them. Hugging them, laughing and crying with them. I love these people. I couldn't love them more if they were related to me by blood.

"I can't believe it," I say as we all settle down and pull Addie in for a hug. "We're going to have a baby."

"Um, I believe *I'll* be having the baby," Tiffany mutters. "But you can hold it."

"And change its diaper," Max adds.

"No way. That's your job." I grin, so happy for them and also trying to stop feeling the ache in my heart for Christina. She and Kevin are trying again this month. "A baby."

"Okay, I'm taking my woman home to celebrate." Max wiggles his eyebrows, making Tiffany laugh. "Have a good night."

"Congratulations," Addie says. "And Tiffany, don't forget to call me."

"Trust me, I won't."

I settle Addie and me back in the chair. "You guys became fast friends."

"She and I went to the same high school," Addie says. "It's a small world."

"Hmm."

"Plus, she's a sweet woman. You can tell that she has a really good heart." There's a sadness in Addie's voice now, making me frown.

"You're definitely right about that," I reply cautiously. Addie's quiet for a long minute. "What's wrong?"

"I don't think I have a good heart," she whispers. "My heart isn't a pretty place, Jake. You should know that before this goes much further."

Oh, baby.

"Why would you think that?"

She shrugs. "Jake, my own parents don't want to be around me much. Men walk all over me. I have wonderful friends, but I don't think I'm particularly lovable."

"You're wrong, you know."

She simply shakes her head. "No, I'm not. My heart's been fucked with too much. I'm callous. I'm cynical."

"So, you're saying you're human," I reply and tilt her chin up so I can look her in the eyes. "Addie, you're a grown woman. Of course you've had life experiences that have broken your heart, made you guarded. I don't need someone with a spotless heart. Give me someone who's been through some shit, who's had to pick herself up, dust herself off, and get on with it."

"I just wish I was less cynical and more kind."

"Stop it. You *are* kind. And you're not necessarily cynical. You're guarded, and that's okay. You're a smart woman. But I see you showing kindness to people all the time. At your job, to your friends, to *my* friends."

She frowns, and I kiss her forehead, then settle her against me again. "Don't be so hard on yourself, sweetheart. It may have taken me a while to break through some of your walls, but here we are. You're wild about me."

"I tolerate you," she replies with a smile in her voice.

"Stop fawning. It's embarrassing."

She throws back her head and laughs, and I'm pleased to have made her smile again. "So, you like to swim?" she asks, tracing the tattoos on my arm.

"Love it. You?"

"I can swim," she says softly. "I learned when I was little."

Suddenly, she stands and strips out of her clothes, leaving me painfully aroused and my jaw dropped.

"I bet I can beat you, from end to end."

"Do you?" I stand and strip out of my own clothes. She cocks a brow at the sight of my hard-on, but I simply shrug. "Your fault, sweetness."

"I didn't do that."

I laugh. "You're breathing. I'm hard. That's how it works."

She smirks and jumps into the deep end of the pool, then comes up treading water. "Are you in or not?"

"What do I get if I win?" I ask and jump in after her.

"Me."

"And what do you get if you win? Which you won't, by the way."

"I get you."

"Sounds like a win-win to me."

She shrugs and braces herself on the edge of the pool. "We'll push off from here. Ready?"

"This is going to be embarrassing for you," I warn her.

"Go!"

I watch her push off and swim away, and then I join her, giving her a three-second handicap.

Because I'm about to crush her in this race.

Just as I pass her, she grabs my ankle, pulling me under. She lets go, but instead of continuing to the other end of the pool, I simply pick her up and throw her toward the deep end.

"Hey!" she sputters as she surfaces. "That's cheating!"

"And pulling me under isn't?" I ask with a laugh.

"You were passing me," she replies primly. "That wasn't fair."

"It was a race. That's what happens when someone is winning."

"You aren't supposed to win," she replies, as if I'm a slow child who just doesn't understand what's being said.

"Sore loser, are you?"

"I like to call it *competitive*." She giggles and swims toward me, wraps her arms and legs around me, and holds on tight, pressing her core against my pelvis. "Sex in the pool always looks fun in the movies," she says, then wrinkles her nose. "But it's not fun in real life."

"No?"

"No." She shakes her head and kisses me. I reach down and guide myself inside her, but stop there, not moving in and out, and walk out of the pool to a chaise lounge in the setting sun and lay her back on it. "But this works."

"This absolutely works," I agree, still seated deep inside her. "God, Addie, you feel amazing."

She's tight. And warm. And fuck me, her skin pressed to mine is the closest to heaven I'll ever be.

I slide in and out slowly, making her wetter, making her moan and writhe beneath me. I fucking love how vocal she is when I'm inside her.

"How do you feel?" I whisper.

"Sexy," she replies as her eyes find mine. "Full. Wet."

I grin and move faster, in short thrusts, rubbing her clit with my pubis each time. She moans, making my dick harden more, if that's even possible.

"You're so fucking incredible." I lean down to pull a puckered nipple into my mouth. "Can't get enough of you."

"You can go harder," she says with a smile.

"You want it rough, baby?"

She nods. I pull out and flip her over, slap her ass, then push inside her from behind and fuck her hard, gripping her hips roughly. I reach down and pull her hair from the scalp and feel my eyes cross when she reaches under to clutch my balls. I'm pounding her. I can't get far enough inside her.

I'm marking her.

The orgasm sneaks up on me and pulls me under quickly. I rock against her perfect ass, coming inside her. She's pushed back against me, spasming around me, coming with me.

"Fucking incredible," I whisper and kiss her shoulder before I pull out and chuckle when she collapses on the chaise, spent. "Tired?"

"Mm."

"Hungry?"

"Mm."

I bite her shoulder. "Ready for a shower?"

"Can't move."

I grin.

"All of this praise for my masculinity is really overboard, babe. Just a simple thank-you is sufficient."

She chuckles and turns onto her side so she can see me.

"Can I please cook you dinner?"

"Cooking twice in one day?"

"I'd like to poke around your kitchen."

I scoop her up and pad, both of us naked, to the house. "You can poke around anything you want, baby."

"Good, because I also want to poke around your bedroom."

"I thought you'd never ask."

Chapter Nine

Addison

"God, I needed this," Kat moans two days later as she and I sit side by side in massaging pedicure chairs, our feet soaking in hot water as we wait for our turns.

"Me too. We spend a lot of time on our feet."

"In heels," she agrees with a nod. "Mia needs this too."

"Mia won't take enough time off to do this." I sigh as the rollers in the chair run up and down my back, on either side of my spine. "She worries me."

"She worries all of us," Kat says. "She's a workaholic."

"We're all workaholics," I remind her. "Mia's a workfanatic."

"Truth," Kat says. "Maybe she needs an intervention."

"I think that's what it'll eventually come down to. And now that we're talking about expanding the restaurant, she's going to need more help. She can't keep firing all of her sous chefs."

"She's a perfectionist. I wouldn't want to work for her."

"She's a tyrant," I reply with a laugh. "I mean, I appreciate that she just wants the customers to have what they asked for, but geez."

"Mia just wants people to come back. She wants them to have the best experience ever. We can't fault her for that."

"No." I shake my head and smile at the woman who sits on a little stool at my feet and begins taking my old polish off. "What's new with you?"

"Oh no," Kat says with a laugh. "We're going to talk about you. Please tell me you and Jake . . . played Parcheesi," she says, wiggling her brows and making me giggle.

"Parcheesi?" I ask with a snort. "Is that what we're calling it?"

"For now it is, yes."

"Yes, we played Parcheesi."

Kat claps her hands and shifts in her seat. "Finally! How was he? Does he know his way around the, um, board?"

"He doesn't need a GPS, that's for sure." I take a sip of my iced latte. "He stayed the night, then took me to his place the next day. It's a nice place."

"I bet it is," Kat replies with shrewd eyes. "What else happened?"

"I met Steve Jennings."

"The rock god, Steven Jennings?" Kat squeals. "Shut the front door!"

"That's the one," I reply with a nod. "He's quite the flirt."

"He's old," she replies with a frown.

"Doesn't mean he's not a flirt. Besides, old or not, I bet he doesn't have to work very hard to get women in his bed."

"True. But back to Jake. Things are going well?"

"I think so."

She turns her head to me, one perfectly sculpted eyebrow raised. "You think so?"

"How do you always have such perfect makeup?" I ask, deliberately trying to change the subject. "I mean, have you found a new setting spray you haven't told me about? Because you need to tell me these things."

"I swear, you two are like kids who don't know what they're doing, and you're too fucking stubborn to admit it."

"We are not like kids," I reply with a frown.

"You *think* things are going well," Kat says. "Are you guys not talking? Or are you just playing Parcheesi?"

"Of course we talk," I reply, getting angry now. "I've only been out with him a handful of times, Kat. We just started sleeping together. We're still learning each other. It's not like we're eight years in and I still *think* it's going well. Did you expect him to put a ring on my finger already?"

Jesus, just the thought of that terrifies me.

"From the look on your face right now, I'll say absolutely not," Kat replies with a chuckle. "I know it's early, and it's totally cool to take your time, Add. In fact, take all the time you want. But you should know if it's going well or not. I mean, does he piss you off? Irritate you? Snore too loud? Use up all the hot water? Is he nice to you?"

"He's very nice to me," I reply softly. "And he doesn't irritate me."

"Good."

"How about you?"

"He definitely doesn't irritate me either, but I'm not the one fucking him."

The woman rubbing Kat's feet whips her head up in surprise, then looks back down.

"I mean, I'm not the one playing Parcheesi with him."

"No, I mean are you seeing anyone?" I close my eyes, enjoying the calf massage I'm getting. God, my heels make my calves hurt so bad.

But they're so worth it.

"Yes," Kat replies dryly. "I'm seeing the wine delivery guy twice a week."

"Isn't he married?"

"Yes, smart-ass, he is." Kat laughs, then sighs in pleasure as her pedicurist hits a good spot on the sole of her foot. "I don't have time to date, Addie."

"Neither do I, but I'm fitting it in somehow."

"I guess if I met someone worth making room for I would. But he's still a myth."

"He exists," I reply confidently. "You'll meet him."

"God help him," Kat says with a laugh. "I'm a handful."

"We all can be." The lady moves to my other leg, twisting her hands around my ankle. God, I love her right now. Seriously, can I just date her?

"What are you doing after this?"

"I'm going home to do some laundry and dishes, then get ready for work. You?"

"Riley is dragging me to yoga," she says, making a face like she just swallowed sour milk. "What did I ever do to her? Why does she want to laugh at me like that?"

"What's up with you and Cami and your aversion to the gym?" I ask with a laugh. "It's a good stress reliever."

"So is stabbing people, but I don't do that either." Her pedicurist looks up at her in horror again. "I just said I don't do that."

"Yoga is fun."

"Why did I choose friends who always want to get together?" she asks grumpily, pursing her bright red lips. "Why can't we all love each other from afar?"

"You love us," I reply, reaching over to pat her arm. "You've loved us since we met at college, and you and Cami were roommates, and you'd miss us if you never saw us."

"Yeah, yeah. Says the girl who gets to go home and be alone today."

"So bail on Riley. She'll understand."

Kat frowns. "No. I won't bail."

"You're a good friend."

"I am where it's earned," she replies, sober now. "And I think the five of us have earned it."

"In spades," I agree.

I HAVE BLOUSES hung all over my condo, drying. I don't ever put them in the dryer because they'll shrink up in the bust area, and while I don't mind showing off the girls now and again, I am not a stripper. They don't need to be in anyone's face.

Well, except Jake's. He seems to like it when they're in his face.

I smirk and fold a pair of panties from La Perla. I only have a few pairs of these, and they are so worth the expense.

Jake loves them.

Jake, Jake, Jake.

He's all I think about these days, and that's starting to irritate even me. Am I one of those annoying women who obsess about a guy and annoy everyone around them?

And is Kat right? Am I too stubborn to admit that I don't know what I'm doing?

Do I know what I'm doing?

"What the fuck are we doing?" I ask the empty room as I fold towels. We're getting to know each other. We're having great sex.

Amazing sex.

The best sex in the history of sex.

But more than that, I like him. Like, really like him. So does this mean that it's going to hurt more when he breaks my heart?

Correction: when he destroys my heart.

Because he will. At this point, if it were to end, I'd be hurt. I'd be sad. It would be another shot to my already Swiss-cheesy heart.

Then again, maybe he really is different from the others. I mean, the only similarity so far is the fact that the man has music running through his veins. He's not like the other wannabe musicians I've dated. He's funny and kind, and although he can be a little cocky, he's not an asshole.

Or is all of that a ruse?

I hang my head, face buried in a clean towel, and moan.

"I don't know what the fuck I'm doing."

Let's be honest, I've never known what I'm doing when it comes to men. Because I've always been drawn to the man who was the exact opposite of what was good for me. Do I feel the need to fix them? To *change* them? To rescue them?

Damned if I know.

But Jake doesn't need to be saved or fixed. He's got his shit together. And I'm still attracted to him.

More attracted than I've ever been in my life.

Maybe I should talk to him. Ask him what he wants.

Except, I'll be mortified when he just stares at me blankly, wondering what the fuck I'm talking about because, after all, this is just sex.

But, it doesn't feel like just sex. It feels like more.

And I don't even know why I'm getting all worked up about it because it's still super-early, and we have lots to learn about each other, and damn Kat for making me think about this shit!

We need to find her a man so she stops worrying about me and mine.

I finish folding the towels and eye the dishes in the sink. There aren't many, so I quickly rinse them and stack them in the dishwasher, then check the time.

I have an hour until I need to get ready for work.

My phone rings, startling me.

"Hi, Mom."

"Aloha, darling," she replies with a smile in her voice. "How is my sweet girl?"

"I'm good." It's so good to hear her voice. I've missed her and Dad both so much. "What are you up to? Is Dad okay?"

"He's just fine," she assures me. "He's napping on the balcony, as usual."

I smile. Every afternoon, my dad sits on the balcony that looks out over the Pacific and falls asleep. He says he's brainstorming lectures for class.

Sure he is.

"And what are you up to?"

"I was just thinking about you. How is the restaurant going?" I hear her munching on something crunchy on the other end of the line.

"It's so great, Mom." I tell her all about hiring Jake, and how our business has boomed in the past two months. "In fact, we're thinking of buying the space next to ours—it's for sale—and expanding. You should come visit! I'd love to show it to you."

"That all sounds fantastic, Addie! I'm so proud of you. You know your dad and I would come visit in a heartbeat, but we were just at your aunt Judy's place in Sacramento, so another trip to the mainland is a few months off yet."

"You were at Aunt Judy's?" I ask with a frown. "When?"

"Oh, just a couple of weeks ago. It was a quick trip."

"It's a thirty-minute flight from me, and you didn't think to let me know you were there? I would have come to see you, or you could have come up here."

"Really, Addie, it was a quick trip. You're being a bit dramatic."

Dramatic? Tears prick my eyes as I sit on the edge of the couch. They were hours from me. I haven't seen them since the grand opening of Seduction more than six months ago, and I miss them.

But I'm being dramatic.

I just want my mama.

"Addie? Are you there, darling?"

"I'm here."

"I see your father stirring. I'd better start making lunch. It was so good to hear your voice. Keep me posted on the expansion, okay?"

"Oh, can I say hi to Daddy real quick?"

"You know how he is after his nap, darling. I'll tell him you send your love."

He doesn't want to talk to me.

"Okay. Love you, Mom."

"I love you too, baby."

I hang up and swipe angrily at the tears falling down my cheek. It's stupid to have my feelings hurt. I'm an adult. They don't have to check in with me every time they come to the mainland, for crying out loud.

But it would have been good to see them. And the fact that they didn't think to call me does hurt my feelings.

Just once in this life I'd like to feel like I'm someone's priority. That I matter.

My parents love me, I know that. But they're doing their own thing now, which is what they should do.

I don't even know why I'm upset. They didn't do anything wrong.

I'm definitely moody. Maybe I'm hormonal. One thing is for sure, for the first time since we opened our doors, I'm not looking forward to work tonight. I don't want to go in. I want to stay home, eat pizza, and watch girl movies.

And why shouldn't I do exactly that? I have hired an excellent staff. I have four partners who know the place inside out. I don't have to be there every damn day.

Before I overthink it, I call Kat.

"Don't ever let me go to yoga again," she says immediately. "They make you fold yourself into poses that just aren't natural. I'm pretty sure I strained an eyebrow."

"An eyebrow?"

"And a calf. Maybe my wrist, I'm not sure."

"There is a point to my call," I say.

"Oh, right. What's up?"

"I'm not coming in to work tonight."

Silence. Finally, after a long pause, she says, "What do you mean?"

"I didn't stutter," I reply and sniffle. "I'm not coming in."

"Hey, does this have anything to do with our conversation earlier? Because after I gave it some thought, I realized that I was pretty hard on you. I'm sorry. I just love you and I want to make sure you're happy."

I love you too. This only makes the tears come harder.

"No, it's not you," I lie. "I just think it's best if I stay home. You guys can handle the front of the house for one night."

"Of course we can," Kat assures me. "I'll call in an extra

bartender so I can bounce back and forth. It won't be a problem at all."

"Thank you."

"Addie? You'd tell me if you're upset because of me, right? Because I don't ever want to hurt your feelings."

"Of course." *Probably not.* "I'm just gonna take some time for myself."

"Okay. Let us know if you need anything."

"Thanks."

I hang up and sigh deeply. First things first. I need a shower, then I'm going to order pizza and break into the emergency tub of chocolate peanut butter ice cream I have in the back of the freezer and settle in to watch movies.

Alone.

So MUCH FOR being alone.

When I got out of the shower, I had four missed calls. Kat clearly can't keep her trap shut.

Since then, they all, and by all I mean *all,* including Cici, have been texting me, asking me if I'm okay. What's wrong. Do I need anything.

They're driving me crazy, and making me love them even more.

It's weird.

I've eaten four slices of New York–style pizza and am thinking about firing up the oven and baking some of the ready-to-bake chocolate chip cookies I have in the fridge when the doorbell rings.

"Are you kidding me right now?"

I pause my movie and stomp across the condo. "Seriously, you didn't have to come! You bitches need to get a life and stop worrying about me."

I yank the door open and stop short when I'm staring at a very broad, very muscular T-shirt-covered chest. My eyes travel up to Jake's face and narrow as a slow, sexy smile spreads over his face.

God, that smile freaking kills me. All he has to do is smile and I'm a pile of mushy goo.

Except, not today.

"Why are you here?"

The smile doesn't leave his face as he leans his shoulder against the doorjamb. His eyes lower to my chest and his smile widens.

I glance down and sigh at the sight of tomato sauce on my white tank top, and then realize that I'm *only* wearing the tank and some red panties.

Because I'm being lazy.

Alone.

I roll my eyes and turn away, walking back into my living room. My blankie is in a wad in the middle of the couch, the pizza box on the ottoman, open, with three empty Diet Coke cans sitting next to the uneaten portion of the pizza.

Which I fully intend to eat before the night is out.

"Look, Jake, I'm not really fit for company tonight."

"It looks like you're having quite the party," he comments as he follows me inside. He's carrying a grocery bag. "I brought ice cream and what I've been told is your favorite wine."

God, I love Kat.

"You didn't have to do that."

"I don't *have* to do anything," he agrees as he saunters all sexy-like into my kitchen and stows the ice cream in the freezer, then finds a wineglass and pours me some wine. "But I don't like the thought of you being here, unhappy, alone."

"I'm not unhappy. I'm moody."

I cross my arms over my chest and glare at Jake. God, I look horrific. Can't a girl have a pity party for one in peace?

"I won't bother you." His eyes have sobered, and he's staring at me now, waiting for me to kick him the hell out.

Which I'm sure I should do. Right now. I have a movie to watch, wine to drink, and pizza to eat.

But instead I sit on the couch and gesture for him to sit on the opposite side.

"I'm watching a girl movie," I inform him. "And I'm not changing it."

"Good plan."

"And I'm eating lots of food, and I'll probably belch. I'm not very pretty tonight."

"You're always gorgeous, and none of that offends me." His lips twitch as he sits, not touching me. His hands are clenching in and out of fists, and I can tell he wants to pull me to him, but he's respecting my need for some space.

So, I resume the movie, offer him a slice of pizza, and we sit in silence as we watch *The Fault in Our Stars.* This movie always makes me cry. Always.

Especially just before the very end. God, it's a shot to the heart.

But Jake pulls my feet into his lap and just rubs them firmly. He doesn't pat my leg and say, "It's only a movie."

He simply stays with me.

When the movie ends, I flip off the TV, wipe my eyes, and turn to look at Jake, who's still rubbing my feet.

"You're good at the girl's-night-in thing."

"My best friend since I was fifteen years old is a girl," he replies with a smile. "I've had a little practice."

I return his smile, finally feeling somewhat better. I'm glad he has Christina. I'm glad that she's been there for him, through everything.

True friends are hard to find.

"She seems nice." I lean my head against the back of the couch and watch his strong hands as they move up and down my legs.

"She's awesome," he replies. "And speaking of her, she wanted me to ask you if you'd like to come for dinner at her house sometime in the next week. I'm supposed to find out what night works best for you."

"Isn't it a bit early to meet the family?" I ask sarcastically, and frantically try to come up with a reason that I shouldn't go. This makes things . . . serious.

"Look at me." I oblige, and immediately feel like a bitch when I see the concern and a little hurt in his amazing green eyes. "What do you have to be afraid of? You've already met her."

"This will be different," I whisper.

"It'll be on her turf instead of yours," he guesses correctly. I simply shrug. "Life happens outside of our comfort zones, sweetness. And she wants to spend some time with you. Not because she's uberprotective of me, but because she loves me and she knows you're important to me, so she wants to get to know you a bit."

"I get it. If the girls didn't get to interact with you at the restaurant, they'd want the same thing. They may want you to hang with us outside of work anyway, now that I think of it."

"Of course they will, they love me." He smiles. "Really, Addie, this isn't a huge deal. She's my friend. We'll just go have dinner and you can get to know each other. You'll like her."

"I already do," I admit, pleating the blanket in my lap. "Both she and Kevin seem really great."

"So what night should I tell her?" he asks with a wink.

"Well, since I'm playing hooky tonight, let's say Sunday night?"

"Works for me," he replies.

"How did the other song go on Monday with Steve?"

He tilts his head in surprise. "It was good. It'll be a hit for him."

"I'm glad." I nod and flip through the movie channels, looking for another girl movie.

"Thank you."

My eyes whip to his. "For what?"

"For asking."

He squeezes my foot once, then lets go and I crawl across the couch to him. I still don't want to be held, but I lay my head in his lap and sigh when he runs his fingers through my hair.

"Thank you," I whisper.

"For what?"

"Being here. Even though I didn't know I wanted you here."

His hand pauses for a moment, then resumes brushing gently through my hair.

"You don't ever have to thank me for being here."

"And you don't ever have to thank me for asking."

Chapter Ten

Jake

She's a mess tonight, and I wish I knew why. I wish I knew what put the sad in her blue eyes. Why are her shoulders slumped? Why does my usually strong girl seem so defeated tonight?

I know her well enough to hold off on the questions. Right now, she just needs me here, and I'm happy to sit through a dozen sappy movies, eat as much pizza as she wants, and simply be here with her until she feels better.

Her hair is soft in my fingers. She's turned on another movie, a romantic comedy with Sandra Bullock and Ryan Reynolds this time. I wonder if she knows that Hard Knox has two songs on this soundtrack?

Probably not.

She laughs when Ryan's character spills coffee all over himself, and makes a coworker trade shirts with him.

God, I love her laugh. She needs to laugh more often.

I saw a vulnerable side to Addie tonight that I'm pretty sure she rarely lets anyone see. It makes sense that she would be nervous to spend time with my best friend away from the comfort of Seduction, but I forget that Addie has a vulnerable side, because she's so good at showing everyone how confident she is.

And I know it's not an act. She *is* confident. But today, something threw her off her game, and it makes my heart hurt for her.

Addie lets out a little snore, making me grin. God, she's adorable. I'm glad she fell asleep. She needs it.

And I'm not staying tonight. Because that's not what she needs from me tonight. She barely wanted me to touch her, and it took everything in me not to simply scoop her up and hold her.

I have a feeling that the foot rubs and hair strokes were a big step for my girl.

I grin down at her blond head and brush my fingers down her smooth neck.

Mine.

Yes, she's mine. Whether that's for the short term, or for the long haul, I'm not sure yet, but I know that the thought of another man putting his hands on her makes me want to punch someone.

And that reaction doesn't happen often for me.

I gently slide out from under Addie and replace my lap with a couch pillow. She stirs and smiles up at me, making my heart catch.

"I'm sorry I fell asleep."

"It's okay, baby." I kiss her forehead and then her cheek as I cover her with the blanket she's been curled up in all night. "Just sleep."

But she's already breathing long and deep, hugging the pillow to her. I turn the TV off, and leave a single lamp burning, in case she wakes up and wants to go in to bed.

Before I walk out the door, I glance back at the woman curled up on the couch and feel my heart catch. God, she's amazing.

And she's *mine*.

Once in my car, I shoot a quick text off to Christina, letting her know that Sunday night works for us, then text Kat to report that Addie is sleeping peacefully.

When I got the call from Kat earlier, she told me that Addie needed ice cream, wine, and me.

And I didn't ask any questions. I simply came. Because staying away isn't an option.

The drive home is quick. Portland is quiet this evening, and the farther I drive out of town toward my house, the more it reminds me of small town America.

Which I love.

My house is dark and silent as I walk through, past the kitchen, to the piano. The song that's been in my head since the day I saw Addie has been nagging at me, so I sit to work on it. This isn't one that I'll offer to another artist.

This is Addie's. She can decide what to do with it, whether I record it for her, or we keep it just for us.

The music came first with this one. Songwriting is never

the same for me. Sometimes the lyrics come first, and sometimes it's the music.

Every time I have her in my arms, this music plays in my head. Sometimes the melody is faster, and sometimes slower, but it's always this melody.

I reach for the sheet music I brought in from the studio last week and begin to write the notes, then grab a notebook to start jotting down lyrics and lose myself in Addie's song.

"YOU'RE LATE," CHRISTINA says with a smile as she answers the door on Sunday night. She takes the flowers from my hands and gestures for us to come inside. "Kevin is manning the grill."

"It's his fault that we're late," Addie says, immediately throwing me under the bus.

"Why was it my fault?" I ask with a frown. "You're the one who couldn't decide what to wear."

"You're the one who kept taking all of my choices off of me," she reminds me with a smile, then links her fingers with mine and gives me a squeeze. This seems to be the form of public affection that she's most comfortable with, and that's fine.

For now.

"If you didn't look hot in everything you wear, I wouldn't have to take you out of it." I glance down at the simple red dress she's wearing now and begin to salivate all over again. I lean in to whisper in her ear, "And I can't wait to get you home so I can strip you out of this one too."

"God, you're such a man," Christina says with a roll of

the eyes as she leads us back to the kitchen. "And welcome, Addie. Next time, you can just come by yourself and leave that one at home."

"*That one?*" I pull Christina into my arms and twirl her around the kitchen in a quick dance. "Admit it, you love me."

"Oh, you mean the one with the ego," Addie says with a nod. "Got it."

"You're crazy about me," I remind her and hand Chris off to Kevin as he comes in the back door with a plate full of grilled steaks. "Take your woman."

"Gladly." Kevin wraps his arms around his wife and kisses her soundly as I reach for Addie and give her a turn around the kitchen.

"Why are we dancing?" she asks with a laugh.

"Because I like to dance," I reply and kiss her nose. "Even though Chris has horrible taste in music."

"Don't start," Christina warns, pointing her finger at me. "You like my music."

I lean in and whisper loudly in Addie's ear, "I tolerate her music."

"I heard that." Christina laughs, then turns to toss the salad, but has to lean against the countertop and presses a hand to her belly. "Ugh, I wish I didn't get so crampy after the doctor visits."

"Are you okay?" I ask just as Addie speaks at the same time.

"You're pregnant too?" Addie asks with an excited smile.

"Too?" Christina raises a brow. "Don't tell me you're pregnant."

"No!" All of the blood leaves Addie's face, and then she laughs. "No."

"Me neither," Christina replies, shaking her head. "But we're trying. I had in vitro today, so now we cross our fingers and hold our breath for a couple of weeks to see if it works."

"Oh, I'll cross mine too," Addie says with a wide smile. "I'm sure it'll work."

I hope so.

"So who's pregnant?" Kevin asks.

"Tiff's pregnant," I reply, watching Addie. How would I feel about having babies with this woman?

Why am I even asking myself that question?

"That's exciting," Kevin says.

"Yeah, seems babies are in the air." I reach to grab a slice of green pepper out of the salad, but Chris slaps my hand. "Ouch!"

"I'll have to call her," Christina says with a smile. "If all goes well, maybe we can go baby shopping together."

Addie joins Christina. "How can I help?"

"Are you any good at chopping tomatoes?"

"I can handle it," Addie replies.

"Good, 'cause I suck at it. They're too slippery." Christina winks at me, and I can almost hear her thoughts. *I like her. She's helpful. She's not lazy.*

I wink at Chris and steal the pepper anyway, chewing happily.

"How did you and Jake meet?" Addie asks her.

"He asked if he could cheat off me on a math test in the tenth grade," she replies automatically.

"And did you let him?"

"No," I reply for her. "She refused, but then offered to tutor me."

"That was nice of you," Addie says as she cuts a cucumber.

"He was pathetic in math," Chris says as she grins at me.

"*Pathetic* is a strong word." I glare at her and cross my arms, but she just rolls her eyes.

"You don't intimidate me."

"Nothing intimidates you," Kevin says as he passes by her, stopping to kiss her on the back of the neck. "That's just one of the reasons that I love you."

"So did you tutor him?" Addie asks.

"Yes. And then I never could shake him loose."

"I think it's the other way around, C. I couldn't shake *you* off. You're a clingy woman."

Christina snorts, then laughs out loud as she pulls salad dressings from the fridge and sets the table. "Maybe we just found that we were kindred spirits."

"The geeks," I clarify for Kevin and Addie. "Let's call it what it was."

"I can't imagine either of you as geeks," Addie says with a shake of the head and smiles at Kevin as he offers her a glass of wine.

"We have the yearbooks to prove it," he says with a smile. "They've come a long way."

"So you grew up in Minnesota too?" Addie asks Christina.

"Yep. It's damn cold there."

"Is your family still there?"

All humor leaves C's face, and Kevin simply slips his arm around her.

"No," she replies, and I expect her to leave it at that. Christina doesn't ever discuss this part of her childhood.

But instead, she shrugs and passes me napkins to add to the table.

"My parents were killed when I was young," she says. "My family is here."

Addie nods politely, but then mumbles under her breath and pulls Christina in for a hug, surprising all of us, most of all Christina. "That fucking sucks and I'm sorry."

"It was a long time ago," Christina reassures her. "But thank you."

"Who's hungry?" Kevin asks.

"Me," we all reply, then laugh and sit down to dig in.

"What about you, Addie?" Kevin asks. "Did you grow up around here?"

"I did," she replies. "My parents live in Hawaii now."

She looks down at her plate, but not before I catch a bit of the sadness I saw in her eyes last week, and I can't help but wonder if that's part of what had her upset.

"Any siblings?" Christina asks.

"Nope, just me," Addie says. "Which was fine. I was a handful."

"Jake must have been a handful too," Kevin says before taking a sip of his wine.

"That's a given," Christina replies.

"Why are you guys giving me so much shit tonight?"

"Because it's fun," Kevin says.

"What he said," Chris adds, but her smile is soft and sweet as she watches me reach for Addie's hand.

When dinner is finished and the dishes have been cleared and the kitchen tidied, Christina catches me by the arm.

"Can you help me out in the garage?"

"In the garage?" I ask.

"Yes, the garage," she repeats between her teeth, as if that's supposed to make me understand better.

It doesn't.

"I think she wants to talk to you alone," Addie says with a laugh. "Go ahead. I'll help Kevin load the dishwasher."

I follow Christina into the garage and smile at her. "You could have just said that you wanted to talk to me."

"I didn't want to sound rude."

"She's not stupid," I reply and feel my face sober. "She's so fucking smart, C."

"I can tell." Her limp is hardly noticeable tonight as she paces back and forth by her Volvo. "And I like her."

"I like her too—"

"I like her," she interrupts me, "but I *love* her for you."

I stop talking and watch my best friend as she tries to find her words. "She's so great for you, J. She doesn't take any crap from you, but she laughs with you. She doesn't hero-worship you."

"Hero-worship me?"

"You know what I mean. She's not all starry-eyed because you're Jake Knox."

"No," I agree, "she isn't."

"But the best part?"

"There's a best part?"

"Oh yes, friend, there is. The best part is, you're *you* again. You're smiling and teasing and you're happy." She has tears in her eyes as she wraps her arms around my middle and hugs me close. "And that makes me happy."

"I like her a lot, C."

"Good. Don't fuck it up."

I laugh and hug her back. "I'll do my best."

"I WAS SO sorry to hear about Christina's parents," Addie says beside me in the car on the way back to her place.

"Yeah, it happened before I met her," I reply.

"How were they killed?"

"Serial killer," I say softly.

"What?" Addie gasps and grips my arm. "Are you serious?"

"I am." I swallow. "She only told me about it once, but then I went and looked up old newspaper articles to get the full story. A man broke into their house late one night after they'd all gone to bed. He'd been terrorizing small towns around ours for months, but they couldn't catch him."

"Oh my God."

Just wait.

"He started in her baby brother's room."

"No." She's shaking her head next to me in horror.

"Yeah, he suffocated the baby in his crib, then went into Chris's room and did the same, but didn't kill her; she passed out, thank God. When she woke up and went looking for her parents, she found them, in their bed, shot to death."

I glance over to see Addie staring at me with her mouth dropped open, one hand covering it, and the other holding tight to my arm.

"She went to live with her grandparents."

"That's the most horrific thing I've ever heard in my life."

I nod in agreement, then unfasten her fingers from my flesh and kiss her hand gently. "She's been through a lot, but she's happy now." She's been through hell and back, most of it because of me, and God, how I wish I could make that right.

"She's with her family," Addie says, finally understanding. "Good for her."

"So, are you glad you went?"

"Yes." She turns in the seat and smiles at me. "I had a great time. They're really nice people. And they love you."

"What's not to love, right?" I toss her a flippant smile, but she just tilts her head to the side, studying me.

"You know, you look good in this car."

I raise a brow at the sudden lust that's burning in her eyes. "Is that right?"

"Mm." She leans over and kisses my shoulder. "Your arms flex just so when you grip the steering wheel, and it makes me crazy."

"My arms?"

"Sexy," she whispers and unfastens her seat belt so she can get closer to me, then kisses my neck, almost making my eyes cross. "And have I mentioned that I love the ink on this arm as well?"

"You didn't have to mention it," I reply with a grin. "You pay enough attention to it for me to know that."

She kisses down my arm as her hand drags up my thigh, and just like that, I'm hard as fucking stone.

Before I can form a complete thought, Addie has my pants undone and my very hard cock out and in her sexy little mouth.

"I'm going to wreck this car, Addison."

"No you won't," she says with a grin before sliding her tongue up my cock, from my balls to the tip. "We're almost there."

"Son of a bitch," I mutter and do my best to concentrate on getting us through Addie's gate and to her building, then throw the car in park and bury my fingers in her soft hair as she works my cock with her hot mouth, sucking me hard, moving up and down in the perfect rhythm.

"Addie, stop."

She barely shakes her head no and keeps going.

"Addie, I don't want to come in your mouth."

She hums, but doesn't stop, and fuck me, I can't stop the orgasm that shudders through me and she pulls away in time for me to come in her hand.

I'm breathing hard. I'm fucking sweating. She sits up, wipes her hand off on a tissue, adjusts her dress, and steps out of the car, while I sit here, chest heaving, wondering what in the fuck just happened.

She just sucked me off in my *car*.

"Where are you going?" I ask as I jump out of the car.

"Home." She turns and grins. "You're welcome. Good night."

"Hold it." My voice is sharp, and I don't do anything to soften it. "Either I'm coming inside with you or I'll get you off right here for all of your neighbors to see. It's up to you. I don't get off and then leave you. That's not how this works."

"Oh." Her eyes are wide, and then a slow, sexy smile spreads over her lips, swollen from my cock.

Her other lips will be swollen from my cock before the night is out too.

She simply turns and walks to her door, unlocks it, and as soon as we're inside, I slam it shut, then slam her up against the door and squat in front of her. I don't have time to undress her, to kiss her.

All I can think about is tasting her.

"God, you smell so fucking good."

I pull the skirt of her dress up around her waist, lift one of her legs onto my shoulder, and yank her panties to the side, exposing her.

"Your pussy is so fucking wet."

"You say *fuck* a lot when you're turned on."

I can't take my eyes off of her. I lean in and swipe my tongue from her opening to her clit, then back down again, and groan in satisfaction when she grips my hair in her fist, moaning and arching her back against the door.

"God, Jake."

I press my thumb to her hard nub as I hollow my cheeks, pull her lips into my mouth, and fuck her with my tongue.

She's squirming, trying to pull me away and press me closer at the same time.

Now I switch, pushing two fingers inside her and sucking on her clit, making her fucking crazy. I'll likely be bald from her yanking on my hair when this is over, but I don't mind in the least.

Finally she stiffens and cries out, coming hard against my mouth. I stay here, kissing and caressing her as she rides out her orgasm, and when I stand, bracing her so she doesn't fall, I kiss her hard, letting her taste herself.

Which has me hard all over again.

"Well, that was fun," she murmurs with glassy eyes.

"Oh, baby, we're just starting."

Chapter Eleven

Addison

"I love the menu changes." I smile at Riley, then look back down at the beautiful menus she designed. "Seriously, these are gorgeous."

"Mia came up with the content, I just designed them," she replies and sips her coffee. We haven't opened for lunch yet, so she and I are sitting at a table in the dining room, going over the menus and catching up. My waitstaff has arrived, and they're bustling about, getting ready for us to open.

One of my full-time waitresses, Daisy, walks past us, pulling on the neckline of her blouse, and smiles. "Good morning."

"Morning," I reply.

"So, we haven't talked in a while," Riley says and settles back in her chair. "Tell me how you're doing. How are you and Jake getting along?"

"I'm great," I reply honestly.

"Even after your minor meltdown a few weeks ago?"

I roll my eyes. "It wasn't a meltdown. God, you guys are dramatic. I just had a bad day."

"And called in sick," she reminds me. "You worried us."

"No need to worry. I'm fine."

"And Jake?"

I sip my latte and lick my lips. "I'm assuming he's fine too."

"Don't be a pain in the ass," Riley says with a sigh. "I don't see you very often. I need to know these things."

"We're good," I reply honestly and watch as Daisy pushes into the restroom. "That's the third time she's gone in the bathroom in the past hour."

"I noticed," Riley says with a nod. "Maybe she has a bladder infection."

"Mm."

"Jake. Don't change the subject."

"The past few weeks have been great. We spend more nights together than apart these days." I wiggle my eyebrows at Riley, and then we both dissolve into a fit of giggles. Just then, Daisy walks back out of the restroom.

"So, he's good in that department."

"Oh, girl. *Good* doesn't begin to cover it. The man should teach classes on the art of cunnilingus."

"I hate you," Riley says with a pout. "You get a rock star *and* he's good at sex? No fair."

"You're not celibate," I remind her.

"I'm not banging any rock stars either," she says with a shake of the head. "But I'm happy for you. I can see that he makes you happy, and that's all any of us want for you."

"Plus, he's not a mooch or an asshole," I add.

"Right. Those things are important too." We raise our cups in cheers and sip them just as Daisy walks past us toward the bathroom again.

"Something's up there," Riley murmurs.

"So, I'm not crazy." I sigh and rub my forehead with my fingertips. "I'll go check on her. She's either got that bladder infection you mentioned or morning sickness."

"Does she have a boyfriend?" Riley asks with surprise.

"I have no idea." I shrug and stand. "These menus are perfect."

"I'll send them off to the printer, then."

"Thanks, Ri."

I march into the bathroom and come to an abrupt halt as I watch, unbelievably, Daisy snort something up her nose. I'm immediately transported back to my modeling days, walking into trailers and bathrooms, even backstage at runway events, watching models snort coke rather than eat a meal, fighting to maintain both their weight and the little sleep they got from partying too much.

"Am I interrupting?" I ask calmly and cross my arms over my chest, standing in front of the door so Daisy can't escape.

"Oh my God," she moans and wipes white residue off her nostrils. "It's not what you think."

"I think you've been coming in here all morning to snort cocaine up your nose," I reply and tilt my head to the side. "Are you going to tell me I'm stupid?"

"No." She hangs her head in defeat and begins to cry. "My mom is really sick."

"I know." Daisy's mom has stage four breast cancer, and Daisy has been caring for her from the beginning. "What does that have to do with you doing drugs in my place?"

"It's so hard," she mumbles. "I'm with her all day and I work here all night, and I'm exhausted. The coke just helps me cope with it all."

"Well, the working-here part is about to change." My voice is hard and cold. Daisy whips her head up to stare at me with wide eyes. "Did you really think that you'd get caught and I *wouldn't* fire you?"

"Please don't," she says, crying harder. "We need this job. I can't lose it."

"We have a zero-tolerance policy here, Daisy. You're dealing with the public and their *food*. You could hurt someone."

"I wouldn't ever hurt anyone," she cries. "Please, give me a chance. I'll stop doing the coke. I promise."

"How long have you been doing it? And don't you *dare* lie to me."

She bites her lip, then sighs. "For a while. At first it was just occasionally, but now it's a lot. I feel like I need it all the time."

"You're taking the rest of the week off."

"But, I need the money!"

"You're lucky you're not losing your job altogether, Daisy." I pull my phone out of my pocket and thumb through my contacts. "I have a friend who works as a drug counselor. I'll ask him to come here to meet you and you two can figure out an outpatient program to get you into so you can still take care of your mom and work for me, but I'm warning you, Daisy, if I so much as see a little sniffle or twitch, you're out of here for good."

"I promise, Addie. I promise, I won't let you down."

I hold my hand out, palm up. "Hand it over."

"ARE YOU TWO okay?" I ask, and pat Daisy's shoulder. She and Cici's brother, Dan, are seated at a table in the corner of the bar, ready to talk.

"We'll be fine," Dan says with a smile.

"Thanks again, Addie." Daisy offers me a watery smile and I turn to walk to the bar for a glass of wine.

It's five o'clock somewhere, for God sake. It's that or go to the gym to work off some of this energy. But when I look up, there's Jake leaning against the bar, watching me with worried eyes.

It seems he worries about me a lot.

"This is a nice surprise," I say with a smile and immediately wrap my arms around him, hugging him tight. "What are you doing here?"

"Thought I'd steal you away for lunch." His voice is soft in my ear, immediately soothing me. "What do you think?"

"Well, I'm not really hungry, but I'd love to get out of here for a while. Somewhere with not a lot of people." *But I don't want to have sex either.* Geez, how do I say that?

"I know a place," he replies with a soft smile. He drags his knuckles down my cheek. "I hate it when your eyes are sad."

"Not here," I say simply and shake my head. "Let's not do this here."

"Okay." He takes my hand in his and links his fingers, squeezing mine in the way that I love, and gives me a reassuring smile. "Let's go."

As we pass through the dining room, I see Riley talking with Cami.

"She okay?" Riley asks.

"I think so," I reply with a nod. "I'm going to take the afternoon off. I'll be back for the dinner shift."

"No problem." Cami nods. "We have this covered."

Jake leads me out to this car, gets me settled, then walks around to the driver's side and gets in. We pull away from the restaurant.

"We have to stop by your place," he says quietly as he maneuvers through traffic.

"Why?"

He glances down at my heels, my brown slacks, and my teal blouse. "Because you'll need something more casual and better shoes."

"Will my workout clothes work?"

"Perfect."

I CHANGED INTO my gym clothes and shoes, but brought my work things with me because I *am* going back to work today. No playing hooky twice in the same month.

Or twice in the same year.

The drive out of Portland has been quiet and perfect. Exactly what I needed to clear my head.

How does he always know what I need?

He pulls off I-84 just about thirty minutes out of the city, then pulls into a parking lot.

"Have you seen Multnomah Falls before?"

"I'm from here," I reply with a laugh. "But I haven't been here since I was a kid."

"I come here all the time. Usually in the off-season, in the middle of the week."

"Less people," I agree. "Well, it's not the off-season, but it is the middle of the week, so it shouldn't be bad."

He nods and takes my hand as we start down the path to the falls. They are magnificent, cascading from hundreds of feet up. The cold mist from the falling water makes it cooler up here, but I barely notice as I take in the scenery.

"It's so green," I breathe.

"Smells good too," he adds, and leads me up a path to get a better view. There aren't many people up here today, which is nice. "Do you know the legend behind the falls?"

"There's a legend?"

"Of course there is." He chuckles and points out a tree limb to step over. "According to Native American lore, it was created to win the heart of a princess who wanted a private place to bathe."

"Of course it's about a princess," I reply sarcastically. "And some dude who wanted to get her naked. But the story I heard as a kid said that the princess threw herself from the falls as a sacrificial act to end a plague killing her tribe and her lover."

"It's supposed to be a romantic story, not a tragic one," he says, barely panting as we climb the few hundred feet up to the bridge that spans the falls, so we can get an even better view.

I'm panting like a whore in church.

Wait. Do whores in church pant?

"I run three times a week," I complain. "How is it that I'm out of breath from this and you're not?"

"Because I'm an awesome example of a man, and you're lucky to have me here?"

"I don't think that's why."

God, he's funny.

"It could be why."

"Or, you're lucky when it comes to genetics and you're just in really good shape."

"It's the swimming," he says simply, shrugging one shoulder. "I'm not an Olympian or anything, but it's good for the lungs."

"Huh." I grin as I remember our own private time in his pool. That was fun. We reach the bridge, and when we're in the middle, staring up at the most beautiful waterfall I've ever seen, I lean against the railing. Jake moves up behind me, presses his chest to my back, and cages me in, his hands resting on the stone bridge on either side of me.

"It's so beautiful," I say.

"You're beautiful," he whispers in my ear. "Are you going to tell me what's bothering you?"

"I'm fine," I automatically reply.

"You're not fine, sweetness. Talk to me."

I lean my head back on his shoulder, turn my face, and

kiss his chin. "Sometimes owning your own business is hard."

He nods and I turn back to the water. "Go on."

"It's a lot more responsibility than I first realized. Don't get me wrong, I *love* it, Jake. It's fulfilling and rewarding and I can't imagine doing anything else."

"Addie, work we love is still work."

"And sometimes people disappoint me, and I need to get over that."

"Why do you need to get over it?" he asks, and circles his arms around my waist, holding me close. "Why aren't you allowed to feel the way you do?"

"Because it interferes with my life. I call in sick at work and take afternoons off with you."

"Seduction isn't your whole life, Addie. It's an important part of it, yes, but you're still a woman. A friend. A human being. Days off are not against the law."

I simply shrug and watch the water fall before me. The mist coming off of it feels so great on my skin. It smells clean, and I can smell the trees nearby as well.

"I usually go to the gym when I need to empty my head." *But this is so much better.*

"Close your eyes."

I glance up at him, then oblige him, standing in his arms, my eyes closed.

"Now just listen," he says in my ear. "Listen to the music of the water, Addie. The birds, the wind in the trees, the beating of your heart. Even your own breath. Listen to it."

It's hypnotic. I bite my lip and simply listen to it all, and suddenly, it's as though a blanket of *calm* is wrapped around me. My mind stills, my shoulders drop. I can even feel the muscles in my face relax.

Jake's arms tighten around me, and this is when I know, without a doubt, that I've fallen in love with this man. It's not necessarily where we are that has soothed me.

It's him.

He knows what I need to make me feel better. He listens without judgment.

For the first time in my life, a man wants to take care of me.

Because he cares *for* me.

And this is new.

"You just melted into me," he murmurs, "like a huge weight was lifted."

Because it was.

I turn in his arms, my back to the water, and tuck my arms against my body as he holds me tight. I'm cocooned in him, soaking him up.

I almost feel guilty for how good he makes me feel.

"Better?"

"Mm." I nod, then lean back so I can look up into his green eyes. "Thank you for this."

"Well, it *is* my special place," he teases, but then sobers and kisses my forehead. "And you're welcome, baby. Your gorgeous eyes don't look so sad anymore."

"You have an amazing way of making me feel better." I

bite my lip again, unable to look him in the face. I've always been a little uncomfortable with telling men how I feel. But he tips my chin up and kisses my lips softly.

"I'm glad." He smiles. "Are you hungry yet?"

At the thought of food, I feel my stomach growl. "I think I'm starving."

"Good. So am I. We can go down to the lodge."

"Can we stay here for just a little longer? Just like this?"

He tucks me under his chin, and simply rocks me slowly back and forth, his nose buried in my hair, and I don't think I've ever felt so safe in my life.

Tell him you love him!

But I don't. It's too new. It's too scary. Instead, I relish in his hands gliding up and down my back, the sound of the water and the wind, and the smell of my man, as he rocks me in his arms.

"I WANT A bacon cheeseburger, well done, with fries and a side of ranch," I tell the pretty waitress at the lodge near the falls. "Oh, and a chocolate milk shake."

"I want the same," Jake says with a grin, then just stares at me for a long minute.

"What?"

"I love the way you eat."

"Trust me, my hips won't love this, but I'm starving and that's what I want." I shrug and sip my water. "I'll go to the gym an extra day this week."

"Your hips are awesome," he says, eyeing the hips in

question. "They're perfect for holding on to while I'm behind you."

Well, that makes me squirm in my chair.

"I'm glad you approve."

"As far as I'm concerned, you're perfect, Addie. If you want to go to the gym to make yourself feel good, then by all means do it, but please don't think that you need to change anything about you."

"Oh," I say as I wave him off and shake my head. "Trust me, that ship has sailed. If that were my intention, it would have happened when certain photographers called me a cow back in the day."

His jaw ticks with agitation, and I can't help but love him for being offended on my behalf.

"I just go now to stay in the shape I am now. I'm perfectly okay with my size, Jake."

Our food is served and I clap my hands gleefully.

"Plus, I love food way too much to ever be a size zero."

"I love food too." He takes a big bite of his burger and sighs. "So good. Tell me more about it."

"About the food?"

"No, smart-ass, the modeling. How did you get into it?"

I pop a french fry in my mouth, thinking back. "I was a freshman in college at Oregon State. Riley was my roommate; that's how I met her."

"I didn't know that," Jake says with a grin. "How did you meet Kat?"

"Kat was Cami's roommate, and coincidentally, Kat and

Riley were good friends already, so we all just became a fivesome. Anyway, my parents paid for school, but not for the extras, and I was prepared to get a part-time job so I had some fun money, but I saw an ad for a talent agency that was coming through Portland."

"And you went."

I shrug, munching my fries. "I'd thought about it off and on through high school. I knew that I had the height, but not the waiflike figure. Cami talked me into just going to the audition, so I did. And I didn't get hired."

"Idiots."

"They take test photos of you at the audition, and somewhere down the line a photographer saw my test photo and said I was perfect for an ad he was doing. This was about six months later, during the summer, and I got a call. And that's where it started."

"Did you go back to school, or did you do the model gig for a while?"

"I put school on hold for one year, and let me tell you, that was an education all on its own. My parents hated it, but I'm stubborn as hell, so—"

"So you did it anyway." He grins. "I like your stubborn streak. What did you learn?"

"To develop a thick skin. Some people are just dicks. But some are really great too. It's not a glamorous life. At all. There are drugs and sex and seedy things that happen behind the scenes, probably just like in anything else."

He cocks his head to the side and eyes me shrewdly. "I can't imagine you getting caught up in the drug scene."

"Trust me, if I'd been the one snorting the coke, I would have been much thinner," I reply with a wave of my hand. "That doesn't interest me. I also met some of the most amazing people, and Cici is in our lives. So, it all worked out in the end."

"And why did you stop doing it?"

"I wanted to stop all the travel. I wanted my friends. I wanted to eat cheeseburgers and go to football games and live a normal life."

"Those all sound like good reasons." He nods and sighs, then changes the subject. "Do you like to cook?"

"Do I like to? Sometimes." I dip a fry in ranch and munch on it. "I'm pretty good at it. I guess I have to be in the mood. I'm no Mia."

"No one but Mia is Mia," Jake says with a smile.

"How about you?"

"I like to cook," he replies and sips his shake. "I don't do it much for just me, but I like to cook for others. In fact, I'd love to cook for you."

"That would be awesome," I reply with a grin. "Can I help you chop stuff?"

"No, but you can sit with a glass of wine and look beautiful."

"That's not a very difficult job."

He shrugs, chewing his fries. "I don't need you to work at my house, baby. I enjoy taking care of you sometimes."

And who knew that I would love him taking care of me?

"I know, it's not really PC to want to take care of a

woman," Jake adds before I can respond. "And I know that you're perfectly capable of taking care of yourself."

"But sometimes it's nice to have someone around that you can lean on," I say. "And I like that you have some old-fashioned values."

"Don't let it get out," he says with a wink. "I don't want it to affect my badass reputation."

"Your secret is safe with me." I laugh and eat my lunch, content with the silence.

"You're very easy to be with," Jake says out of the blue. "And I don't always find it easy to just *be* with anyone."

"Thank you." I grin and steal one of his fries. "You can just be with me, whenever you like."

"Not if you're going to keep stealing my fries."

"Suck it up, Keller."

Chapter Twelve

Jake

"Are you sure you want to go?" Addie asks from the passenger seat of my car, fidgeting with the ruffles on the front of her sleeveless blouse. "I mean, I would understand if you don't."

We're on our way to Mia's parents' house in southwest Portland for a barbecue. Mia's older brother, Landon, is home on leave from the navy.

"Addie, you've spent time with Max and Christina. I haven't had a chance to spend time with the people you love outside of the restaurant. But if you don't want me to go, just say so."

"No." Her head whips over to mine. "I do want you to go, I just don't want you to feel obligated."

I shake my head with a chuckle, following the directions on the GPS. "Sweetheart, I don't feel obligated to do anything where you're concerned. I simply want to be with you."

Her smile softens. "Okay. It'll be good to see Mia's parents. Just Cami and I are going because Riley and Kat don't know Landon well, so they're holding down the fort at the restaurant."

We pull up to the house in the upscale neighborhood of the city and cut the engine. Addie smiles when she hears the commotion coming from the backyard.

"Let's go find them."

"Let's do it," I reply and let her lead me by the hand around the house. There's a fire pit in the back corner of the expansive yard with chairs set up around it. It's not lit yet, but the grill on the covered patio is sizzling, sending the aroma of cooking meat into the air.

"You're here!" Mia exclaims and runs over to hug us both. "Dad won't let me cook."

"Good," I reply before Addie can. "You should just relax and enjoy this evening."

"Mia doesn't understand the meaning of those words," a tall man says as he approaches us. He's dark, just like Mia, but where Mia is short and curvy, her brother is tall and lean. "I'm Landon. You must be Jake."

I nod and shake his hand. "Pleasure."

His smile widens when he turns to Addie. "Hey, blondie."

"It's about time you came home, handsome." He hugs her tightly and lifts her up off her feet. "I missed you."

"Missed you more," he murmurs, then sets her down and ruffles her hair, the way someone would do to their sibling.

"You're messing up my hair!"

"Sorry. Not sorry."

"For someone who flies trillion-dollar planes for the government, you're sure immature," she says and sticks her tongue out at him.

"Is that what you do?" I ask as he laughs at Addie.

"They're not trillions of dollars, but yes. I fly jets for the navy. Currently stationed in Europe."

"That's amazing; welcome home. How long do you get to stay?"

"A few days," Mia says with a pout. "He thought it would be fun to visit friends in Scotland before he came home this time."

"Rude," Addie says, glaring at Landon. "How dare you have a life?"

"How do you deal with these women?" he asks me.

"It's a hardship, that's for sure," I reply and tug Addie against me so I can kiss her temple. She smells like fresh apples today. Her hair has purple highlights and is pulled back into a loose braid that falls to the middle of her back. She's dressed simply, in a tank top with a ruffled front and a long black skirt with sandals.

She's as comfortable as I've ever seen her. This is her family.

"You haven't been home in eighteen months," she says primly. "You didn't even come home for our grand opening."

Landon cringes. "I'm sorry. I couldn't get home for it. But I'm coming for dinner tomorrow night."

"If you stayed through the weekend, you'd get to hear Jake sing," Mia says, batting her eyes.

"It's called AWOL, Mia," he reminds her. "I don't get to decide how long my leave is." Then he turns to me and tilts his head. "I thought I recognized you. Jake Knox, right?"

I nod, surprised that Mia didn't already tell her brother that I've been playing at her restaurant.

"I liked your stuff," Landon says and snatches a carrot off a nearby table. "I prefer the stuff you produce now."

I cock a brow. Most people don't know that I produce.

"Stop acting like you don't know he's part of our circle." Mia rolls her eyes. "He's been doing the big-brother thing and had a background check done on you."

Now both eyebrows climb into my hairline. "Really?"

"You're working with my sister and sleeping with a woman I love as if she were also my sister. You bet your ass I did." He smiles and claps me on the shoulder. "But you came out clean."

"That's a relief."

"Either you're an upstanding citizen, or you haven't been caught yet," he says while chewing his carrot.

"Did you really just say that?" Addie demands, but Landon just continues to stare at me, and the message is crystal clear:

Fuck with them and I'll kill you and make it look like an accident.

"You don't have anything to worry about from me," I assure him soberly. "This one"—I point to Mia—"worships the ground I walk on, and this one"—I point to Addie—"can't get enough of me. It's embarrassing how they dote on me."

"He's delusional," Addie says dryly as Mia simply rolls her eyes and runs off to greet several guys who just walked into the backyard. Three of them are carrying guitars.

"Did you hire a band?" I ask in surprise.

"No, my friends just like to jam around the fire." Landon grins and flicks Addie's nose as he walks by to greet his friends. "Maybe you can play with us later."

"I didn't bring a guitar," I call out to him.

"I have a few you can borrow."

"You totally don't have to play," Addie says and shakes her head. "But knowing his friends, they'll go all fangirl on you when they meet you. Sorry."

"It's fine. After five minutes they'll be normal again."

She nods and then smiles as an older couple come out the back door of the house, arms loaded with plates and bowls.

"Let us help," Addie says and steps forward, but the small, dark woman simply shakes her head and sets the bowl on a table.

"You're a guest, *mi amore.*" She cups Addie's face in her hands and tugs her down so she can kiss both of Addie's cheeks. "You stay away too long."

"I'm sorry, Mama, we've just been busy with the restaurant."

"Our Mia says the same," the tall man replies sternly. "You work too hard."

"Mama, Papa, this is Jake. These are Mia and Landon's parents, Noemi and Giovanni Palazzo."

"Pleasure to meet you," I say, shaking Giovanni's hand, and then suddenly, my own cheeks are being tugged down so Noemi can kiss my cheeks as well.

"You're handsome," she says with a wink. "You're keeping our Addison on her toes, yes?"

"I'm trying," I reply with a laugh. "But I think she's keeping me on *my* toes."

"Good girl," she says with another wink. "You be at home here, Jake. Eat, or I'll feed you myself."

"Yes, ma'am."

"I'm here!" Cami announces as she joins us, getting hugs from Mia's parents, then snatches a cookie from the table. "God, I'm hungry."

"Thanks," Landon says, gripping Cami's wrist in his fist and guiding her cookie to his own mouth, biting off at least half of it. "I'm hungry too." He winks and walks away, chatting with some friends.

Cami simply swallows hard, clenches her eyes closed, takes a deep breath, and then eats the remainder of her cookie.

"You okay?" Addie asks her softly.

"Never better. Is there liquor?"

"I see some coolers over by the fire pit," I reply and grab Addie's hand in mine as we follow Cami toward the chairs. "How long has she been in love with him?"

Addie's gaze whips up to mine, then back to Cami. "Our whole lives."

"It shows."

"Not to him," Addie replies as we both watch Landon

wrap Cami in a bear hug, then ruffle her hair, the same way he did Addie's. "See?"

"Maybe he sees it but doesn't know what to do about it?"

Addie shrugs. "Maybe it's none of our business." She chuckles as we sit next to each other. "Thanks for coming."

"Thanks for inviting me."

DINNER WAS AMAZING. I can see where Mia gets her culinary skills. It has to be embedded in her genetic makeup.

We're in a large semicircle around the now-lit fire. Cami and Addie are roasting marshmallows. Two of the three friends of Landon—Mike and Corey—are playing guitar and singing some old Johnny Cash songs.

They're not half-bad.

Corey stops playing halfway into "Ring of Fire" and says, "It feels weird to sing songs with Jake Knox sitting here with us. Play with us, man."

"I don't have—"

"I have a guitar for you to play," Landon says and dashes into the house to retrieve it.

"You don't have to," Addie says with worried eyes, but I just smile and brush my hand down her long braid.

"It'll be fun. Maybe they'll teach me a thing or two."

"Right." Mike snorts.

Landon passes me the guitar, a Gretsch, which is gorgeous. "Nice guitar, man."

He grins and sits on a bench next to Cami. "I know."

"Let's do 'Ring of Fire' again, from the top," Mike says and we all break into the song. I sing along with the guys, enjoying myself. I haven't jammed just for fun in a very long time.

We play three more songs, and then conversation takes over. S'mores are made, jokes are told. I begin to strum the melody that won't leave me alone lately. I've only ever played it on the piano, but it sounds just as sweet on the guitar.

"That's pretty," Addie murmurs next to me. "I don't recognize it."

It's yours.

"It's just something I've been fiddling with," I reply honestly.

"Oh my God, Addie!" Mike calls from across the fire. "I can't play 'Margaritaville' without thinking about that time you and I went on that weekend trip to the beach."

Addie chuckles beside me. "You mean the time I went when my parents said I couldn't and I got grounded for a month when we got home?"

"Hey, it's not my fault that you were a disobedient teenager," Mike replies with a smile. "Addie and I used to date in high school," he informs me. I glance down at Addie, who simply laughs.

"*Date* is a strong word, Mike. I think you used to annoy the hell out of me in high school is more accurate."

"Right," Mike says with a sarcastic nod. "You just keep telling yourself that."

"Addie was quite the naughty girl when we were younger," Mia informs me as she takes a bite of her s'more.

"Oh, do tell." I set the guitar aside and lean in, already fascinated.

"Remember that time we had a kegger out on old man Mathewson's property when we were seniors?" Corey asks. "That means Addie, Mia, and Cami were sophomores."

"Oh God," Addie groans and then laughs out loud. "Why are you doing this to me?"

"She got so drunk," Cami says with a shake of the head. "So, so drunk."

"So drunk that she stripped naked and jumped in the lake," Landon says, laughing. "It was March, I think."

"February," Addie mutters. "It was so fucking cold!"

"Sobered you right up," Mia adds. "But then, when she tried to get dressed, she couldn't find her panties. Turns out, she'd flung them over her head, and they got stuck on a tree branch about twenty feet in the air."

The girls are doubled over in laughter, wiping tears from their eyes.

"Hey, I retrieved them for her!" Corey says. "I climbed that damn tree and got pitch all over me."

"Poor baby," Addie says, then sighs as the laughter subsides. "Ah, the good ol' days."

"Wait," Cami says with a frown. "Was that twelve years ago, or last week, because she'd totally still do that."

"Not in February," Addie says, laughing all over again.

"Blondie!" Landon slaps his leg, then points to Addie. "Remember the summer after you graduated, and I came home on leave, and we went camping?"

"Uhh . . ." Addie replies, but Mia jumps in.

"The sad old man!" Mia exclaims.

"Sad old man?" I ask, enthralled.

"Addie saw this old man at a campsite next to ours, and she decided he looked sad," Mia explains.

"So, she went over to the edge of his site and flashed him," Cami finishes, rolling with laughter again.

"Did you ever keep your clothes on?" I ask her.

"Not if I could help it," she admits with a naughty grin. "Why would anyone do that?"

I'm going to fuck the hell out of her when we get home.

She glances up at me and frowns. "What's wrong?"

"Absolutely nothing."

Her eyes narrow. "What are you thinking?"

I smile and she swallows hard, then I lean in and whisper in her ear, "I'm thinking about being behind you later and fucking you until you can't remember your name."

I pull away and she blinks rapidly. "Oh."

"Oh," I agree.

"Do you leave tomorrow?" Addie asks.

"In the morning, yes, but I'll only be gone for twenty-four hours." She nods grimly, but smiles bravely. "You're going to miss me."

"You're only going to be gone for twenty-four hours," she says and rolls her eyes. "I think I'll survive it. What are you going to L.A. for again?"

"I'm presenting Steve Jennings with a lifetime achievement award," I reply. "It's a big deal."

"Definitely." She nods and follows me into my house. "That's exciting for him. My friends liked you," Addie says as we make our way up the stairs to my bedroom. "I could tell."

"How could you tell?"

"They didn't try to beat you up," she says with a laugh.

"I liked them too," I reply and pull the covers back on the bed, then tug my shirt over my head and throw it on the floor. I reach out for Addie, to help her out of her sexy clothes, but she shakes her head.

"Just have a seat."

"Excuse me?" I lift a brow and brace my hands on my hips.

"You heard me," she says with a coy smile. "Sit on the bed. Please."

"Since you asked nicely." I sit on the bed and almost swallow my tongue when she turns her back to me and slowly lifts her top over her head, then lets it fall to the floor.

She's wearing a flesh-colored strapless bra, which is quickly unfastened and joins her top on the floor.

God, her back is gorgeous.

She tosses me a flirty smile over her shoulder and pushes her thumbs into the waist of her skirt, and with just a couple of tugs over her hips, it floats to the floor, leaving her completely bare.

She turns slowly, tilts her hip out to the side, and the wide smile on her gorgeous face is nothing but pure sin.

"Come here."

She walks slowly toward me, and when she reaches a hand out to me, I catch it in my own grip and pull her onto the bed, rolling us until she's beneath me.

"You have no idea how fast my heart races when I look at you," I whisper, my lips mere inches from hers. "You turn me inside out, Addison."

"You do the same to me," she murmurs. Her fingertip is tracing the ink on my arm in long, lazy strokes.

"I was going to fuck you hard tonight." My voice is calm. Matter-of-fact. "But that's not what I need right now."

"What do you need?" she asks.

"I need," I kiss the corner of her mouth, "to make," then the other corner, "love to you." My fingertips brush down her neck to her breast, where they tease her nipple until it's hard, and then travel farther south, over her barely rounded belly to the most beautiful pussy I've ever seen in my fucking life.

"You're already wet."

"You're already hard," she replies and circles her hips, grazing over my still-jean-covered hard-on.

"Sweetheart, I've been hard since the first moment I saw you."

"That must be very uncomfortable for you," she whispers before she bites my lower lip. She reaches between us and unzips my pants, tugging them down my hips, and when my cock springs free, she immediately guides me to her wetness.

"Addie, we don't have to rush."

"I'm not rushing." She shakes her head and sighs when just the tip slides inside her. "I just need this with you."

"Why?"

She opens her big blue eyes, and I can see it there. She loves me.

And God, I love her so much it hurts.

How am I just now realizing this? She's as important to

me now as breathing, and there isn't anything I wouldn't do to make sure she's safe. That she's happy.

"Because, I—"

"You what, baby?"

"I just do."

She tips her forehead against my shoulder, hiding. It's the sweetest thing I've ever seen. I sink all the way inside her and rest there. We're both panting harder now, and sweat is beaded on my forehead at the energy it's taking me to hold back from pounding the fuck out of her.

"You scare me a little," she admits softly.

"You scare me a lot," I reply with a grin. "I think that if it wasn't scary it wouldn't mean as much."

She smiles slowly and circles her hips again, making my eyes cross.

"God, baby, you feel so fucking good."

"So good," she agrees and clings to me as I begin to thrust in and out, in a long, slow rhythm. I don't want to rush it. I don't want it to be over yet.

I want to savor every fucking second with her.

I push one of her legs up over my shoulder, opening her to me, so I can sink in even deeper. She cries out and digs her nails into my ass, pulling me in.

And I almost come, right here.

But I bite my lip and hold on, riding her, watching her face as her own orgasm begins to wash over her.

"So close," she whispers. "So close."

"So beautiful." I kiss her lips and press my forehead against hers. Her tight pussy is clenching me now, almost desperately, and her already strong grip tightens on my ass as she comes spectacularly.

"That's right, baby," I croon, brushing loose pieces of hair off of her damp cheeks. "Let go."

"Come with me."

"I'm right here with you," I assure her and let go, exploding inside her, around her. She holds me close until the aftershocks subside, and I roll us to our sides, facing each other.

"It always feels like the first time," she says, almost shyly.

I smile and kiss her nose, her lips, her cheek. "It's all you, sweetness."

"No, it's us."

Chapter Thirteen

Addison

"Hey, blondie."

I twirl at the sound of Landon's voice in my ear, and am instantly caught up in a big bear hug. "What are you doing here, handsome?"

"My flight leaves in a few hours, so I thought I'd stop in here before the place got hopping for lunch to say goodbye to my best girls."

My heart sinks at the thought of Landon leaving. It could be another year before we see him again.

"I hate that you're stationed way the hell over in Europe," I reply with a pout. "Aren't there naval bases in the States?"

He just smirks and shrugs. "I like it there."

"Well, stop waiting so long between visits home," I scold him as we walk toward the bar.

"Now you sound like my mother," he replies with a laugh just as his eyes land on Cami, who's sitting at the bar, spreadsheets laid out before her. She's biting her lip as her fingers fly over a ten-key calculator.

"I'll grab Mia," I murmur and saunter toward the kitchen. Maybe Jake's right. Maybe Landon isn't as immune to Cami as we all think he is.

He's just a stubborn man, which is entirely typical.

"Mia?"

"Yeah?" she calls from inside the walk-in refrigerator.

"Landon's here to say goodbye." Mia walks out of the fridge, carrying a tray of chicken.

"In the bar?" she asks.

"Yep."

"Be right there."

I nod and return to the bar, where Cami and Landon are laughing and Kat is pouring them each some coffee.

Mia walks in behind me.

"Your flight doesn't leave until this afternoon," she says with a frown.

"I thought I'd stop in before you opened for lunch," he says as he hugs his sister close. "Gonna miss you, brat."

"No you won't. You're too busy flying planes and failing at staying out of trouble to miss me." She has tears in her eyes as she leans her head on his chest and hugs him tightly.

"I always have time to miss you," he says. "You should come visit me."

"Sure." She laughs and steps away, wiping at her eyes. "I'll do that as soon as I get a vacation."

"You work too hard," he says, but Mia is already shaking her head at him.

"We had this conversation already. It's closed."

"I didn't close it," he begins, but stops when she glares at him. "Fine."

"How long will you be traveling?" Kat asks, changing the subject.

"About twelve hours," he says, as if it's a short flight to Seattle. "I'll sleep most of it."

Kat stares at him in horror. "How can you stand it? Oh my God, I'd have a stroke. I'd lose my mind."

"Kat is afraid of flying," Cami informs Landon dryly.

"If God had intended for us to fly," Kat says, "He would have given us wings."

"He did," Landon replies with that cocky smile we all love so much. "Metal ones."

Kat shivers and shakes her head. "No thanks."

"You're safer in a plane than—" Landon begins, but she cuts him off midsentence.

"Yeah, yeah, I know. I've heard the statistics. I still don't like it."

"You'd feel safe if you flew with me," he says confidently.

"No offense, and I'm sure you're an excellent pilot, but bullshit," Kat says with a sweet smile, making us all laugh.

"Okay," he says, holding his hands up in surrender. "It was good to see you again, Kat."

"You, too."

I'm watching Cami, who's fidgeting with her pen and looking down at her spreadsheets.

She looks so damn sad, and it breaks my heart.

"Come here, chameleon," he says to Cami as he pulls her in for a hug. He's called her that since we were in grade school. *Cami the chameleon.* "Stay safe," he whispers to her and takes a deep breath, smelling her hair.

Mia and I share a quick glance, but don't say anything as he pulls away, waves at Kat, and grins at me. "Be good, blondie."

"I'm always good," I reply, batting my eyelashes. "Take your own advice, please. Stay safe *and* be good."

"I'll be fine," he replies with a nod. "Love you, ladies."

And with that, he walks out. When we hear the front door close, Cami dissolves into tears, resting her head on her arm.

"I'll get the chocolate," Kat says, rushing toward the kitchen as Mia and I flank Cami, rubbing her back and speaking softly to her.

"I'm so sorry, Cam," I say.

"Don't cry," Mia croons, running her hand over Cami's pretty blond hair. "He's a big dork."

Cami laughs through the tears. "I'm stupid."

"No, you're not." Kat sets a plate of chocolate cake on the bar. "How long have you loved him, Cami?"

"I don't remember not loving him," she replies honestly. She sits up and takes the napkin Kat offers her to blow her nose. "And I'm ridiculous. I love a man who doesn't love me back. He thinks of me like a sister."

I'm not so sure of that.

But rather than say that out loud, I just sit next to her and let her vent. "I mean, how pathetic am I? I'll tell you." Cami points at Kat, on a roll now, still crying. "I was so desperate to forget him, I married someone *completely* wrong for me. I *ruined* a perfectly good man's life."

"I think *ruined* is a bit strong," Mia says, earning a glare from Cami.

"Brian is a great man, and I broke his heart, all because I'm in love with your stupid fighter-pilot brother."

"Hey, it's not my fault," Mia says and shakes her head. "I think my brother is stupid too."

"I think you should go home for the day," Kat says, taking a bite of Cami's cake. "Or go get a massage or something."

"She's right," I say with a nod. "Go be sad for a few hours, and then pull yourself back together. You deserve a day to yourself."

"Absolutely," Mia says.

Cami just shrugs and wipes her nose on the back of her hand. "I guess. I won't get any more work done today anyway."

"Someone will drop dinner off to you later," Mia says, but Cami shakes her head.

"I'll order in Chinese and watch movies."

"Atta girl."

"Speaking of men who suck," Mia says, turning to me. "How are you doing?"

I look around like she's talking to someone behind me. "Me?"

"She hasn't seen it?" Mia asks the others, who shake their heads.

"Landon got here just as I was going to show her," Kat says quietly.

"Show me what?"

"So, I follow the old Hard Knox page on Facebook," Kat says and pulls her phone out of her pocket, taps the screen, and hands it to me. "And they posted this this morning."

My heart stops as I stare at a photo of Jake on a red carpet, dressed in a sexy black suit. Unfortunately, his lips are planted on the cheek of Karina, a famous singer who has her hand on his chest, leaning her ample bosom against him.

Don't they look just motherfucking cozy?

Rather than throw the phone across the bar the way I want to, I pass it back to Kat and turn to walk away.

"Addie?" Mia calls out.

"I'm fine," I reply with a wave of my hand and keep walking.

Except, I'm not fine. I'm not even in the realm of fine. I'm pissed and I'm hurt and I've just been reminded, again, that I can't count on men. They aren't loyal. They aren't trust-worthy.

Even my own father doesn't want to take the time to talk to me.

The only person I can count on is me, and it's about time I got my head out of my pants and remembered that.

"Uh, Addie," Riley says as she comes into our office less than an hour later, "Jeremy is in the bar asking for you."

"What?" I scowl and shake my head. "What the hell is he doing here?"

"Well, given that I'm not psychic, I'm not sure." She rolls her eyes and sits at her desk. "But you should go see."

"Smart-ass," I mutter as I walk through the still mostly empty dining room toward the bar. Cami left about an hour ago, and we've barely opened for the day. I mentally cross my fingers, hoping the bar is still empty as well so I don't have to kick Jeremy's ass in front of customers.

"What do you want, Jeremy?" I ask as I walk briskly into the bar, my heels clicking on the floor.

"Fucking hell, you're beautiful, Addie."

"Cut the shit," I reply coldly. "What do you want?"

"I want to apologize," he says with sad brown eyes. I'd believe him, if he wasn't such a lying piece of shit. "You know that I would never intentionally hurt you."

"Your fist cocked back to deck me said otherwise," I reply and cross my arms over my chest, and I hear Kat gasp behind me.

Damn it, I never told them that part.

"I wouldn't have hit you," he says and shakes his head. "Never. I love you."

I bust out laughing. "Right."

"I want you back, Addie. I miss you so much."

Kat's watching with interest from behind the bar as Jeremy steps toward me and I take a step back, out of his reach.

I don't want his hands on me.

"Have you been thrown out of wherever you've been staying?"

His eyes lower, and I know I've hit the nail on the head. "I could use a place to crash, yeah."

Unbelievable. "Do I have *doormat* tattooed on my fore-head?" I ask incredulously.

"That's not it at all," he says, again stepping toward me.

"Touch me and I'll have you arrested for assault."

His eyes narrow. "I'm trying apologize here, Addie. I truly am sorry."

"Okay. You've apologized. Goodbye, Jeremy."

"I just need—"

"Whatever it is you need, you're not getting it from me," I interrupt him, my voice sharp.

"Addie." Jeremy's shoulders sag.

"You heard her." Jake's voice comes from behind me, sur-prising me, and washing emotion over me all at once. Fear, betrayal, and anger, but I don't show any reaction in front of Jeremy, who finally marches out, passing by me without another word.

"Are you okay?" Jake asks and I whirl around, glaring at him.

"I'd like to see you in my office, please." I'm proud of how even I'm able to keep my voice when I want to rage. My hands are shaking, my heart pounding.

"What did I do?" he asks, hands out at his sides, but I ignore him and stomp to the office. Thankfully, Riley isn't in here, and I shut the door behind us, then whirl on him again.

"I didn't need your help back there, Jake. I had it handled just fine."

"Look, he hurt you before, Addie. Do you think that if

I see a man threatening my girl I'm not going to make it known that I'll do whatever it is I need to to defend her?"

"Why do men have to have pissing contests over every damn thing?" I ask the room at large and pace back and forth. "I'm not a damsel in distress, Jake. I did just fine before you, and I'll do fine after you."

"After me?" he asks with a raised brow.

"After you," I repeat, glaring at him. My heart is pounding and my hands are shaking and I want to smack him and kiss him all at the same time. "Did you think I wouldn't find out?"

"Addie," Riley says, coming into the office without knocking. "Daisy is here and says she's clean and wants to talk to you about putting her back on the schedule."

"Clean?" Jake asks.

"Daisy's the one that Addie found snorting coke in the bathroom," Riley says, making me cringe. Jake pins me in a glare.

"Tell Daisy I'll call her later," I say to Riley, who simply nods and backs out of the office.

"You have drug addicts working for you?"

"You don't know anything about it," I reply.

"You're right. Because you didn't *tell me*."

"This is my job, Jake. My business. I don't have to tell you every little thing that happens here. Just like, apparently, you don't have to tell me about the women you hook up with when you're working."

His eyes narrow and nostrils flare as he clenches his jaw.

"I'm going to start with the first comment, and then we'll deal with the other. Finding someone snorting coke in your bathroom isn't a little thing."

"Are you going to try to protect me from that too?" I ask with exasperation.

"I'd really like to know why you're putting her back on the schedule," he says, hands on his hips. "This place is too classy to employ junkies."

That does it. "Why are you here, Jake?"

"I thought I'd surprise you and take you out for lunch or something."

"Well, I don't have time," I reply, wanting this whole episode over. "I have an appointment this afternoon, and I have to work tonight." I grab my handbag and turn back to him, but my bag snags on the corner of the desk, spilling its contents on the ground.

Before I can reach for anything, Jake bends over and picks up Daisy's vial of coke.

"Tell me this isn't yours."

"What if it is?"

"What the fuck, Addison?" Now his eyes just look *hurt*, and he doesn't have any right to be hurt with me.

Not one.

"It was Daisy's, Jake. I took it away from her when I caught her with it in the bathroom and forgot to flush it. I told you before, I don't do that shit. I don't lie. Unlike you."

"Okay, point number two. What the fuck are you talking about?"

"You, hooking up with Karina at the awards show last night."

He scowls. "I presented an award with her."

"Right." I blindly grab handfuls of purse stuff and shove them back in. "I'm sure that's exactly what you were doing on the red carpet when your lips were all over her."

"I kissed her *cheek,* and that was it, Addie."

"Okay." I need to get the hell out of here. "I don't want you here when I get back."

"You don't believe me."

"No. I don't."

"Then we're going to talk about this until you do. I'm not lying to you. I don't want to fight with you."

"Well, I'll just fight with you, then," I reply and slam the door behind me as I stalk out of the office.

"I WAS THINKING about trying a new color on you today," Cici says as she removes my old polish off my toes. "What do you think?"

"Do whatever you want," I reply with a frown.

"Well, aren't we just two scoops of bitchy in a bowl full of grouchy this afternoon?" Cici says. "What crawled up your ass?"

"Men suck."

"Well, that's true," she says. I come in every other week for a mani-pedi and for some girl talk with Cici. If it hadn't been last minute, I would have canceled today though. I just don't want to talk about it. "What did he do?"

"He tried to come to my rescue when I didn't need it."

"Hmm."

"And I have photographic proof that he had his hands and lips on another woman last night."

Cici stops cold and stares at me with her jaw dropped. "Excuse me?"

"He says that nothing happened and that it was a photo for the press, but I don't give a shit. He shouldn't have kissed her."

"Was it the kind of kiss where it looked like he was about to eat her face, or was it a peck?"

"He was kissing her cheek."

She sits back and blinks at me, frowning. "Okay."

"He's constantly butting in, trying to 'help' me," I say, using the air quotes. "As if I'm not an adult and need his help."

"They do have a tendency to be very testosteroney," she says with a nod.

"Right! I mean, I'm an intelligent woman. He doesn't always have to come save the day."

"Micah does that all the time too," Cici says, smiling as she thinks of her husband. "But it's just because he loves me."

"But it drives you batty," I insist.

"Yes." She nods and rubs my feet, just as my phone lights up in my hand. *Jake.* I roll my eyes and toss my phone into my handbag.

"That him?"

"Yeah. He can just go to voice mail." I sigh, thinking of all the things that completely annoy me about Jake. "You know what else he does? He'll drink almost all of the juice or milk or whatever, and put the last few drops back in the fridge."

"Ugh, I hate that!" Cici chuckles. "Or when you ask them what they want for dinner, and they say 'I don't care,' but when you start suggesting things, they don't want any of the suggestions."

"Yes!" I point at Cici in agreement. "I hate that! Or when they put the new toilet paper roll on, with the flap facing the wall. I mean, *who does that*?"

"Exactly," Cici says with a nod, switching feet. "And why can't they actually put dirty dishes *in* the sink? Why do they put them on the counter beside the sink?"

"Actually, I can't complain about that because Jake will put his dishes in the dishwasher."

"Oh my God," she says, staring at me with wide eyes. "I thought the dishwasher-loading man was a myth."

"Nope, I found one in his natural habitat."

"Impressive." We're quiet for a moment while she continues to rub my feet, then cleans off my nails to paint them. "At least Micah doesn't pee all over the bathroom, and he's teaching our sons not to either."

"That's good," I reply softly. "Also, I really do love it when Jake cuddles with me."

"Seriously? You hate to cuddle!"

"I know." I smile, then laugh. "I used to hate to cuddle. But Jake is really good at it. And sometimes, he'll cuddle me and not expect sex after."

"I love it when that happens," Cici says. "I mean, I love the sex too. Obviously because I have four kids."

"I was wondering if you knew where those come from," I say and watch as she applies the top coat over my robin's-egg-blue polish.

"Micah brings me coffee in bed every morning. And I do mean *every single morning*, no matter what."

"Even when he has to get up super-early for work?"

"Yep." She smiles softly. "It's our quiet time together before the kids get up and life gets crazy."

"That's so sweet." We move over to the manicure station and get settled. "Jake brought me wine and ice cream when I had a bad day a few weeks ago," I say softly. "It made me feel really special."

"Aww," she says and smiles up at me. "That would make me feel special too. He sounds like a really nice guy, Addie."

I sigh. "He is. Except the kissing other girls part. And speaking of the sex, damn girl."

"Good?"

"The best. Ever."

"Ever?" She pauses filing my nails, surprised. "Better than that photographer in the Bahamas?"

I nod.

"Better than the drummer when we were shooting in New York that one summer?"

I cringe. Geez, I don't need to be reminded of all the guys I've had sex with. "The best."

"Is it the best every time?" she asks skeptically.

"Of course not." I roll my eyes. "But it's always intimate, even when it's rougher, you know?"

"I do."

"And he always makes me feel sexy. He says I'm sexiest when my hair's a mess and I have no makeup on."

"Keep him," she says immediately, making us both laugh. "Seriously, Addie, when was the last time you were with a guy who even *wanted* to help you?"

It's true, I've never dated the white knight before. "Probably never."

"It's okay for the guy you love to want to defend you."

I pause, frowning. "Who said anything about love?"

"Oh come on," she says with a snort. "I've known you all of your adult life. Love is written all over you in permanent marker. And also, he kissed her cheek, Addie. You don't have photos of him fucking some chick."

I bite my lip and watch as she paints my nails. "Loving him scares me."

"As it should." She screws the brush on the bottle of polish and sits back in her chair. "Love is fucking terrifying."

"It's fucking bullshit," I mutter.

"No it's not." She smiles and pats my arm. "But I understand the sentiment."

"I wasn't very nice to him earlier." I cringe and blow on my fingers. "He was just trying to get Jeremy off my ass."

"You skipped that part," Cici says. "What did Jeremy want?"

"A free ride," I reply. "Under the disguise of *I want you back, I was stupid, blah blah blah.*"

"Idiot."

"Big-time. And everyone tried to warn me, but I didn't listen."

"That's pretty typical for women whose loins are attracted to someone."

"*Loins?*" I smirk. "My *loins* were attracted to him?"

"Seriously, was there anything else there?"

I think back on my time with Jeremy and shrug. "No. You're right."

"And what do you find attractive about Jake?"

"Well, my loins are certainly attracted to him." I giggle. "But it's more than that for sure. I love watching him work. He's seriously good at it, and he *loves* it. It's not just what he does, it's who he is."

I tilt my head to the side, thinking. "He's thoughtful. He's nice to my friends. And when he smiles, I'm telling you, my panties burst into flames."

"You must spend a lot of money on lingerie," she says with a laugh. "I like him for you, Addie. You deserve to be with someone that makes you happy."

"We all do." I chew my lip. "I may have overreacted this afternoon."

"It happens. At least you know it, and you can work on making it up to him."

"I think a blow job is in his very near future."

"I think you'll be forgiven quickly."

Chapter Fourteen

Jake

*W*hat just happened?

I stare at the door that Addie just slammed, and am dumbfounded. We just had our first argument, and she walked away.

She walked away.

I sigh and push my hand through my hair in exasperation, just as Riley walks back into the office.

"Oh, sorry. I thought you guys left."

"Addie left," I reply. Riley tilts her dark blond head to the side and frowns.

"Is everything okay?"

"I think they will be," I reply honestly, shoving the vial of coke into my pocket, then chuckle in frustration. "We argued, and she left."

"Ah." Riley nods and walks behind her desk. "Typical Addie."

I simply raise a brow, waiting for her to continue.

"Addie's great at confrontation, when it comes to strangers or people she doesn't love," she says carefully. "But when her heart is invested, whether it be family, or friends, or a man, she's not good at confrontation at all. She never has been."

"An argument isn't confrontation," I reply and shake my head. "It's a heated conversation."

"For some," she says simply. "For others it's scary. Not that she would ever, *ever* admit that. She has abandonment issues."

Of course she wouldn't admit it. "Who abandoned her?"

"Her parents. They're good people, but they're pretty selfish. Not really around when she needs them. She grew up and they pretty much washed their hands of her. Men don't stick around when they don't get what they want from her. She's learned to guard her heart, Jake."

She and I need to talk. "I guess I'll head home and get some work done."

"Don't worry, she'll cool off, and by this time tomorrow, she won't even remember that you fought." Riley offers me a supportive smile. "But that photo of you with Karina? Not cool, man."

"I didn't fuck Karina!"

"I didn't say that you did, but Addie has a history with musicians who didn't think twice about fucking around on her, so just seeing that photo of you from last night would be enough to make her run. She'll come around."

"Thanks." I wave and leave, still completely confused. I'd planned to come pick Addie up and take her somewhere nearby for a quick lunch, see how her day is going. Hell, I just wanted to see her. Because I'm a selfish bastard.

I'm addicted to her.

But when I arrived, Jeremy was leaning toward her, about to put his motherfucking hands on her, and I saw red. I *know* she can handle herself, but damn it, she doesn't have to. Not with me around.

Maybe I overstepped when it came to finding out that one of the waitresses was using, but damn it, why does she have a junkie working for her?

It's none of your damn business, Keller.

I tighten my grip on the steering wheel as I drive through the tunnel and up the Sunset Highway, heading west of Portland. This highway is curvy, and hilly. People go way too fast up this thing.

So how am I going to fix this? How am I going to convince her that she needs to run *toward* me rather than *from* me?

Because I'll be damned if I'll let her turn her back and walk out on me again. I'll put her over my fucking knee.

Just as I reach the Portland Zoo exit, I see a wrecking crew, and a Jetta, crumpled from rolling.

My heart speeds up as I realize it's the same color as Addie's car.

Is that Addie's car?

I pull up behind a cop car, and race out of my car toward the first officer I see.

"Where is she?"

"You can't stop here," he says sternly. "This is the scene of an accident."

"Who was in the car?" *Please, for the love of Christ, tell me some guy was in the car.*

"A woman was in the car," a female officer replies. "She's already been transported to the hospital."

I watch in horror as what I'm sure is Addie's car is loaded onto the bed of a tow truck.

I run back to my car and peel out into traffic, desperate to get to the hospital. I call Addie's number, praying that by the grace of God it wasn't her, but it just rings and rings and finally dumps me into voice mail.

Sonofabitch.

I try one more time, cursing more as I get the voice mail again, then I try Kat.

"Seduction, this is Kat."

"This is Jake. Did Addie come back there?"

Please say yes.

"No, she had an appointment with Cici this afternoon. Why?"

"I just came up on a wreck on the Sunset," I reply grimly. "Same car as hers, same color. The person in the car has already been taken to the hospital. I'm on my way there. I tried her cell and she's not answering."

"I'm sure she's fine," she says, but her voice is shaky now. "Let me call Cici's phone and make sure she's there."

She clicks off, but calls back in less than thirty seconds. "Cici didn't answer."

"Fuck."

"But her phone might be off," she says quickly. "She usually turns it off when she has a client."

"I'm pulling into the hospital now. I'll call you when I have information."

I hang up, thank the parking gods when I find a spot close to the door of the emergency room, and run inside.

"I'm looking for Addison Wade," I say breathlessly as I approach a receptionist. "She's been in an accident, and would have been brought in by ambulance." *I think.*

The young woman clicks the keyboard, frowning.

"I don't see anyone by that name."

That's a good sign.

"But if she was just brought in, we might not have her in the system yet. Go ahead and have a seat. I'll keep an eye out and ask around." She smiles kindly, but she doesn't make me feel any better.

The woman I love so much it hurts could be broken back there right now.

The thought makes me want to scream. And throw up.

I sit, leaning my elbows on my knees, and curse myself as every kind of selfish bastard there is. What am I doing?

I destroy the people around me. The ones I love suffer because of me. My parents. My band. Christina.

And now Addie.

Addie deserves so much better than me.

After thirty minutes of waiting, I glance up at the receptionist, making eye contact, but she only shakes her head, silently telling me that there is still no word.

My phone rings in my pocket. "Kat. Tell me you found her."

"She's fine," she says, leaving me weak with relief. "She and Cici both had their ringers off. She's safe, Jake."

I nod, not even caring that Kat can't see me, and hang up the phone. I scrub my fingers through my hair and stand, on autopilot as I return to my car and drive toward my house.

She's safe.

She didn't run out, upset, and get hurt the way Christina did.

She's going to be just fine.

But what happens next time I screw up? I obviously fucked up big-time last night. It didn't even occur to me how it would look to kiss Karina's cheek. It's her goddamn *cheek*.

But I should have thought about it. Jesus, even when I had my lips planted against Karina's face, all I could think was that Addie smells better and I wish she'd been my date.

Instead of just thinking of myself, I should have also realized that the photos wouldn't look as innocent as it was.

I pull into my driveway and bypass the house, headed for the studio.

"You know, you were much more punctual before you had a girlfriend," Max says with a grin as I walk inside, but when he sees my face, he sobers. "What's wrong."

I shake my head and sit in my office chair. "What am I doing, man?"

"Well, right now you're freaking me out," he replies and

walks toward me, dropping into the chair on the other side of my desk. "Who died?"

"That's not funny."

"I didn't mean it to be funny."

I pick up a pen and tap it on the desk, turning it from end to end. "No one's dead." I tell him about the argument and coming up on the crash and waiting at the hospital for what felt like hours.

"She's not Christina," he says softly.

"I fucking know that."

"But it scared you."

I nod. "It was five years ago, all over again. And then I felt like such an asshole."

"Because you were worried that she might have been in an accident?" Max asks with a scowl. "Yeah, that's a real dick move."

"No, because I started this relationship with an amazing woman. Because I'm playing music every weekend again, and I'm loving it. And I don't deserve any of it, Max. I walked away from performing for a reason. I don't do the relationship thing for a reason."

Max sighs. "You know, I never really understood what exactly those reasons are."

I narrow my eyes on my best friend, not afraid to deck him if I need to. "People around me get hurt."

"Bullshit."

"How can you say that? You were there five years ago. Before that." I stand and pace. "Christina lost her leg because of *me*."

"As she has said, many times, bullshit."

I shake my head. "It's not bullshit. And that could have been Addie today. She could have been hurt. She could have been *killed*."

My blood runs cold at the thought. I lower myself into the chair and stare at Max. "She deserves so much better than me, man."

"Maybe she should be the one to decide what she deserves."

"I have to quit performing."

"You're an idiot."

"Boy, that's the truth."

"And you're being a selfish asshole."

I stare at Max in disbelief just as my phone pings with a text.

Addie:

> Kat says you were worried about me. I'm okay. I'm sorry that you were worried. Let's talk tomorrow, okay?

"First of all, five years ago was an *accident*. It wasn't your fault, but you've convinced yourself that it was. So the band broke up, which I don't have too much resentment over anymore. I mean, we probably would have broken up at some point anyway, and this writing and producing gig is awesome.

"But you've become a hermit. And Addie was bringing you out of that. You deserve to be loved, you know."

I shake my head, but he interrupts me before I can speak. "You do. Everyone does. You deserve to fall in love and have a dozen babies and do what you love. If you love to sing for a couple hundred people every weekend in a pretty cool restaurant, then do it."

I don't respond. I simply nod and stand and walk out of the studio. I need some time in the pool.

I need Addie. Everything in me is screaming at me to go find her, to hug her and make sure that she's really safe and whole.

But Addie doesn't need me.

Chapter Fifteen

Addison

"It's going to be another stellar day in Portland, Bill."

"Indeed it is, Shelley."

I glance out the window and smile at the sunshine. The newspeople are right; it's going to be another beautiful day in Portland.

I reach my arms high above me, stretching, and then bend over to touch my toes. Even in heels, I can touch my toes.

Not bad, if I do say so myself.

I feel great today. I slept like the freaking dead, although I would have slept better if I'd been wrapped around a certain sexy rock star, but I think it was good to have a night away from each other. My chat with Cici helped a lot. I know that there will be times that we get on each other's nerves, but we're just human. It happens.

And whether I like it or not, he's a celebrity, and there will be times that he's gone, around other famous people, and photos will be taken. The press is a son of a bitch who likes to start rumors, and I need to learn to trust.

Because I don't really believe that he'd hurt me. Not on purpose.

In fact, I miss him. I reach for my phone, but stop with my thumb hovering over his name. What am I going to say? *I'm sorry* seems trite.

But I am sorry.

Just as I'm about to tap on his name, the doorbell rings, and I can't help but smile and rush to the door, butterflies taking flight in my belly.

I hope it's Jake.

I'm not disappointed when I fling the door wide open. He's leaning on the jamb, and when his eyes meet mine, I see relief in their green depths.

I grip his hand in mine and pull him inside, then launch myself into his arms, holding him tightly around the neck.

"I was just about to call you! Jake, I'm so sorry for yesterday. I totally overreacted. I think I was thrown off and irritated by Jeremy showing up, and then you surprised me, and I really just reacted poorly." I kiss his cheek and bury my face in his neck. God, he feels so damn good. "But I talked with Cici for a while yesterday and she helped me come to my senses. Sometimes I just let my emotions get the best of me. I'm sorry."

I kiss his neck and wiggle even closer to him, soaking up his warmth and his clean, amazing scent. "I'm really sorry you thought I was a part of that accident. From now on, I'll keep my ringer on."

He suddenly stiffens against me, and it occurs to me that he hasn't said a single word since he got here.

"Are you okay?"

"No." He grips my shoulders in his hands and sets me away from him, then walks to my window, facing away from me. He shoves his hands in his pockets. "No, Addie, I'm not okay."

"Is this about yesterday?"

I frown and watch him as he stands perfectly still. He's not looking at me. He's completely closed off. He simply shakes his head no and sighs.

"Are you not speaking to me?" I ask incredulously.

He sighs again and turns to me now, looking at me with resigned, bloodshot eyes.

"Have you slept?" I ask, frowning.

"No," he replies.

"Why not?"

His hands are still in his pockets. I walk to him, but he immediately walks away, out of my reach. "Why won't you let me touch you?"

He shakes his head and sighs. "My life is busy, Addie."

"All of our lives are busy, Jake." He rubs his hand over his lips, then turns to me and all I see is a stranger. I don't know this man staring at me with empty, emotionless eyes. "Are you saying you need time away from me? We have been spending a lot of time together—"

"I don't *want* time away from you," he whispers.

"I know you're attracted to me." Why is my voice shaking? And why do I want to beg him to stay? I fucking hate this!

"Look at you," he murmurs, with a sad half smile, gesturing at my outfit. "That red blouse shows off your tits perfectly, without actually *showing* me your tits. How the fuck do you do that? Did you learn that from modeling?"

I simply nod.

"I thought so. But you're beautiful no matter what you wear. You could wear a burlap sack and my dick would be clamoring for you."

"Thanks. I think."

Pure emotion is rolling off him in waves. "That's not our issue at all, Addison."

"What is our issue, Jake?" I approach him now, grip his shoulders, and look him in the eye.

"I can't do this," he murmurs.

"What can't you do?" *Are you fucking kidding me?* He's bailing. He doesn't even have to say the words, I can see it written all over his face. I love him. I gave him everything, learned to trust, and he's bailing.

"I can't do us."

"Well then, you'll need to leave." I keep my face perfectly clear of any emotion and my body doesn't move, until he's gone and I shut the door behind him.

I sit blindly at the dining room table and brace my head in my hands. I'm too stunned for even tears to come, and I'm not even sure *why*. Why does this surprise me? This is what happens. People leave.

The only person I can depend on is me.

"Pass me the bottle," I say, reaching toward Kat for the bottle of tequila she just opened. All five of us are sitting on Cami's living room floor, getting drunk. We each have a shot glass, and a fork for the chocolate cake sitting in the middle of us. "Thanks for coming, guys."

"Hey, we have rules," Riley says, watching me pour some tequila in my glass. "If there is a death, a birth, or a breakup, we come. No questions asked."

I nod, then throw back the shot, enjoying the way it burns down my throat.

"Besides," Cami says with a grin as she takes a bite of cake, "I enjoy our *she-woman-man-haters club* nights."

"I'm not a man hater," I say with a shake of the head. "The one I love is just dumb."

"Totally dumb," Kat says, raising her glass in salute, then shoots the liquor back.

"Did he say why he was dumping you?" Mia asks. She's lying flat on the floor, staring at the ceiling, her long, dark hair spread out around her like a halo.

"Not really." I shrug, and take the bottle back from Riley. "He ranted for a while about having to be away from work too much, and some other stuff that I didn't quite under-stand, and then he just said he couldn't do *us* and left."

"That doesn't make any sense," Cami says with a frown.

"You keep that bottle," Kat says and returns to Cami's kitchen for more liquor.

"Is there any of that whipped vodka in there?" Mia calls out. "I want something sweet."

"Yes," Kat says with a grin as she returns with the bottle Mia asked for, along with a can of whipped cream. "There's this too. It has alcohol in it." She sprays some of the whip in her mouth and hands it off to Cami, who takes a bite of cake, sprays some whip on it, and stuffs it all in her mouth.

"I hate it when men are dicks," Riley says with a frown. "Like, why do they have to be dicks?"

"Because that's what they're thinking with. Their dicks," Mia says with a sigh, then swigs directly from the bottle before passing it back to Kat. "It's like they don't know any better."

"Bullshit. They know better." Cami points her fork at Mia. "Dickery is a chosen attitude."

"Dickery." I snort, then laugh out loud. God, I can't feel my lips. I shrug and take a swig of tequila out of the bottle. "I just hate it when they just leave." I fling my arm out, driving my point home. "They just leave, and you don't know *why*. There is no reason. I mean . . ." I scrunch up my face, trying to find my words. "Maybe there's a reason, but they don't tell you."

"Exactly," Riley says with a nod. "Because they're chickenshit."

"And there's the dickery." Cami stuffs more cake in her mouth. "Fucking dickery."

"Sometimes their dickeries are fun," Kat says with a wink. "Lots of fun." She points at Cami and squirts more alcoholic whip in her mouth. "God, this is strong."

"God bless the man who put alcohol in whipped cream," Mia says.

"It was probably a woman," I reply. "On a night like this."

"Well, God bless her," Mia repeats, then stares at me with one eye clenched shut. "Did you know that if you close one eye, then switch to the other, it looks like stuff moves around, but it *doesn't*."

"Mia's drunk!" Cami announces and she and I clink our bottles in celebration.

I dive for the cake, stuffing way too much in my mouth, making me cough and spew chocolate pieces all over the carpet. "Sorry, Cami."

"Meh." She shrugs. "I'll vacuum tomorrow."

"I have good friends," I say with a sigh, after I swallow the cake and take a swig of tequila. God, this shit is good. "Like, the best friends *ever*. I don't just have a person, I have *people*. How many bitches can say that?"

"Four others that I know of," Riley says with a laugh. "We are lucky to have a tribe."

"We so are," I say, patting her pretty hair. "Your hair is so soft."

"You know who has soft hair?" Cami asks, her voice *really* loud. "Landon."

"Are we talking about Landon?" Kat asks. "I thought he was still off-limits."

"It's a dumb-man party," I point out. "I say let's talk about all the dumb men."

"Except, he's not dumb," Cami says sadly. "He's really, really, really smart. He was the valedictorian of his class."

"That doesn't make him smart," I reply, but then frown. "Wait. Maybe it does."

"He's dumb for hurting you," Mia says. "But he doesn't even know he's doing it, which makes him doubly dumb."

"I think he might now," Cami says softly, tears forming in her eyes. "But I think he just doesn't care."

"Landon would care," I say with a frown. "Landon is a good person. He wouldn't be dickery with you. He loves you."

"But he doesn't *love* me, and that's the problem."

We all nod, understanding what Cami means perfectly.

"Well, I'm gonna text Jake," I decide with a nod. "I think I should. He shouldn't get the last word."

"Do it!" Mia says, clapping her hands. "Let us take a picture of your tits and you can send him those too, so he remembers what he's missing out on."

"No," Riley says, shaking her head emphatically. "All of that is a very bad idea."

"You're right." I nod and smile at Riley innocently. "I won't send him a picture of my tits. But I can still text him and tell him his dick is too small."

"Is it small?" Mia asks, shooting up into a sitting position, then nearly falling over again. "Whoa!"

"No. It's actually really good-sized."

"Damn," Kat mutters. "And he's good with it. You told me that, I think."

"Really good with it," I confirm. "I'd never had an orgasm from penetration before."

"That exists?" Cami asks in surprise.

"You mean, Brian never did that for you?" I ask her.

"Unfortunately, Brian is not as gifted in the dickery as Jake." She snorts, then starts to laugh, and we all join her, finding this news *hilarious.* "I need to know what all the fuss is about."

"So, Brian's nice, but he's not great in the sack," I say, now petting Cami's hair. "Your hair is soft too."

"Why are you petting everyone?" Kat asks.

"It's soothing," I whisper loudly to her. Geesh, she is not maternal *at all.*

"Brian is good with his tongue," Cami says thoughtfully. "But the rest? Meh."

"Then why are you constantly trying to set the man up?" Mia asks.

"Well, what was *meh* to me might be *wowza* to someone else. It's all subjective."

We nod in agreement. I mean, she makes perfect sense. And then I remember that I was going to text Jake.

"I have to text Jake." I crawl across the room to fetch my handbag, and Kat comes after me.

"No, you don't." She reaches around me, fumbling for my phone, but I hold it close to my belly and bend over, out of her reach. "Give me your phone, Addison."

"Let her text him," Mia yells.

"No, she should *not* text him," Riley says.

Kat tickles me and I squirm, losing my grip on my phone, and she plucks it out of my hand.

"You're strong for someone who thinks the gym is a weapon of mass extinction."

"Mass destruction," Cami corrects me, still eating cake.

"That's what I said." I turn back to Kat and hold my hand out. "Give me my phone."

"No."

"Yes!"

"Addie, look at me." There are two of her. "You will regret this tomorrow. Do *not* text him. Don't give him the satisfaction of that. He broke up with you, sweetie. You can't text him: it makes you look weak and pathetic."

I stare at her, blinking rapidly as the tears begin to come. "I never told him that I love him."

"Ah, baby," Kat says and pulls me in for a hug.

"I trusted him. I let my guard down with him." I pull out of Kat's arms and plop down on the floor in defeat. "I told him *everything* about the modeling days."

"Everything?" Cami asks in surprise.

"Everything. I told him about my parents, and I let myself be vulnerable with him. I snuggled with him, for fuck sake, and I hate to snuggle!"

"Boy, don't we know it," Riley mutters and swigs her vodka.

The sobs are coming hard now, making me shake with every breath I take. I'm pretty sure snot is running down my chin.

And I don't freaking care.

"I fell so hard for him! Most of the time I don't give any fucks. Not one. But this time I gave fucks," I say to Cami, who nods with wide eyes. "I gave lots of fucks, Cam. I'm a prostitute of feelings."

"I don't think you need to call yourself a feeling hooker," Mia says wisely. "Having feelings is good."

"Having feelings fucking sucks," Kat mutters with a shake of the head. "Especially when it comes to men, because when we care, we give them the power to stomp our hearts into dust."

"We do," I say between broken sobs. "And it hurts so much, you guys. I didn't know I could hurt like this." I shake my head violently. "I didn't know."

"This is why you can't text him," Kat says and brushes my hair back over my shoulder. "Because he'll respond, and then it'll just keep hurting."

"I don't want it to hurt anymore," I whisper and wipe at my eyes, then stare at the mascara smeared across the back of my hand. "I'm so tired of hurting. I'm so tired of being thrown away as if I'm nothing."

"You're not nothing," Riley says, her voice hard and angry.

"But they toss me aside like I'm nothing," I reply, wiping at the other eye.

"Who are *they*?" Mia asks.

"Men. My parents." I swallow hard. "Jake. Jake tossed me aside like I'm nothing. And that one hurts the most because I could see a future with him, you guys. I'm not saying that I'd picked out a dress or anything, but he was just so easy to be with, that when I thought about being with him forever, it didn't scare the piss out of me."

"That's so sweet," Cami says, wiping at her own eyes.

"I know." I sniffle and wipe my nose with the back of my hand. "Are there tissues?"

"I think we're all too drunk to try to go find some," Mia says. So I just wipe my nose again on my shirt, then lie down flat on the carpet, my face cradled on the back of my hand.

"I miss him already."

It's REALLY, *REALLY* bright in here. And my eyes are closed. I groan and open one eye, just a slit, to find that all of the lights are still on in Cami's living room, and all of my friends are passed out on the floor and the couch. Actually, it looks like Cami and Riley are cuddling on the couch, both snoring.

At least I'm not the only one who snores.

I roll onto my back and the first wave of nausea kicks in violently.

So violently, that I stand up and run for the bathroom, then when I get there I fall to my knees and throw up into the toilet. So much that I'm pretty sure I just lost some vital organs.

Suddenly, someone presses a cold washcloth to my neck, but I can't even look back to see who as I continue to hurl. My stomach is heaving so hard I can't breathe and I can feel my face going beat red.

God, this hurts.

Everything hurts.

"Oh my God," I wail when I'm able to take a breath, my face still halfway into the bowl.

"I'm so sorry, Add," Mia whispers, rubbing big circles around my back. She flips the cloth over so I get the cool side on my skin. "I'm so very sorry."

"Make it stop, Mia." I'm begging and sobbing, and then throwing up some more. I can't stop throwing up.

I can't stop hurting.

"It'll get better," she croons, holding my hair back. "I know it hurts so much now that you want to die, but it'll get better. I promise."

Mia would know. Mia's been here.

I lay my cheek on the toilet seat and try not to think about the fact that my cheek is on a toilet seat. I don't think it's wise to move yet.

"He said he couldn't do it, and when I asked him what he couldn't do, he said he couldn't do *us*."

"Bastard."

"But he didn't tell me *why* and that hurts almost as much because I don't know what I did wrong."

"Oh sweetie, I don't think you did anything wrong." She's brushing her fingers through my hair, soothing me.

"I must have done something, Mia. You don't dump someone for no reason."

"Dickery," she whispers, making me chuckle.

"The thing is, he's not a dick. But I guess he's not my problem anymore." That makes me tear up all over again. "I miss him."

"I know."

"I loved the way he touched me. He made me feel important, Mia."

I hear her sniffle, making me cry harder. I'm so fucking sick of crying. "And I hate sounding so damn whiny, because I'm not a whiner."

"You're entitled. It hasn't even been twenty-four hours yet."

I nod, but that makes me nauseated all over again, so I spend the next five minutes, which feels like at least an hour, heaving into the toilet.

Finally, I'm gripping on to the lip of the toilet weakly, my shoulders shaking. "I don't think I have anything left in me."

"Are you sure?" Mia asks.

"Yeah."

"Okay, stay put, I'm going to get this rag cold again and I'll help you to Cami's spare bedroom."

"Mia?" I grip onto her hand before she can back away.

"Yeah."

"Love you."

"I love you too, friend."

Chapter Sixteen

Jake

$\mathcal{I}$ couldn't go home. I'd just get lectured by Max, or worse, I'd deck him and fuck that friendship up, and that would just add more shit to an already shitty day.

Maybe the worst day of my life.

Because I had to let *her* go, and it was the hardest fucking thing I've ever done. When I close my eyes, all I can see is the heartbreak on her gorgeous face and it makes me feel like a grade-A piece of shit.

Which, I am.

But it's better to hurt her now, before we get in too deep and before I do something that does far more than just hurt her feelings.

No, I couldn't go home. Instead I came to a bar on the outskirts of Hillsboro, not far from my house. I've been here all morning. I think it must be sometime in the afternoon by now because a new bartender came on shift, replacing the young redhead who served me all morning.

I don't really fucking know what time it is. Or care.

The middle-aged bartender wipes down the bar with a white rag and nods toward my glass. "Get you another?"

I nod. "Jack and Coke."

He turns to fetch my drink, then slides it over to me, and just as I'm lifting the glass to my lips, I hear next to me, "Well aren't you the sexiest thing I've seen in here in a while."

The stranger's voice is rough from too many years of cigarettes. I ignore her, sipping my drink, hoping she'll just take the hint and go away.

But she doesn't. Damn it.

"I don't think I've seen you here before," she tries again.

No, you haven't. I sip my drink again, still ignoring her.

"Hey," she says and lays her hand on my arm. "Are you okay?"

Finally, I glance over at her, barely taking in blond hair and bright red lips. I shake my head and raise my glass to my lips. "I'm not interested in whatever it is you're offering."

"How do you know?" she asks, still touching my arm. "I like your tattoos. Why don't you tell me what you *are* looking for?"

I turn on my stool, getting a good look at the bad dye job on her blond head, with at least two inches of brown showing at the roots. She's tried too hard with her makeup, probably taking the same amount of time as Addie to get ready, but instead of looking natural and classy, her heavy hand with eyeliner and blush just makes her look trashy.

Her white T-shirt is too tight, her denim skirt too short.

"You wanna know what I'm interested in, honey?" I ask her.

She bites her lip, twirls a strand of hair around her finger, and nods.

"She's about five foot ten, with natural blond hair the color of morning sunshine and eyes so blue you could drown in them. She's got curves for days, and her legs are so long they make a man sit up and beg for her to wrap them around his waist. She's sassy and kind, and has the wittiest comebacks of anyone I've ever met."

"She sounds impressive," the woman replies, then smiles. "But I bet I can make you forget her."

"No." I turn back to the bar and lift my glass, knock back what's left, and signal for the bartender to give me a refill. "You're wasting your time here."

"Well, I'll be right over there if you change your mind."

Her heels click as she walks away, and I don't even give her a second glance. Did I really used to think that women like her were attractive? Because there was a day when I would have taken her up on her offer. I would have taken her into the bathroom, locked the door—or not, I didn't give a fuck—and fucked her brains out, then gone about my way.

It's been a very long time since those days, but they existed.

And the thought of it now makes me sick.

"Turned her down, huh?" the bartender says as he passes me a new drink.

"Not what I want," I reply curtly.

"No, I heard what you want. That's what we all want, kid." He snickers and washes glasses in the sink in front of me. "I'm Bill."

"Jake. Yeah, well, I can want her all day long, and I do, but I can't have her."

"So she exists?"

I laugh and nod. "Oh yeah. She exists." I pull my phone out of my pocket and thumb through my photos, until I come to the selfie we took at the falls. I'm kissing her cheek and she's smiling brightly for the camera.

"She's a knockout," he says with a low whistle. "Fucked it up, did you?"

I just nod and tuck my phone back in my pocket.

"My Marion, she was a knockout when I met her, thirty-three years ago last February." He pulls his wallet out of his back pocket and shows me a photo of a beautiful redhead with big green eyes and a pretty smile.

"She's definitely a knockout," I agree with a nod. "Are you married?"

"For thirty-three years this August," he confirms with a wink. "I knew a good thing when I found it and I snatched her up before anyone else could."

"Kids?" I swallow the rest of my drink and nudge it toward him for another.

"Nah." His eyes dim as he shrugs and pours my drink. "Tried. Didn't work out for us."

"Sorry to hear that." I toss half of the new drink back, my chest heavy with sympathy. Fuck, I need to call Christina. When does she find out if the last round of IVF worked?

"I have her." He grins. "That's all that matters."

I'm fucking jealous of a guy double my age and his pretty wife. Because he has what I want. He has the woman of his dreams for the rest of his life.

I toss back the rest of my drink. "Another."

"You better slow down, son. It's barely four in the afternoon."

Is it that late already? I've been here, brooding, longer than I thought.

"Just keep them coming."

"Is this going to be a *fuck my life* kind of drunk, or a *I just want to forget* kind of drunk?"

I smirk. "Honestly, I think it's both." I slide off the stool. "You pour, I'll be back."

I stumble—Jesus, I can't be drunk yet—to the men's room and piss. After zipping my fly, I push my hand in my pocket, and come out with the small vial of coke that Addie had in her purse.

Fuck me.

Alcohol always was my gateway to the coke, and staring at it now, I want it more than I want my next breath.

Who would care if I got high one more time? Who would it hurt? I mean, I've already completely obliterated the no-alcohol rule, so I'll do this one last time and call it quits.

I look at myself in the mirror, lean on the counter, and swear a blue streak as I turn the water on, open the coke and wash it down the drain, then toss the vial in the trash.

I'm not a junkie, and I'll be fucking damned if I'll snort

that shit up my nose now just because I'm pouting over Addie.

But I'm going to drink every bottle of Jack Daniel's in this place.

THE BAR HAS filled up this evening. There are kids playing pool and sinking dollars into a jukebox, choosing some good music, but mostly shitty music.

Or maybe I'm just not in the mood for happy songs.

They played a Hard Knox song, and that only made me want to deck someone.

I forgot that alcohol makes me aggressive, and that's only one of the reasons I gave it up long ago.

"Do you want to close your tab, Jake?" Bill asks as he hands me a drink. I've been steadily getting more and more drunk all day. And it feels fucking fantastic.

"No. I'll need another."

"I think I'm cutting you off, pal," he replies. "It's almost midnight, and you've been drinking all day."

"Are you the fucking alcohol police?" I ask with a frown.

"Yeah, actually, I am." He smirks. "Who can I call for you?"

"Why would you call anyone for me?" God, my words are all fucking slurred.

"Because you're not driving home. I can call a friend or a cab, which is it?"

"Call Addie." I pull my phone out of my pocket and then bark out a laugh. "Wait. You can't call her." I slide my phone across the bar at him. "She hates me. Call Christina."

"Are you sure?" he asks with a grin. "Or is there another woman's name you want to toss out?"

"Christina," I repeat and lay my head down on my arm, suddenly very tired. When did I get so fucking tired?

"This is Bill at the Yellow Rose bar in Hillsboro."

I'm at the Yellow Rose? Huh.

"I have Jake here, and he's going to need a ride home. He told me to call you."

I don't need a ride home. I have a fucking car. As soon as I sleep off this bender in the backseat, I can drive myself home.

God, it feels like I'm spinning. The kids playing pool are laughing. The music is loud.

"You okay, Jake?"

"Yeah, Bill, I'm good," I answer him without opening my eyes. "I can just sleep here."

"No, you can't." He laughs and I suddenly smell coffee. "Have some of this."

"No thanks."

"Suit yourself."

I haven't had the spins since . . . hell, since before the band broke up. Since before Christina's accident. I frown and shake my head, trying to clear it. Why in the hell am I thinking about that? It was a long time ago. It has nothing to do with now.

I feel a hand on my back.

"I told you, sweetheart, unless your name is Addison, I'm not going to fuck you. I'm sure one of the guys playing pool will take you out back and rock your world, just ask them."

"I'm relieved to hear that."

Christina.

"Hey." I open my eyes and try to focus on the three Christinas standing beside me. "How did you get here?"

"I drove here, Einstein. Has he paid his tab?"

"I have it here," Bill says, handing Christina my debit card and passing me a pen to sign the receipt. I give him a five-hundred-dollar tip. He's earned it. "Here's his phone."

"Thanks."

"You didn't have to come." I step off the stool, and Chris tucks herself into my side, helping me toward the door. "Thanks, Bill! Have a good one!"

"Obviously, I did have to come," she says as she leads me to her car. "You're hammered."

"Thank fuck."

I drop into her car and put the seat back, immediately closing my eyes.

"Spinning?" she asks as she pulls out of the parking lot.

"Yeah."

"If you're gonna throw up, warn me so I can pull over."

"Not gonna throw up." I take a deep breath through my nose and will myself not to throw up. "Fucked up."

"What happened?"

I swallow the bile rising in the back of my throat. "Addie's gone." I feel her turn off the freeway and brace myself as she turns right. "God, slow down. This isn't a fucking race."

"What do you mean Addie's gone? Where did she go?"

"Broke it off," I reply. We come to a stop, and I push out of the car and hurl on the grass, unable to keep it in anymore.

"At least you didn't do it in my car," Chris says from behind me. "Come on, jackass."

Man's arms pick me up, and I look over at Kevin, who smiles happily. "How did you get here?" I ask him.

"I live here."

"You don't live with me. Christina wouldn't like that, and I don't swing that way, man."

"Oh my God," Chris says with a laugh, leading us to the front door. "We're not at your house."

"Oh." Before I know it, we're in the guest bedroom. "I fucked up, C."

"Why did you break it off?" she asks quietly and helps me out of my shoes.

"Because I fuck up everyone's lives," I say and lie back on the bed. At least throwing up made everything stop spinning.

"You're an expert at fucking up your own life," C mumbles, but then the lights go out, and I let sleep take over.

BACON. I CAN smell bacon. I turn onto my side and moan. *Fucking hell, I should never drink like that.*

Thing is, I *don't* ever drink like that. I'm too old for that shit.

"Jake! Get your ass out of bed!"

Christina is yelling from the kitchen, and it makes me smile. Back in the day, before the fame and all the bullshit, she used to make me breakfast to get over a hangover. A four-egg omelet with bacon and more cheese than any one person should eat in one day.

Except, I don't want to move. My head feels like ten people are sitting on it, and I'm pretty sure I no longer have a functioning liver.

"Jake," Christina snaps as she opens the door to the bedroom. "Don't make me throw water on you."

"You wouldn't." Is that even my voice?

"Oh, you know as well as I do that I would. And have. And will again if I have to. So get your hungover ass out of bed."

She slams the door, which makes me grab my head, needing to stabilize it.

When did she get mean?

I roll to the side of the bed and lift myself into a sitting position, moaning. God, I did a number on myself yesterday.

And Addie's gone.

Fuck me.

I shuffle out to the kitchen, still in yesterday's clothes, and most likely smelling like the booze-filled bar I spent the day in, and almost run into Christina, who's on her way back to the bedroom with a glass full of water.

"You got mean."

"It's noon," she replies with a roll of her eyes, and leads me to the kitchen. "And your omelet is ready."

"This omelet is why we're friends."

"No, me picking you up last night is why we're friends." She smirks and sits at the breakfast table with me, watching as I devour the omelet. "At least you have an appetite."

"I need something in my stomach. It feels raw."

"It probably is," she replies with a soft smile. "Want to talk about it?"

"Do I have a choice?"

She shrugs and looks out the window, which gives us a beautiful view of Mount Hood. "You always have a choice, but I won't stop badgering you until you talk, so you might as well make it easier on both of us and do it willingly. You broke up with Addie."

"How do you know that?" My head whips up to stare at her.

"You told me last night."

"I was so fucking drunk." I lower my head into my hand.

"Yeah, you gave the whole bar quite a show, lip-synching to Cyndi Lauper, and stripping down to your underwear and all."

"I'm not wearing underwear," I mutter, slightly mortified.

"Yuck." She scrunches up her nose, then laughs. "I'm kidding. It sounds like you were just broody."

I nod and take the last bite of the omelet.

"Here." She hands me four ibuprofen and a tall glass of orange juice.

"Thanks for taking care of me."

"I'm practicing." She grins and rubs her belly.

I stop cold and stare at her. "For what?"

"For having a baby." Her eyes well up. "It worked. I'm pregnant."

"Oh my God, C!" I pull her into my arms and hug her close. "I'm so fucking happy for you. When did you find out?"

"Yesterday." She pulls away and smiles happily. "I would have told you last night, but I was hauling your drunk ass around."

"You didn't have to do that."

"You didn't see yourself last night. You're lucky you made it to the grass to throw up."

"Oh God. I'm sorry."

She shrugs and takes a sip of my juice. "So tell me why you broke it off with the best thing that ever happened to you."

I stare at my empty plate, and all the grief from the past twenty-four hours comes crashing back down on me. "Because I'm not right for her."

"Why do you think that? Seemed to me that you guys were great together."

"We weren't going to work out for the long haul."

"So, you're just not interested?" She nods. "It happens. I mean, she seems nice enough, and God knows she's beautiful, but that's only skin deep. Maybe's she's not as great as she led me to believe."

"She's amazing," I whisper. "She's better than you know."

Chris is quiet, watching me, and finally takes my hand in hers, holding on tight. I need this, this connection with her.

"Then why aren't you with her, J?"

"The other day, after she and I had an argument and she stormed off, frustrated with me, I drove up on an accident on the freeway. Same car as Addie's."

Christina's eyes narrow, but she doesn't say anything.

"I thought for sure it was her. I thought that she'd been angry, and she got into an accident, and that she'd been hurt. God, C, for about an hour there, when I didn't know for sure if it was her, I thought that I'd killed her."

"What are you talking about?"

I shake my head, staring at our linked hands. "I can't continue a relationship with her. Yes, she's the best thing that ever happened to me, but don't you get it? I'll only fuck up her life."

She's scowling at me now, shaking her head. "I'm not following you at all, Jake."

"I hurt people. I disappoint people." I swallow hard. "I didn't care for my dad the way I should have the last few years of his life."

"You were doing exactly what your dad wanted you to be doing, Jake. He was so proud of you, he was bursting with it."

"How do you know?"

"Who do you think gave him regular updates on you? I spoke to him all the time. Do you know how many times I heard *I'm so proud of that boy?*" A tear slips down her cheek. "He wanted you to chase after the music, Jake. It would have pissed him off if you'd done anything else."

"I know," I whisper. She's right. He would have. But fuck, how I miss him. I wish I'd been the one to call him regularly, to tell him about my life. "And there's you."

"Me?" She raises her brows.

"You." I shake my head slowly. "I'm so sorry, C."

"For what? For being a douche bag?"

"For the accident." I meet her gaze now, surprised to find so much confusion in her pretty eyes. "For you losing your leg. For the horrible things I said to you before you drove off in that car that night. For it taking you so damn long to get pregnant."

"Yeah, let's talk about this, Jake. You've been dodging me on this for five damn years, and it's time you and I have this conversation."

"I don't want to talk about it," I reply. "I just wanted to apologize for it."

"I don't want your fucking apology!" she shouts, slamming her hand on the table. "I want you to *listen to me!*"

I sit back, stunned. She's never, *never* yelled at me before. Not like this.

"You're so damn stubborn," she mutters and takes a deep breath. "First of all, I want to know, what do you think it was that you said to me before the accident?"

"You know what I said. I told you that if you didn't like the lifestyle I'd chosen you could get the fuck out of it. I didn't need you."

"No you didn't." She's frowning, shaking her head. "Jake, I don't remember much about the accident itself, but I remember everything about that conversation. You were drunk as fuck, and you might have been on something, who knows."

I cringe.

"And I was lecturing you, telling you to grow the hell up. You were drinking too much, experimenting with drugs, fucking a lot of women. I was telling you to get a grip on your life."

"And I told you to fuck off."

"No. You didn't. You didn't say much of anything at all. Maybe you were saying those things in your head, but I couldn't get you to say anything, so I told you I'd talk to you the next day after you sobered up, and I left. Jake, do you really think I'd let you tell me that you didn't need me and to get out of your life? I'd have kicked your ass."

I smirk, then sober up again. "It doesn't matter, the end result was the same. You were upset at me, and because of that you got in that accident."

"Bullshit."

I throw my hands up in frustration. "Now who's stubborn?"

"You wouldn't listen to anyone, Jake. The accident wasn't my fault. It wasn't anyone's fault. I was merging onto the freeway, and the car ahead of me lost a tire. It came bouncing straight at my car, hit me, and made me lose control. I was pinned in that car because a tire fell off, not because I was so upset at you that I lost control."

What?

I blink at her for a moment, then stand up and pace away.

"Is that why you broke up the band, J? Because you thought that you'd somehow fuck up their lives too?"

"No," I reply honestly. "That might have been part of it, but your accident messed me up, C. I couldn't perform for a long time after it. It was a wake-up call for sure, and I'm thankful for that because it made me take a look at myself and cut out everything toxic in my life. A lot of those toxins were because of the band. But damn, I missed the music."

"And now you have it again," she replies. "You make a good living doing what you love and you get to perform for people too. It's a pretty great gig."

I nod.

"And you have Addie."

"No, I don't."

But, oh God, how I want her.

"Do you love her?"

"More than I can tell you," I reply immediately. "But I told her that I can't do a relationship with her. I hurt us both pretty badly, C."

"Well, then we're just going to have to figure out a way for you to *untell* her. She brought the best of you back to life, Jake, and I don't want to lose that again."

I grin, hope blooming in my chest for the first time in a long time. "Do you think it'll work?"

"Only one way to find out."

Chapter Seventeen

Addison

$\mathcal{J}$ couldn't hack it. Last night was the first night that Jake performed at Seduction since he decided to be a dirtbag and slice my heart open with a rusty knife.

Yes, I've become a bit dramatic over the past few days, but that's exactly what it feels like. I feel bled out. I'm tired, probably because I'm not sleeping, and I'm weak, most likely because I can't keep food down.

I'm just sad.

And that really pisses me off. I hate that he has that kind of power over me, that he's affected my mood like this.

So he dumped me. So what? I mean, life goes on.

But last night, when he began playing "Sad," one of my favorite Maroon 5 songs, I just couldn't do it. I turned around, waved at Kat, and walked right out the back.

It's bad enough that I've stayed away for the hour or two before he shows up to play so I don't run into him before he takes the stage. Just the sound of his voice made me panic.

I have Jake PTSD.

"You're not going to do that tonight," I say to my reflection in the bathroom mirror as I check my lip gloss and smooth my hands down my high-waisted pencil skirt. "Jake brings in a lot of money every weekend. Like it or not, it's best having him here for business." I point at myself and narrow my eyes. "You're a grown woman. You're a professional. So pull up your big-girl panties and deal with it."

"Is that working?" Riley asks as she comes out of the stall behind me.

"I think so."

She smirks and washes her hands. "You don't have to be here, Addie. The rest of us can handle it here."

"I'll be fine."

"Addie—"

"This is my place too," I interrupt her with a shake of my head. "I made the bad mistake of falling for an employee, and now I'm paying the consequences. Lesson learned."

"If you need *anything,* all four of us are here."

"I know." I hug Riley tight. "Thank you." The fact that my friends have come in when they don't have to, just because they know that being faced with Jake is hard on me, makes me more grateful than I can say.

"He asked me to give this to you." She pulls a small white envelope out of her pocket.

"You can rip it up and throw it away."

"Come on, Addie. Just read it."

I roll my eyes and take the note.

> *Addie—*
>> *I miss you. Just talk to me.*
>>> *—Jake*

We can hear applause from the dining room. "He's on," Riley says. "It's safe for you to go out there now."

"I don't know what you mean." I sniff and put my nose in the air as I fold the note and shove it in my bra, then walk out of the bathroom, purposefully not looking in Jake's direction, and begin to make my rounds through the dining room, asking diners if they're happy with their dinners, and if anyone needs anything else.

I may be avoiding looking at him, but there is no way to avoid hearing him. God, I love his voice. He's singing a Gavin Degraw song, and his voice washes over me. It's the most amazing and the most hurtful thing, all at the same time.

But I force a smile as someone asks for another glass of wine and I try to block out that the love of my life is currently on my stage. He won't take me home tonight and touch me or make love to me. Or simply smile at me or make me laugh.

There is nothing there, yet I can hear him, and it's my own private hell.

"You okay?" Cami asks as she passes by me on the way to the bar.

"Yes. Can you please get another glass of house white for table fourteen?"

"On it." She nods and bustles away, as if she waitresses every night. I turn at the sound of my name and smile when I see Christina and Kevin sitting at a table in the heart of the dining room.

"Hi, guys. How are you?"

"We're fine," Christina replies, her eyes shrewd as she watches me. "How are you?"

"I'm great." *Fake it till you make it, girl.* I smile brightly. "Can I get you anything?"

"We're great," Kevin replies kindly. "It's good to see you, Addie."

"You too." I smile again. "I need to check on an order from the bar." I need to get away from them. It's too soon to see people that I'd come to really care about who I don't get to keep in my life. Just as I reach the back of the room, Jake begins to talk.

"This next song is for someone special." That's all he says before he begins to sing a cover of "Thinking Out Loud."

Darling I will be loving you till we're seventy.

I can't do this.

My heart literally aches as it beats out of control. I march straight back to the bar, where Kat and Cami are filling drink orders.

"I can't."

"Addie—" Cami's eyes are worried.

"No. I can't do this. I thought I was strong enough, but I'm not. This is his last night. I'll find someone else." I take a deep breath, trying to keep my tears at bay. "I have to go."

"Go." Kat tips her chin toward the back door as she pours a beer from tap. "You shouldn't be here anyway."

I nod and fetch my purse, then walk straight out the door without looking in Jake's direction.

I consider that a win.

I've had "Thinking Out Loud" on repeat in my condo all damn day. It's my one day off, and I'm doing exactly what I want to do: housework and laundry. I have a green mask on my face, my hair in a towel, letting the deep conditioner do its job.

I might shave my legs later, just to make me feel better.

I mean, my heart may be broken, but that's no reason for a girl to let herself go.

Cami and I met for breakfast this morning, and she told me that before they could tell Jake that he was fired, he quit after his set. That made me sad, which I don't understand *at all*.

But really, I don't understand many of my feelings this week.

Just as I'm about to go rinse my face and my hair, there's a knock on the door.

"Ms. Wade?" a young woman asks. She's holding a big white box with a red ribbon around it.

"Yes."

"This is for you." She's smiling widely as she hands it to me. The bottom of it is warm.

"Is it going to explode?"

"No, ma'am," she replies with a laugh. "Enjoy."

"Thanks."

I carry the box to my kitchen counter, pull the red ribbon apart, and open the box, frowning at the contents.

There's another white box with a red ribbon and a brown paper bag with the most delicious smells coming from it.

I pull everything out, toss the big box aside, and open the bag first. A burger and fries from the lodge at Multnomah Falls.

They deliver?

Inside the smaller box is a framed photo of the selfie that Jake and I took at the falls. He's kissing my cheek.

On the frame is engraved ALWAYS KISS ME GOOD NIGHT.

And there's a note.

A—

This was at my second favorite place with my very favorite person. I miss you.

—J

I miss him too, but I'm completely confused. Is he trying to get me back? Or is he just playing with my emotions?

I set the photo on the windowsill above the kitchen sink and lean against the countertop, eating the burger. And how did he get this to me still piping hot? Did he helicopter it in?

And how did he know that I'd be home?

"I HAVE A delivery for Addison Wade."

I frown at the flower delivery boy who just walked into Seduction. We aren't even open yet for the day.

"That's me."

"Oh, look how beautiful those are," Daisy says beside me. She's all heart-eyed as I take the bouquet of yellow roses.

They smell so damn good.

What is he doing?

"There's a card," Daisy says as Riley joins us.

"Got flowers?" Riley asks.

"No, I got chicken pox," I mutter and pull the card from its envelope.

> *A—*
>
> *Sixty-three yellow roses. One for every day our friendship grew. I miss you.*
>
> *—J*

"Damn, that's the sweetest thing I've ever read," Cami says from behind me, startling me.

"Where did you come from?"

"I heard Riley say that you got flowers. That's very sweet of him, Addie."

I shrug and carry the beautiful roses back to our office, Cami, Riley, and Daisy following me like little ducklings.

"He's sending me things," I mutter with a frown.

"This isn't your first delivery?" Cami asks, trading glances with Riley.

"No." I tell them about the photo and the food from yesterday.

"He's obviously trying to woo you," Cami says with a romantic sigh.

"Well, it's not going to work," I say, not with nearly as much conviction as I'd like.

"Why?" Daisy asks. "He's hot and, like, totally into you."

I shake my head. *No way.*

"You could just talk to him," Riley says.

"I'll pass. Kat said it best the other night. The more I talk to him, the more it'll keep hurting. It hurts enough already. He'll give up and go away." I shrug, as though it's no big deal, but I want to curl up and cry.

And I refuse to give him even one more tear. I have a life to get on with.

"So, HOW ARE you really?" Cici asks the next day as she takes my nail polish off.

"I'm really sick of answering that question," I reply, glaring at my friend. "Seriously, we all need to move on."

"Hey, I haven't seen you since it all went down, so I get to ask."

"I'm hurting and I'm tired and I'm pretty sure everyone hates hanging out with me these days because I'm a bitch." I smile sweetly. "But I'm fantastic."

"Well, you're still a smart-ass, so that's a good sign."

"A good sign of what?"

"I don't know, it just sounded like a good thing to say."

I chuckle and shake my head. "You're funny."

"And your nails look like you've been clawing at the walls."

"I cleaned my condo on Sunday from top to bottom with no gloves." I shrug. "I clean when I'm stressed out."

"Next time, come clean my house."

"You have four kids. I wouldn't even clean your house with gloves on."

We're both laughing as Cici's husband comes into her studio carrying a huge bouquet of pink roses. "Sorry to interrupt, but these were just delivered for you, Addie."

"Wow," Cici says with wide eyes. "You don't send *me* flowers like that."

"I don't think I screw up as big as this guy must have," he replies with a wink and returns to the main house.

"There are a lot of flowers here," I mutter, staring at the beautiful pink blooms. "He sent sixty-three yesterday, and there's more than that here."

"He sent flowers yesterday too?" Cici asks.

"Yeah."

She pulls the card out of its plastic holder and passes it to me before burying her nose in the fragrant blooms. "Seriously, my husband needs to pick up his game."

A—

A pink rose for when I think of kissing your gorgeous lips. Not one for every time because they'd never all fit in one room, but a hundred is a start. I miss you.

—J

"Marry him. Right now."

I shake my head and tuck the card in my purse, next to the other three notes from Jake. "He's not mine."

"But it's clear that he could be. Aren't you being stubborn?"

"Yes." I nod and sit back in the chair. "And you know why? Because when I forgive, I just get my heart trampled on again and again, and I'm not settling for that again. He tossed me away. He doesn't get me back."

"I'M GOING TO lock you out of the kitchen," I warn Mia the next afternoon, right before we open for lunch. "I'm serious, Mia, you need a day off."

"I took last Tuesday off," she says stubbornly, glaring at Kat and me. "I need to check on the new appetizer menu."

"No. You don't." Kat crosses her arms over her chest. "Go home, Mia."

Mia's dark brown eyes are furious as she spins and stomps out of the restaurant, slamming the door behind her.

"I hate that she won't voluntarily take days off," I murmur. "Even one day a week."

"I know," Kat replies, her eyes widening at something over my shoulder. "Um, I think those are for you."

I spin around and am met with a smiling delivery boy—the same one from Monday—and more white roses than I can count.

"For me?" I ask.

"Yes, ma'am."

"You can just put them on the bar."

He complies, grins again, then leaves, mentally counting his tips from all the deliveries he's making to me, I'm sure.

"This is crazy," I mutter as I press my nose against one of the soft blooms.

"Read the card," Kat says with a grin. All of the girls have come to love his cards, most likely because of the sweet way he has with words.

No wonder he's won Grammys for the songs he's written.

> A—
>
> *These smell the best, and when I touch them, they remind me of the softness of your sweet skin. I don't know how many there are, I told them to just send them all. I miss you, so much.*
>
> —J

I simply rest my head on the bar, right against the wood, and let the tears come.

"I have to tell him to stop," I cry. "I can't do this anymore, Kat. I just can't. You were right: the more I hear from him, the more it hurts."

"Wow, Jake," I hear from behind me. I quickly wipe my cheeks and turn to find Christina gaping at the display of white roses. "He might have gone a little crazy with this one."

I nod, mortified that she heard my crying. The only thing worse would be if Jake himself heard me.

And I'll be damned if that ever happens.

"What can I do for you, Christina?"

"I was hoping that you'd have time for me to take you to lunch. I'd really love to chat with you."

"I don't really—"

"Sure you do," Kat says with an innocent smile. "Go ahead and go."

I glare at her, then turn back to Christina. "So, here's the thing. I'd love to chat with you, but I don't want to talk about Jake."

"Perfect." She smiles and leads me out into the sunny Portland afternoon. "Actually, do you mind if we just walk down to the park?"

"Works for me."

We walk in silence. I didn't realize how nice it would be to be out in the fresh air. It feels good.

"How's Kevin? It was good to see you guys the other night," I begin, breaking the silence.

"We both know that's bullshit," Christina replies with a kind smile. "Seeing us was salt to an open wound, and I'm sorry for that."

I shrug. "It is what it is. You're always welcome in my restaurant, and I'd like it if you came often. I like both of you very much."

"We like you too." Christina clears her throat. "Jake says that you still haven't contacted him."

"No." I shake my head. "And I don't plan to. His efforts are flattering, but I'm just trying to move on."

"So, you don't believe in second chances, then?" she asks, putting my guard right up.

"You don't know anything about me," I reply coldly. "You

don't know how many second chances I've given to people who have thrown me away like I'm trash, and it turns out Jake was no different than the rest of them. So, no, I don't believe in second chances anymore because I'm the one who ends up disappointed."

"He definitely doesn't think you're trash," Christina begins, but I hold my hand up, stopping her.

"I said I would come if we didn't talk about Jake."

She takes a deep breath. "You're right. Instead, let's talk about me."

I raise a brow. "Okay."

"Did Jake tell you how I lost my leg?"

I shake my head, not sure how much I should say, and definitely keeping my guard up.

"I was in a car accident, after Jake and I had a pretty brutal argument. I was irritated with him, but that's not what caused the accident. It was simply that: a freak accident, and I ended up upside down at the side of a freeway, my leg trapped between the steering wheel and the seat, and the doctors couldn't save it.

"It was no one's fault, but Jake stupidly shouldered the blame for a very long time. He was convinced that it was his stupid actions that made me lose my leg. And there are other factors there that he should probably be the one to tell you about."

"Not that I'm not sympathetic, but why are you telling me all of this?"

"Because I think you're good for my friend, and I just wanted to give you some insight into why Jake reacts the way he does sometimes. Thinking that you might have been in that accident last week after you'd argued put him in a bad head space. I think he's trying to make up for that now."

"Look." I stand up and begin to walk away. "I understand what you're saying. I do. I'm sorry that all of you went through that time. But honestly, I feel like I'm being punished for the past. I didn't do anything wrong, but I was punished anyway, and frankly, I *can't* give him the opportunity to do it again."

I shrug, holding my hands out at my sides as I back away from Christina, who simply looks sad. "I wish you nothing but the best," I tell her. And with that, I walk away, not looking back.

Chapter Eighteen

Jake

$\mathcal{I}$'m sitting on the bench next to Max at the piano, singing the final few lines of Addie's song. I finished writing it yesterday and asked Max to come in the studio with me to fine-tune, as only he can. The man is amazing when it comes to the melody, and he took my good song and made it fucking perfect.

Tiffany, Cami, and Mia are sitting nearby, watching with matching expressions of wide eyes and surprise as they take in the lyrics and melody. I was surprised when Mia and Cami accepted my invitation to come listen to Addie's song. They've been nice enough to help me out over the past week, giving me a heads-up on where Addie was so I could have the flowers delivered directly to her, but now they're going above and beyond, and I appreciate them.

Addie has some amazing people in her life.

And having them here is like having a piece of Addie here too, and I don't give even one fuck about how silly that sounds. I'm desperate these days.

I hope their dropped jaws are a good sign. I know it's a great song. I feel it in my bones, the way I do when I know that a song is going to be a hit. This song is that good, but will Addie like it? Because that's the most important thing.

When the last note fades, all three girls stand, applauding. Cami wipes a tear from her cheek.

"Yeah?" I ask, hope surging in my chest.

"Oh yeah," Cami says with a nod.

"Not just yes, but hell yes," Mia agrees. "It's so beautiful, Jake."

"You know," Tiffany says as all three girls approach the piano and lean against the side. "I've heard your love songs before. You've written songs that have won Grammys that were *gorgeous* love songs—"

"But they never felt like this," Max finishes for her, smiling at her. "That's what I told him too."

"It's special," Cami says with a nod. "She's going to love it, Jake."

I nod, relieved. "I hope so. This has to work. It's my last option." I glance at Mia. "Did you talk to Mike?"

Mia, Cami, and Addie's friend Mike have agreed to take on the weekend gig at Seduction until they're able to replace me with someone steady.

"Yep, and he said that he'll play 'Drops of Jupiter,' and you can come up onstage after that. He'll be ready for you, and you can use his guitar." Mia grins, then shakes her head.

"I can't believe you roped us into helping you so much this past week."

"I couldn't have done it without you," I reply honestly.

"We're doing it because we think you're perfect for her," Cami says. "And when she finds out, we might all be killed."

"Let's hope it doesn't go that way," Tiffany says with a laugh.

"I have to warn you," Mia adds. "Don't expect a scene out of a romance novel, Jake. This song is awesome, and all of your gestures have been very romantic, but it may take her a little while to process it all."

"So he shouldn't expect her to run up on the stage and throw herself into his arms?" Tiffany asks, raising a brow.

God, I should be so lucky.

"Probably not," Cami says with a cringe. "I mean, we could be wrong, and she might run dramatically up on-stage, throw herself into his arms, and pledge her undying love to him."

"You know her the best. That's why I asked for your help in the first place." I look down at the keys and take a deep breath. "I just hope she doesn't run off screaming in the other direction."

"Or punch you," Max suggests. "I mean, this could just piss her off."

"Thanks, man." I glare at my best friend. "Thanks for the encouragement."

"She won't hit you," Cami says, but her face doesn't look too confident. "She's not usually the violent type."

"She did hit Robert Valenetti in the fourth grade when he stole her pencil sharpener," Mia reminds her.

"Well, Robert had it coming."

I probably have it coming too. "Right now, I'd settle for any kind of communication from her. I haven't heard one peep from her. How is she?"

Mia and Cami share a glance.

"She's good," Cami says with a smile.

"She's sad," Mia says with a shrug, earning a glare from Cami. "I won't lie to you, Jake. She's sad. But she's okay. And Jake? You need to know that whether she's with you, or without you, she will continue to be okay. Because that's who Addie is."

"And that's just one more thing that I love about her, Mia. I wouldn't have it any other way. I want her to be more than okay. But I hope she chooses to be awesome *with* me, because we will be so much better together than we would be apart."

"Wait." Max grips my shoulder. "Are those *feelings* coming out of your mouth?"

"I love her." I shrug. "It's as simple and as terrifying as that."

"Well then, win your girl, handsome." Tiffany smiles and pats her belly. "Because I like her. And I want her to stick around."

I kiss Tiff's cheek. "Me too, friend. Me too."

I'M SO FUCKING nervous I can't see straight.

"I don't think I've ever seen you like this," Christina says with a frown as she watches me pace in the parking lot of Seduction, pushing my hands through my hair. "I mean, I know that you sometimes get a *little* nervous, but not like this."

"Is that sweat on your lip?" Max asks, then breaks out in laughter. He's going to bust my balls for this. "Mr. Cool and Collected has stage fright."

"Fuck you." I glare at Max, then take a deep breath and laugh. "Yeah, you're right. I do. My palms are sweaty. And for the first time in my life, I think I might need to throw up."

"The song is awesome," Tiffany reminds me. "Seriously, Jake, it's so beautiful. You have no reason to be nervous."

"I don't think he's nervous about the song," Kevin says. His arm is wrapped around Christina's shoulders. "It's the woman he's singing it for."

"It's going to be great." Christina gives me a smile. The one she used to give me before gigs in our early days, when I still let the nerves take over. "I can't wait to hear it."

"We'd better get inside," Max says, clapping my shoulder as he passes by. "You got this, bro. And if you need it, I'll ask for an ice bucket so I can pass it to you onstage when you toss your lunch."

"Very funny, asshole. Thanks." I nod and watch my friends walk in the front door, then jog around to the back. When I walk into the kitchen, Mia grins and winks at me. "How is she?"

"Grouchier than I expected," she says thoughtfully.

"Crap. That's not good."

"Actually, I think she's grouchy because *you* aren't here." Her smile widens. "So I'd say it's a great sign."

"Did she say anything about me?"

"Not in study hall, but I might see her before choir," Mia replies, rolling her eyes, then laughs. "No, she didn't say anything, but I don't expect her to. She's in moving-on mode."

"Let's see if we can stall moving-on mode and instead kick her into forgiveness gear."

Mike begins to sing "Drops of Jupiter," and my heart immediately begins to race. I let out a gusty breath and rub my hands together. When he reaches the bridge, I walk into the dining room, sticking close to the outer edges of the tables where it's a bit darker so Addie doesn't see me.

But I can see her. She's standing at a table, smiling at customers, nodding, one hand on a man's shoulder. God, she's gorgeous. I feel like it's been years since I last saw her, rather than it being two weeks.

Two of the longest weeks of my fucking life.

Her hair is pinned up tonight, with loose curls hanging around her face. She's wearing those fucking sexy black-rimmed glasses that I learned she only wears when she's been battling a headache, along with a flowy red dress and black heels that beg for a man to bend her over the closest surface and fuck her blind.

I pray she gives me the opportunity to do just that later tonight.

Right after I tell her how much I love her and explore every inch of her incredible body.

Mike finishes his song and, without a single word, passes his guitar to me and leaves the stage. The room quiets as customers watch, wondering what I'm doing. I glance up to see Max, Tiff, Chris, and Kevin at a table in the center of the room, but my eyes skim the tables, looking for Addie.

And there she is, at the right side of the room, watching me with a scowl.

"Good evening, folks. Don't worry, Mike will be back out in just a few minutes. I thought I'd give him a break and sing a song for someone special." My eyes are pinned to Addie's. Her hands are clenched at her waist as she watches me. "I hurt someone I care about very much. Okay, I'll be honest, I fucked up." I shrug, playing the audience. "But I would regret it the rest of my life if I didn't sing this song to her. I've been writing it since the day we met."

A woman nearby lets out a loud "Awww!" I laugh and nod. "Yeah, I guess you could say that I felt that *click* the minute I first saw her. I don't know that I believe in love at first sight, but boy do I ever believe in that *click*. So, this is for you, Addie. It's called 'If I Had Never Met You.'"

My fingers begin to strum the strings as Riley, Cami, Kat, and Mia join Addie, holding her hands and smiling in encouragement. I'm soon swept up in the lyrics, singing just to her as the rest of the room fades away, and I'm just looking into her beautiful face as the song comes pouring out of me.

If I had never met you, what would I be now?
I'd be incomplete and wasted, a man who lived without
I would not have seen the sunrise Monday mornin'

And I would not have smelled your hair as the sun was risin'
You take what's broken, touch it softly, and make it better
You're the stream of light that keeps on pushing,
gently breaking through
Into the darkest room

I watch as a single tear rolls down her cheek, and she reaches up mindlessly to brush it away. I want nothing more than to pull her into my arms and apologize. To tell her that everything is going to be okay.

But I'm not so sure that they are.

And if I had never met you, where would I be now?
I'd be searching, lost, and aimless, not knowing when, or how
I'd be looking for my happy ending story
I'd be staring down the broken road before me

You came into my life and saved me
From my wicked self and gave me
A reason to believe that there might be a bigger plan
All my fingers ache to play you
Both my arms have got to hold you
We will make sweet music like this Fender in my hands
What if I had never met you, where would I be now?

The song ends and the audience erupts into applause. I smile and nod, but then sober quickly as my worst nightmare comes true.

Addie says something to Kat, then turns away and runs

out of the room, into the kitchen, and I'm sure right out the back door.

Fuck.

I pass Mike his guitar and weave through tables to where my friends are sitting, clapping and smiling.

"It's over."

"What happened?"

I don't answer as I continue out the front door of the restaurant and to my car. I need to get out of here.

"Jake, stop!" Kevin calls. I turn to find not just all four of Addie's friends but mine as well marching out after me.

"She left," I say, my heart aching. "It's over. She doesn't want me."

"I was watching her," Tiffany says, shaking her head. "Jake, that was not the face of a woman who doesn't want you."

"She's right," Mia says. "I told you it wasn't going to be pretty, remember?"

"Addie runs," Cami says with a nod. "You have to go after her."

"I'm done begging." I'm so fucking frustrated.

"She doesn't want you to *beg*, you idiot," Kat says, rolling her eyes. "God, artists are so dramatic. Just go after her. Have a real conversation with her. Tell her what you want."

"Go," Christina says, nodding emphatically. "You've come this far, don't give up now."

"COME ON, ADDIE, answer," I plead through the white door. "I know you're home."

I've knocked four times and she won't answer.

"Take a hint, Jake," her voice comes through the door. I close my eyes in relief and lean against the jamb.

"If you won't open up, just listen to me. I have no problem talking through this door, Addie. And I don't give a fuck if the neighbors can hear." I swallow hard, gathering my thoughts. "God, I miss you, baby. It was so good to see you tonight. And I know that missing you is my fault. I fucked up big-time."

I shake my head, and I think I hear her say, "No shit."

"I got scared, Addison. I mean, there are all of these reasons for why I reacted the way I did, like thinking that I would somehow end up ruining your life, or disappointing you, but in the end, I realize that it was just pure fear. When I thought it was you in that accident, well, I didn't know that I could feel terror like that. It put me in a bad place, sweetness."

I'm quiet for a moment when she says, "Keep going."

"Good, you're still listening." I grin. "I knew from the minute I first saw you that you were incredible. You're so fucking beautiful, Addie. But more than that, you're . . . *you*. Smart, kind, funny. When you smile, your whole being lights up, and you make everyone around you light up with you." I lean my forehead on the door. "Open up, Addie."

Nothing. So, I keep talking.

"So yes, from that first moment, I had plans, baby. I planned to spend as much time with you as you'd give me. I planned to get to know you, inside and out. And I found more in you than I ever expected to.

"You showed me what I need in a woman, Addison. I need someone who calls me out on my bullshit. I need someone who sees the fire in my eyes and wants to play with it, not try to extinguish it. I need someone who challenges me; in the bedroom, in my career, in my crazy head. And you know what? I found all of that in you."

Still nothing, and it's fucking killing me. I want to hold her while I tell her all of this. I don't want to say it through this fucking door.

"I don't know how else to say that I'm so sorry for how I acted. I should have come to you, shared my fears with you, rather than run. I should have trusted *us* as much as you did."

I swallow hard. God, it really is over. What am I going to do without her?

"You know what, Addie? I learned more about myself in the two months I had with you than I did in my whole life. So, if nothing else, I have to thank you for that. I am so thankful, whether I'm a part of your life or not. And you're probably right, you do deserve better than me. You deserve so much greatness. Please open this door, Addie. Please let me look you in the eyes so I can tell you how I feel about you."

There's a long pause, but finally, *finally*, she cracks the door, just so I can see her face. She's not inviting me in.

"Thank you for all of that," she says quietly. Her eyes are red, but she's not crying now. "Thank you for the apology."

"Can I please come inside?"

She chews her lip. "I don't think so, Jake. I do appreciate

your apology. It's more than I've received before, and I didn't realize how much I needed it until just now."

"I've been apologizing to you all week, sweetheart."

"No." She shakes her head, looking resigned. "No, you've sent me pretty things and said that you missed me, which was also nice, don't get me wrong, but that's very different from an apology."

I frown, shaking my head. "Addie—"

"No, I'm not saying this to guilt you," she says. "Did it ever occur to you that while you were sending me expensive flowers and cheeseburgers, what I really wanted was *you*? Just you." She smiles softly, taking in my hair, face, and chest. "I've never cared about the rest, Jake. The money, or the fame, or the cool house. Those are just the extras. I wanted *you*, because I felt that click too."

"Addie—" I try again, but she interrupts me.

"I had an amazing time with you. You are a wonderful man, and you deserve so much greatness too. More than you give yourself credit for, I think."

"I want *you*." I lean in close, able to smell her now. "Just you."

"You had me," she replies softly. "And you hurt me."

"I know. I'm so sorry."

"The thing is, Jake, I've forgiven before, and it usually ends up the same in the end anyway. I get tossed aside for something else, whatever that may be. I don't think I would survive it twice with you."

"Let me inside, Addison."

"No." She swallows. "I want nothing but the best for you, Jake Keller."

"You're the best for me."

"No, I'm not. Goodbye, Jake."

She closes the door softly, and I'm stunned. What just happened? She's saying *goodbye*?

"No. No, Addison, this is not goodbye. Damn it." I pace away, pushing my hands through my hair, then back again, hoping that I'm wrong, that she's opened the door and has come to her senses, but it's shut and dark.

Jesus.

I didn't realize that it's true what they say, that when your heart is truly broken you can feel the moment it cracks. Until just now.

I'm pretty sure I'm bleeding out, right here on Addie's doorstep.

And that's fucking dramatic. But I don't care.

No.

Chapter Nineteen

Addison

$\mathcal{I}$ can't stop the tears, and I can't have him see them. I'm leaning on the door as I hear his footsteps walk away. I push off and begin pacing around my living room, crying.

Damn it, I've shed enough tears over Jake Keller! And this mascara is expensive.

Why can't he just go? I think I've made it very clear that I can't trust him enough to take him back, and I can't keep doing this. I can't have constant reminders of him, practically every damn day!

He didn't come to me. He didn't *try* to talk to me.

I wipe the tears off my cheeks, and then stop dead in my tracks.

"Jesus, Addie, you're being such a fucking hypocrite."

He came to me tonight.

He apologized, and told me that he's missed me, and he wrote me that incredible song.

And all the while, I've been punishing him for the way other men in my past have treated me. And that's what I've accused him of: punishing *me* for what happened in his past.

I'm a goddamn hypocrite.

Oh my God.

Yes, he was scared, and he made a rash decision. It's not like I've never done that. Yeah, I've done that plenty.

He's gone to great lengths to make it up to me, and I've acted like a spoiled, wounded bear, licking my wounds.

I grab my handbag and slip my bare feet into flip-flops. I have to follow him. I pray he's still willing to talk.

Please let him be willing to talk.

I shut my door behind me and turn to lock the dead bolt. It's difficult to see through the dark and my tears.

"God, it tears me up to see you cry."

I whirl, startled, and breathe a sigh of relief when I see Jake leaning against the wall beside my door.

"You're here," I breathe.

"I was trying to figure out a way to get you to let me in." That smile. Even in the dark I can see it spread across his face, and I can't stand it anymore. I just walk right into his arms, rest my head on his chest, and begin to cry in earnest.

"I'm sorry, Jake."

"I'm the one who's sorry," he whispers, his face pressed into my hair. His arms are so tight around me it almost hurts, but there's no way in hell I'm going to ask him to let me go. His hands rub soothingly up and down my back, as though he can't believe I'm in his arms. "God, you feel good."

I tip my head back and cup his cheek in my hand. The

stubble is rough, but what makes me gasp is the wetness I feel on his skin. "Don't go away."

"I'm not going anywhere, sweetness."

He leans his forehead against mine. "Addie, I love you so much it hurts."

Just when my tears were drying up, he goes and says that.

"I feel like I've loved you for a long time," I admit softly. "I think that's why I was so stubborn this week. I let myself fall in love with you, and when you hurt me, I knew that I'd never survive it if it happened again."

"Ah, baby." He plants his lips on my forehead and takes a long, deep breath. "Let's go inside. I'd rather the neighbors weren't privy to the entire conversation."

I grin and nod. "Good idea."

I lead him into my condo, to the couch, where he sits and tugs me into his lap, wrapping his arms around me again. "I thought I'd lost you forever," he murmurs, his voice rough with unshed tears. "I don't ever want to feel that way again, Addie."

"Me too." I drag my fingertips down his face, his neck, and back up into his hair. "You need to understand, Jake, that you could never ruin my life, as long as you're in it. You bring a lot of good to people."

He begins to interrupt, but I lay my finger over his lips, stopping him.

"You. Are. Wonderful. You're surrounded by people who care about you very much. You're not going to ruin my life, Jake."

"I know that now," he says quietly. "And I realize that it was pretty egotistical of me to think so." He shrugs, embarrassed. "I just always linked my bad decisions to my loved ones hurting, and I didn't want to chance ever doing that to you."

"And running away from me is what hurt me. Ironic, huh?"

He shakes his head. "I'm so sorry."

"I owe you an apology too. The first time you asked me to talk with you, I should have. But I have my own baggage, because you don't get to be our age, have life experiences, and not have the baggage that goes with it."

"I'd like to help you unpack," he says, kissing my forehead.

"I'd like that too." I bury my face in his neck, kiss his smooth skin, and take the first deep breath I've taken since before our fight at the restaurant. "Jake, there isn't one person in this world that I want more than I want you."

He stills, then rubs his hands up and down my back, to my waist, and then simply hugs me close. "Not even one?"

"I might think twice if Scott Eastwood were to make me a proposition."

Oh, how I've missed this!

"Who is Scott Eastwood?" he asks with a growl.

"You know, the actor. Clint's son."

"Hmm." He narrows his eyes. "I've already been replaced by an Eastwood? I'm clearly off my game."

"I haven't replaced you yet," I say with a laugh, combing my fingers through his soft hair. "I'm just saying, you're all

I want. Unless Scott crooks his finger at me. And even then, I'd probably still choose you."

"Probably?" He kisses my forehead, then nuzzles my nose with his.

"Most likely." He nibbles the corner of my mouth, down my jaw to my neck, and then sucks the skin between his lips, releasing it with a loud *pop*.

"Are you sure?" he whispers against my ear, and every hair on my body stands on end.

"I'm not so sure of my name right now," I reply breathlessly. God, how does he turn me on with just one little touch?

"I think I can make you forget all about that Eastwood guy," he says as he moves me effortlessly onto my back, laying me across the couch, hovering over me, kissing down my chest where my dress dips to show my cleavage. He's dragging his nose down the crease, barely touching me, yet making me squirm beneath him.

"Jake, get me naked."

"Not yet." He grins, and I know I'm in trouble.

The best trouble ever.

I'm clawing at his black T-shirt, trying to drag it up his torso, but he's keeping himself just out of my reach, frustrating the hell out of me.

"Please," I whisper. He drags his lips, his tongue, back up my chest and neck, lowers himself against me, and buries his hands in my hair, brushing it gently.

"We are not going to take this fast, baby." He nibbles my lips. "I'm going to make love to you, as slowly as possible.

I didn't think we'd be here again, and I want to savor you."

"It's no wonder you win Grammys," I murmur. "You have such a way with words."

He shakes his head and chuckles. "Every word is true." He skims his nose down mine, sending goose bumps down my arms. "I know that our love isn't perfect, Addie. But I do know that I will fight for us, I will protect you."

"Even though I'm a wreck sometimes?" I whisper.

"In spite of it. I love your chaos, sweetheart." He kisses me now, truly kisses me, taking it long and slow, in that perfect way that Jake does. This man has a gift when it comes to his mouth.

He's plucking pins out of my hair, letting it down, and then his fingertips scrub my scalp, making me purr.

"That feels nice," I say against his lips.

"I love your hair," he says with a grin. "I love your style. And I love that I never know from one day to the next what you'll look like. I have so much fun with you."

"That might be the best compliment anyone has ever paid me," I say, surprised. "Most people just see the boobs or the legs. They don't pay attention to anything else."

"I see you," he says as his lips take a journey down my neck. His hands are pulling on my dress at my shoulders, pulling it down far enough to reveal my breasts. "Not that your tits aren't absolutely gorgeous." He grins up at me as he takes my already hard nipple into his mouth, teasing it with the tip of his tongue. My hips surge up, but he's holding me firmly.

And he's hard.

He moves to the other side, paying it the same attention. I try to pull his shirt up again, and this time he helps me pull it over his head and tosses it aside, then resumes showing my breasts just how much he missed them.

And I get to touch his smooth skin, skimming my fingers up either side of his spine, into his hair, and down again. He's low enough that I can hook my feet into the back pockets of his jeans and give a little tug. "I'd love it if you were naked right now."

"I'd like to get you there first," he replies, and helps me shimmy out of my dress and bra; then, with just my panties remaining, he plants his hand flat on my chest and pushes me back down onto the couch. "God, you take my breath away."

I smile brightly as his gaze rakes down my body, then back up to my face. "Thank you."

He leaves wet, openmouthed kisses down my torso, on my belly button, my hip. He hooks his thumbs into my panties and guides them down my hips and legs, kissing every inch of me as he slowly peels them off of me.

He tosses them aside, and kisses the arch of my foot. I'm lying here, bare as the day I was born, open wide for him, and he's still taking his sweet time, kissing me, gazing at me.

Making me fucking crazy.

"Your skin is so soft," he murmurs, then takes my other foot in his hand and begins his journey back up my leg.

I jump when his tongue grazes the back of my knee.

"Ticklish?" he asks.

"I had no idea that was an erogenous zone," I breathe. He raises a brow and skims his tongue over the sensitive skin again. I tip my head back and moan, then gasp as he kisses up my inner thigh.

"I will never get enough of your pussy," he whispers as he pulls my lips apart with his thumbs and leans in to swipe his tongue from my opening to my clit in one long, fluid motion, sending me reeling. "So pink, so responsive."

I bury my fingers in his hair and tug, but he's stronger than me. He just grins up at me and continues to wreak havoc on every nerve in my body with that amazing mouth of his, pulling my lips into his mouth and sucking gently, his tongue massaging and driving me out of my ever-loving mind.

"Jake!"

"Yes, baby." He slides his hands under my ass and tilts me up. "You taste so sweet."

"You're going to make me come." I can't breathe, and I don't care.

"That's the goal," he says with a chuckle, then blows on me, making the wet skin cool. He gently pushes two fingers inside me and wraps his lips around my clit, sucking in little pulses.

And that's it. I'm done. I cry out as my world explodes into a million tiny pieces. My body is on fire. I can't think. I can't do anything except *feel*.

As I come down from the high, Jake kisses the sensitive crease between my thigh and pussy, then up my body, covering me again. I reach between us and unfasten his jeans, tugging them down his hips, and when he springs free, I cup him in my hand and guide the tip to where his mouth was just moments ago.

"Addie," he whispers, his amazing green eyes pinned to mine.

"Jake."

He's barely inside me, but oh God, it feels so fucking good. I'm still gripping the shaft, and urge him in farther, until he's buried completely inside me and we both sigh.

I clench my muscles, squeezing him, and he groans. "I missed you so much."

"Me too."

He begins to move slowly, in long, steady strokes. He's not pounding me, he's not fucking me.

He's enjoying me. Every inch of me.

I've never felt so beautiful in my life.

He links our fingers and pins my hands over my head as he moves a little faster, just a little harder, as though he just can't help it.

"Is this okay?" he whispers.

"So much more than okay," I reply, watching him. I can't stop watching him. His muscles are all flexed tight, and his stomach as he moves in and out is just . . . well, it should be fucking illegal.

"You are so sexy," I moan.

And that does it. He swears under his breath, releases my hands, and buries his face in my neck as he comes, pushing in one last, hard time as he lets go.

My hands are skimming up his back and down his sides, my feet resting on his calves.

"God, what you do to me," he whispers in my ear, kisses my neck, and pushes up to smile down at me. "I love you."

"I love you."

"This is good," Jake says, his mouth full of grilled cheese with turkey and tomato. He passes me the bag of Doritos.

After we snuggled—I can't believe I'm a freaking snuggler—and cleaned up, we decided we were starving. I don't remember the last meal I had. So I made us the hearty sandwiches and we piled back onto the couch with our food.

"I think the sun is about to come up," I say, gazing out the window. "How long did we snuggle?"

"For a while. You're so crazy about me, you couldn't bare to let me up," he says with a shake of his head. "You should be so embarrassed."

"You're hilarious," I reply dryly and roll my eyes. "That's some ego you have there, Keller."

"It's not ego if it's all true."

I smirk, then shrug. "Okay, I guess it's true. I might like you. A little."

He sighs deeply, chewing on the last bite of his sandwich. He's sitting on the opposite side of the couch, in just his jeans, and I can't take my eyes off his tanned, toned torso.

And then I giggle at the alliteration in my head.

"What?"

"Nothing." I nibble my sandwich as he sets his empty plate aside and begins to rub my feet, his thumb digging into my sole. "I think I love you for this alone."

"Yeah, my thumb skills are impressive."

I send him a smug grin. Yes, he's good at planting that thumb against my clit and making my world explode. "I should know."

"You're such a naughty girl," he says with a smile. "I love it."

"I warned you a long time ago that I was."

"And you weren't lying."

"I don't lie. About anything." Finished with my sandwich, I set my plate aside and settle back to enjoy the massage. "It's a waste of time, and then you have to try to remember what you said."

"It's a good policy to have."

"I also don't waste my time with liars." I'm looking him in the face now, hoping he understands what I'm saying. He stops rubbing my foot, reaches for my hand, and tugs me into his lap, cradling me close.

"I'm not a liar either, sweetness." I wrap my arms around his neck and hold on tight. Is he really here? Is this real? His hands are firm and warm over his T-shirt as he rubs them up and down my back. "But I do notice that you're a thief, always stealing my shirts."

"I like them," I mumble against his neck.

"Addie, I can't promise you that there won't be times I fuck up or that things won't ever feel broken." His voice is a shaky whisper, his mouth planted against my temple. "But I can promise you that I will never walk away from us."

Us.

Not me. Us.

I hug him tighter as tears form at the corners of my eyes. "That's the best promise you can make."

My eyes are getting heavy. His arms are strong around me, his breathing is long and steady, and before long, I feel myself drifting.

The next thing I know, he's lifting me and carrying me through the condo, turning off lights and checking that the door is locked before carrying me into bed. He lays me gently on the bed, then shucks out of his jeans and joins me, turning me away from him so he can spoon up behind me.

But I want to see him, so I turn around and thread my legs through his, hugging him around the middle and burying my face in his chest.

"Just go to sleep, baby," he whispers against my forehead.

"I don't want to."

He tips my face up, frowning down at me in the darkness. "Why?"

"Because what if I wake up and you're not really here? What if this is just the best dream I've ever had?"

"I'm here," he replies softly. "I'm here for as long as you'll let me stay."

Forever.

I'm not ready to say that out loud yet, but damn this feels so good. So *right*. I missed him so much.

"Sleep," he says again, and I can't resist it. My eyes close, and I fall asleep with Jake's heartbeat in my ear and his arms locked around me.

Chapter 20

Jake

I have to convince her that I'm sorry, and that I love her. I need her with me, always.

God, I miss her so much.

I wake, the anguish washing over me, just as it has every day since I stupidly walked out of Addie's apartment, and then I take a long, deep breath.

I can smell her.

I open my eyes and sit up, looking around the brightly lit bedroom and grin. I'm in Addie's condo.

And I held her all night while she slept. Well, technically all morning because we didn't fall asleep until very early this morning, but who's counting.

She's mine.

And if I have anything to say about it, she's going to be mine for the rest of her gorgeous little life.

But first things first . . . where the fuck is she?

I pad out of the bedroom and find her in the kitchen, still wearing my shirt, pulling pans out of a cupboard.

"Did I say that you could get out of bed?" I ask sternly. Her head jerks up, those blue eyes round in surprise.

"It's two in the afternoon, Jake."

"I don't give a fuck," I reply and take her hand in mine, abandoning the pans, and the eggs and bacon sitting on the countertop, and lead her back to the bedroom.

"I'm hungry." I glance back to see her purse her lips in a pout.

I'm going to take that pout right off her pretty face.

Once next to her bed, I lift my shirt off her and toss it aside, then inhale sharply, taking in her amazing, naked body. "Beautiful."

Her hands drift down my chest to my cock, and I step out of her reach. "Lie on your back."

"Bossy," she says with a raise of a brow, but her breathing has increased and I know she's turned on.

"Do I have to tell you again?"

"No, you don't." She lies in the middle of the bed, on her back, crosses her hands over her belly, and watches me with humor-filled eyes. "Now what?"

Oh, baby, just wait.

I don't answer her. I just smile and watch as she bites her lip, already anticipating my next move.

I spread her legs wide and lean in to kiss her breasts. "Grab your ankles."

"I'm sorry?"

I lift my head, looking in her eyes. "I want you to grab your ankles."

"Do you ever say *please*?"

I blink at her. "Not right now."

She narrows her eyes, trying to decide if she's going to trust me with this much control, and finally she complies, gripping on to her ankles as her legs are spread.

"Good girl."

She giggles. *"Good girl?"*

"Mmm." I suck a nipple into my mouth, then lick up her neck and kiss her lips, biting that bottom lip myself. "I understand why you always bite this lip. It's delicious."

"You're in a really interesting mood this morning."

"It's afternoon."

"Whatever."

I kiss her again, and then with my lips still pressed to hers, I say, "Now I want you to count to twenty. If you let go of your ankles, I'm going to spank you. Hard."

The muscles in her neck work as she swallows, eyes pinned to mine.

"Do you understand?"

She nods.

"Words, Addie."

"I won't let go."

I trace her body with my tongue, working my way down, but instead of eating her pussy, I push two fingers inside her. "Count."

"One, two—"

And I begin to finger-fuck her, roughly, my thumb

pressing on her clit. Her back arches and she releases her ankles.

"You let go."

"Wait!" She laughs, shaking her head. "Let me try again."

I tilt my head to the side. "Okay, we'll call that practice. Grab your ankles."

She complies.

"Count."

"One, two, three, shit, shit, shit . . ."

"Shit isn't counting. Start over." I don't slow my hand, and she groans.

"One, oh my God."

"He's not here, baby. Count." She glares at me, but doesn't let go.

"One, two, three, four . . ."

"Slower."

She whimpers, but slows her counting and I resume driving her mad with my hand, watching as her body flushes, tightens, makes me abso-fucking-lutely hard.

She reaches twenty without letting go, and I stop the torture as she sighs in relief.

"Very good."

She smiles triumphantly.

"Okay, let's try this."

"Can I let go of my ankles now?"

I smirk. "Yes, you may. You're catching on."

"I had no idea this could be so much fun. I thought it was just dirty, maybe a little toxic to a relationship."

"What, dominance?"

She nods.

"Nothing toxic ever comes from genuine love and trust. Ever. Remember that, baby."

"I do trust you," she whispers shyly, making me soften.

I'll never abuse that trust.

I reward her with a long, sweet, wet kiss and wrap her legs around my waist, sliding into her warm wetness.

"Fuck, you feel good."

"Mmm," she moans.

"Now you're going to talk to me," I say. Her eyes open in surprise, a little V forming as she frowns at me.

"About what?"

"About this." I slide out, then let my cock skim up her folds, the head tickling her clit. "I want you to tell me how this feels."

"It feels good."

"Be more specific." I bite her lower lip and feel sweat break out on my forehead when her little tongue peeks out to glide over the spot I just bit. "Tell me what you're feeling."

"I'm warm."

"And?" I rear back and slide my cock back inside her. Her ass feels full and perfect as I grip it, pulling her even closer against me.

"And turned on."

"I need more, Addie."

"I feel excited. Your cock hits this spot that sends zings up my spine."

"Good girl." I nuzzle her nipple with my nose. "What else?"

"Your fingertips on my ass."

"Yes?"

"I want them to leave bruises so I can see them later when I take a shower."

I feel a smile spread over my face at the thought of marking her.

Because she's fucking mine.

"I love that. Good one."

"I like the way the hair on your leg feels under my foot."

"Mmm. I love it when you drag your foot up my leg."

She does it again, making me smile.

"Your weight feels good on me," she whispers, then catches her breath when I pound into her, just a little harder. "And when you do that—"

"What, baby?"

"When you do that, it feels like you're buried so deep, I don't know where you end and I begin."

"I love you so fucking much."

Her smile lights up the room. "I love you too. And I love how much you say 'fuck' when you're turned on."

I pull out and kiss down her body to her pussy, pulling her lips into my mouth, sucking hard, then kiss back up and plunge inside her.

"You're the sweetest damn thing," I growl.

"Jake?"

"Yes, baby."

"Am I still talking?"

"Absolutely." I push one of her legs up over my shoulder, spreading her wider, going deeper, making her gasp.

"I feel open."

"Yeah, this position opens you up nicely."

"No," she breathes as she shakes her head. "I feel vulnerable. I trust you. I love you. I feel open."

I stop fucking her hard and stare down into her eyes, lower her leg, and cover her with my body. "I'm right here with you."

"And I feel like I'm going to come."

Her lips are tickling mine as she speaks. My eyes cross as she squeezes down on me, hard.

"Still with you," I groan as my spine tingles, and I feel the orgasm shoot through me, almost violently.

"So good," she sighs, lazily dragging her hands down my back to my ass. "And such a hot ass."

I smirk and roll us to the side so my weight is off of her, but I can still see her and touch her.

"So, did you wait until I told you I love you to break out the dominant side?" she asks playfully, but I can see that the question is honest.

"No, I just haven't shown you all my tricks yet. Sometimes I'm in this mood. Especially when . . . well, never mind."

"When what?"

I swallow, kiss her forehead. "You won't be offended?"

"I didn't say that," she says with a laugh.

"I get this way when I feel like I'm marking my territory."

Her eyes narrow, and I think she's going to yell at me, but then she hugs me tight. "I kind of like that. But don't tell anyone I said that."

"I'm not in a habit of telling people about my sex life," I reply dryly. "I think your secret is safe with me."

"Are you hungry?" she asks sweetly.

"A little." But I don't want to leave this bed. "You?"

"Not really."

"You were hungry thirty minutes ago," I remind her as she scoots closer.

"Yeah, but now you're awake, and I'm in your arms, and this is comfortable."

"Let's be lazy then." I cuddle her close and breathe her in. She smells like her citrusy shampoo and sex.

Sexiest fucking smell in this world.

"We should check our phones." She sighs and reaches over to the bedside table for her phone, and I do the same. "Has yours been blowing up?"

"Yep." We roll back together as we thumb through our phones. "I had six calls and, holy shit, eight texts."

"I've had four calls and twenty-two texts," she says, giggling. "The girls are persistent."

"Yeah, Christina and Max both want to know what's going on. I'll call Max real quick and he can call Christina."

"I'll call Cami," she says with a nod.

"You're alive," Max says when he answers. "I thought maybe she took you out somewhere and offed you."

"Not yet," I reply. "We're good, man."

"Yeah?"

"Yeah. Things are good here. Will you call Christina and let her know? She's been blowing up my phone."

"Sure, she's been blowing up mine too. I don't know

why, it's not like we're having an orgy or anything, and I'm not psychic."

"She's like a mother hen," I reply, watching Addie as she laughs and tells Cami that we're just being lazy in bed. "I appreciate it."

"No problem. And I'm happy for you, Jake."

"Thanks." I hang up, toss my phone aside, and listen unabashedly to Addie's conversation.

She presses her finger to her lips, telling me to stay quiet, and puts her phone on speaker, laying it on the bed between us.

"I mean, you were so darn stubborn, Addie, and he was so sweet. It's a good thing he had me and Mia helping him, so he knew where to send flowers and stuff. Isn't he sweet?"

"The sweetest," Addie says, rolling her eyes.

"He really is. And boy does he love you. I mean, what's not to love, right? But that man is head over heels gone over you. And you so deserve that, Add." She sniffles and Addie shakes her head in resignation. "You deserve someone who pretty much worships the ground you walk on. And he does." More sniffles. "I know you have a lot of baggage, but I really think that Jake is completely different from any of the assholes from your past. I'm glad you pulled your head out of your ass and realized that he was just a stupid man who made a mistake."

I scowl at the *stupid man* comment, glaring at the phone. "Hey! I'm not stupid."

Addie sighs and Cami goes quiet.

"I'm on speaker?" she demands.

"Hi, Cami," I say with a grin. "I think you're sweet too."

"Well, I guess it's good that I was saying nice things about you," she says. "Hey, Jake, do you have any single women friends that I can hook up with Brian?"

"Cami! Stop it," Addie says in exasperation. "Seriously, let the man find his own date."

"He's bad at it," she says with a sigh. "Okay, you guys go have sex, because really, someone should be getting laid. I'm gonna go see if I can help at the restaurant."

"Do they need me today?" Addie asks, but I'm already shaking my head.

"Nope. We're just fine. You enjoy each other today and make up for lost time. Love you both!"

She clicks off and Addie worries her lip.

"You heard her. They're fine."

"Yeah. I'm sure you're right."

"I know I'm right. You girls are damn good at your jobs, and they'll survive without you today. Besides, I want to take you somewhere."

"Where?"

I kiss her lightly, then slap her ass and roll out of bed. "You'll see. Stop being so lazy and needy and let my dick rest for a while. Seriously, Addie, I can barely keep up with you."

"You are not as funny as you think you are." She sniffs and rolls out of bed, but can't disguise the humor in her eyes.

"Sweetheart, I'm fucking hilarious."

"ARE WE GOING to go get burgers after this?" she asks.

"Of course."

"I love it here," Addie sighs as she leans back on me

and watches the water fall down Multnomah Falls. "It's so peaceful."

"Mmm." I kiss her head, breathing in her sweet scent. We're sitting on a rock at the base of the falls. She's sitting between my legs, leaning back on my chest. This is the calmest I've felt in . . . well, since the last time we were here.

"Are you okay?" I ask, whispering in her ear.

"Of course." She looks up at me with a confused frown. "Why wouldn't I be?"

"I'm just checking in. I want to tread carefully."

"Jake, you don't have to treat me like I'm made of glass. I'm fantastic. I'm with you."

I drag my fingertips down her cheek and kiss her nose. "I'm fantastic when I'm with you too."

"You know, the last time you brought me here is when I had kind of a lightbulb moment."

"Really?" She settles back against me, watching the water. "What was it?"

"We were standing on that bridge, and your arms were around me. I'd been having a rough few days, remember?"

"I remember." I remember feeling helpless because I didn't know how to make her feel better.

"You told me to close my eyes and to listen to the falls. And I did. It was beautiful, but it wasn't what calmed me."

"What did?"

"The man whose arms were around me," she says and smiles up at me. "You're the one who calms me."

Jesus. She'd felt safe with me, and I ripped that out from under her. I'm so fucking lucky that she took me back.

"I'm sorry, Addie."

"Hey, I didn't say that to make you feel guilty." She turns in my arms and cups my face in her hands. "It's a happy memory, Jake. I think I loved you then; I was just too stubborn to admit it."

"I'll never forget the moment I realized that I love you." I smile down into her eyes as she lifts her chin, offering her lips for a kiss.

I happily oblige her.

"That night, after the cookout at Mia's parents' house."

"That was some good sex," she says with a nod.

"That night changed my world," I reply automatically. "I'd been falling in love with you for weeks, but in that moment, I knew that I was lost to you, Addison."

"You make me happy," she says simply. "And I love my song. Thank you for it."

"You're welcome. It sort of wrote itself." She tilts her head in question. "I started hearing the melody the night I first saw you. That *click* is a powerful thing."

"Must be," she says with a nod.

"I worked on it almost every day, whenever I wasn't with you or working."

"So you didn't write it just because we'd broken up?"

"No way." I laugh and hug her tight. "That song gripped me by the throat and wouldn't let go."

"It's our song," she says softly.

"No, baby, it's *your* song. We don't need a song. We *are* a song."

She takes a long, shaky breath before kissing me sweetly. "Thank you."

"You're welcome." We sit for a long while, quietly watching the water, listening to the wind in the trees and enjoying the sunshine as it breaks through the leaves above, when something occurs to me. "Hey, does this mean I can have my job back?"

"Do you want it back?"

"Yes. I enjoy watching the audience as they sing along with the songs. Max and I get a kick out of playing harmonies and just giving each other shit onstage. And I love being close to you, and that's just another way that I can do that."

"Well, then the job is yours. It was always yours."

"I'll always be *yours*," I reply softly. "For as long as you'll have me."

"Good." She kisses the underside of my chin. "Because I plan to keep you pretty much forever."

"Excellent idea."

Epilogue

Addison

Three Months Later . . .

"*I* can't believe it," Kat says with a scowl as she eats a croissant with strawberry jam. The five of us are having brunch on a Sunday morning. It's a beautiful early fall day, and the patio out here in northwest Portland is perfect this morning.

"I need to see it again," Riley says, motioning for me to shove my hand across the table so she can get another look at the ring. "I mean, this is *impressive*, Addie."

"Thanks." I grin happily and take a bite of bacon. Jake outdid himself with this ring.

But the best part was the proposal.

"I can't believe that he shared just about every aspect of your relationship with us, meeting you in the restaurant, enlisting our help to get you back, and then he did the proposal all by himself!" Kat scowls. "That's not fair."

"How did he do it?" Cami asks, resting her chin in her hand and smiling dreamily. God, that girl is such a romantic.

"He just asked me to marry him," I reply simply. Jake and I agreed that the details would be left between us. It was a surprise. He took me to our place, the falls, late in the day when it would be pretty much deserted. I thought we were just going up there for a little peace and quiet. We were standing on the bridge, exactly like that first day that he took me there.

But suddenly, he lowered himself to one knee and held up a little blue box.

"I fall for you every day, Addison. Not just because you're beautiful and smart and so damn funny you make me laugh until I cry, although you definitely are all of those things. I want you because there is simply no one else in this world like you. I know there's no one better than you, or more right for me than you, and I don't ever want to start a day without you in it. You are my happy place. You are my safe place. Please marry me. Go on this adventure with me."

"Earth to Addie," Mia says, waving her hand in front of my face. "Are you going to join us?"

"Sorry."

"So you're not going to tell us how he did it," Riley says, disappointed. "That sucks."

"I'm allowed to have something just for me," I say with a smile. "But, I will say that it was incredibly romantic and that he made me cry. But in a good way this time."

"Okay, I can live with that," Kat says with a sigh.

"And, get this, he called my parents and is flying them in

for our engagement party. Mom's going to help me plan the wedding."

"That's awesome!" Mia says with a smile. "I know you miss them."

"Brian went out on a date!" Cami exclaims and claps her hands. "I set him up with my neighbor's daughter, and it sounds like they had a good time."

"You're so weird," Mia says, shaking her head. "You really need to let the man find his own woman."

"Maybe he doesn't want another woman," Riley says quietly. "Maybe he still wants you."

Cami swallows hard. "He can't have me."

Mia's phone rings, and she frowns down at it. "Mom doesn't usually call me this early in the day. Hello?"

"He'll move on," I assure Cami.

"What do you mean?" Mia demands, making us all freeze and listen. "Well, when will we know? Oh my God, Mama."

"It's Landon," Cami whispers hoarsely.

"Call me, as soon as you know. Do we need to go there?" Mia's eyes find mine.

Oh, friend. What's happening?

"Okay. I love you too."

Cami's hand grips tightly to mine.

"What's happened?" Cami demands as soon as Mia ends the call.

"Landon's been hurt." Mia's eyes are full of fear as she wipes tears away. "We don't know how badly yet."

"But he's alive," Cami says. It's not a question.

Mia's eyes meet hers. "He's alive."

"When will we know more?" I ask.

"She didn't know." Mia buries her face in her hands and lets the tears come. I wrap an arm around Cami, but she just stares straight ahead.

"He's going to be okay," I murmur to her. "Landon's a fighter."

"He's okay," Cami repeats, then shakes her head, as though she's coming out of a fog. She turns her eyes to mine. "He has to be okay."

Recipes

FIRST COURSE

Roasted Red Grape and Brie crostini drizzled with
honey and sprinkled with sea salt and fresh thyme

Ovum Off the Grid Riesling

SECOND COURSE

Cheese Fondue

Accompanied by: bread cubes (sourdough &
pumpernickel), **artichoke** hearts, garlic, olive oil, and
rosemary marinated beef cubes and fresh apple slices

Grilled **Asparagus**

Charles Smith Viognier or Eyrie Pinot Gris

DESSERT

Sinfully Delicious **Chocolate** cake with rich,
warm ganache and fresh **raspberries**

Clear Creek Distillery Eaux de Vie, Framboise

ROASTED RED GRAPE CROSTINI

Components

1 lb. red grapes
1 T. olive oil
1 t. thyme, roughly chopped
½ baguette
Garlic olive oil for brushing on top of toasts
8 oz. brie
Honey for drizzling
Sea salt for sprinkling
Additional fresh thyme to top finished crostini

To make Roasted Grapes and Crostini:

1. Preheat oven to 400°F. Place grapes on foil-lined baking sheet and drizzle with olive oil, sprinkle with salt and roughly chopped thyme. Set aside.
2. Prepare the toasts by cutting the bread into ½-inch slices. Arrange on foil-lined baking sheet and lightly brush the top with the garlic olive oil.
3. Place the grapes on the top rack and the toasts on the bottom rack and set the timer for 15 minutes. Check the toasts first; they should be crisp and slightly golden brown around the edges.
4. Roast the grapes for an additional 5 minutes or until the skins are slightly wrinkled.
5. After both have been taken from the oven, set aside.

To assemble:

1. Cut brie into thin slices and place on top of toasts on the foil-lined sheet tray.

2. Top with prepared grapes and move to serving platter carefully.

3. Drizzle with honey, sprinkle with sea salt and fresh thyme.

FONDUE

Components:
Garlic, olive oil, and rosemary marinated beef cubes
Cheese fondue
Artichoke hearts, canned or marinated
Bread cubes (pumpernickel or sourdough)
Apple or pear slices

To make Beef Cubes:
1 lb. sirloin steak, cut into 2-by-2-inch chunks
3 T. olive oil
1–2 cloves of Garlic, minced
2 t. fresh rosemary, chopped
Salt & black pepper to taste

1. Place beef cubes, 2 T. olive oil, garlic, and rosemary in large plastic storage bag. Keep in the refrigerator for 1–2 hours (or up to 6).
2. Preheat a nonstick skillet on high heat. Add 1 T. of olive oil, sear the beef tips in the hot oil until they are a deep golden brown on the outside and cooked in the center, 3–4 minutes in the pan.
3. Take out of pan and rest until all other accompaniments are prepared.

To make Cheese Fondue:
½ cup white wine
1 garlic clove, cut in half
¼ lb. Emmentaler cheese, grated
¼ lb. Gruyère cheese, grated
½ t. cornstarch
Salt & white pepper to taste

1. For double boiler: Bring water to boil in sauce pan. Top with aluminum bowl that covers the top of the sauce pan with ample room and does not touch the top of the boiling water.
2. Rub the aluminum bowl with the garlic clove.
3. Add the wine and bring to a simmer (this is when small bubbles form around the edge of the bowl).
4. Combine the grated cheese in a separate bowl and coat with cornstarch.
5. After the wine has come to a simmer, add the cheese in handfuls and whisk until cheese has fully melted before adding anymore. Repeat until all cheese has been added to the fondue mixture.
6. Turn off heat under double boiler. Add salt and white pepper to taste. Enjoy immediately.

To assemble Fondue Plate:
Make sure all components are assembled or cooked prior to making the cheese fondue. Place all accompaniments artfully on a platter to serve. Fondue can be served in bowl or in heated fondue pot.

GRILLED ASPARAGUS

1 bunch asparagus
1 T. olive oil
Salt & black pepper to taste

To make Grilled Asparagus:

1. Cut 1–2 inches off the bottom of one bunch of asparagus.
2. Coat with 1 T. of olive oil and sprinkle with salt and pepper.
3. Place onto hot grill and cook, turning once, for 5 minutes, just to get enough char on the outside for flavor and for the asparagus to turn bright green.

CHOCOLATE BROWNIE CAKE

Components:
Brownie Cake
Chocolate Ganache
Fresh Raspberries

To make Brownie Cake:
1 stick butter, melted
1 cup sugar
2 eggs
1 t. vanilla
⅓ cup cocoa
½ cup all purpose flour
¼ t. baking powder
¼ t. salt

1. Preheat oven to 350°F. Liberally grease a muffin tin with either shortening or pan release spray.
2. In a bowl, stir together the melted butter, sugar, vanilla, and cocoa. Add eggs one at a time, beating well after each addition.
3. Combine flour, baking powder, and salt in a separate bowl; gradually add to butter mixture, mixing until blended.
4. Scoop into prepared muffin tin using a ¼ cup measure; brownie should fill cup a little over halfway.

5. Bake for 16–18 minutes or until brownies have a firm top and toothpick inserted in center comes out clean. Remove from muffin tin after brownie cakes have completely cooled.

To make Chocolate Ganache:

1 cup heavy cream
1 cup semisweet chocolate chips

1. Heat heavy cream in sauce pan over medium heat to a simmer.
2. Place chocolate chips in aluminum bowl. After cream has heated, pour over the top of the chocolate.
3. Mix gently until the chocolate and the heavy cream have completely combined to create a rich, smooth sauce.

To assemble Dessert:

1. Place warm brownie cake on the center of a plate.
2. Top with chocolate ganache and fresh raspberries.
3. Sprinkle with powdered sugar and serve with a scoop of creamy vanilla bean ice cream.

About the Author

New York Times and *USA Today* bestselling author **KRISTEN PROBY** is the author of the bestselling With Me in Seattle and Love Under the Big Sky series. She has a passion for a good love story and humorous characters with a strong sense of loyalty and family. Her men are the alpha type, fiercely protective and a bit bossy; and her ladies are fun and not afraid to stand up for themselves.

Kristen lives in Montana, where she enjoys coffee, chocolate, and sunshine. And naps.

CLOSE TO YOU

Camilla, "Cami," LaRue was five years old when she first fell in love with Landon Palazzo. Everyone told her the puppy love would fade—they clearly never met Landon. When he left after graduation without a backward glance, she was heartbroken. But Cami grew up, moved on, and became part-owner of wildly popular restaurant, Seduction. She has everything she could want . . . or so she thinks.

After spending the last twelve years as a Navy fighter pilot, Landon returns to Portland to take over the family construction business. When he catches a glimpse at little Cami LaRue, he realizes she's not so little any more. He always had a soft spot for his little sister's best friend, but nothing is soft now when he's around the gorgeous restauranteur.

Landon isn't going to pass up the chance to make the girl-next-door his. She's never been one for romance, but he's just the one to change her mind. Will seduction be just the name of her restaurant or will Cami let him get close enough to fulfill all her fantasies?

Coming August 2016

BOOKS BY KRISTEN PROBY

LISTEN TO ME
A Fusion Novel
Book One

Seduction is quickly becoming the hottest new restaurant in Portland, and Addison Wade is proud to claim her share of the credit. But when former rock star Jake Keller swaggers through the doors to apply for the weekend gig, she knows she's in trouble. He's all bad boy . . . exactly her type and exactly what she doesn't need.

CLOSE TO YOU
A Fusion Novel
Book Two

Since the day she met Landon Palazzo, Camilla LaRue, part owner of the wildly popular restaurant Seduction, has been head-over-heels in love. And when Landon joined the Navy right after high school, Cami thought her heart would never recover. But it did, and all these years later, she's managed to not only survive, but thrive. But now, Landon is back and he looks better than ever.